LOVE SONGS FOR A LOST CONTINENT

Stories

ANITA FELICELLI

stillhouse press

CRAFT PUBLISHING FOR ARDENT SPIRITS

FAIRFAX, VIRGINIA

All inquiries may be directed to:
    Stillhouse Press
    4400 University Drive, 3E4
    Fairfax, VA 22030
    www.stillhousepress.org

Stillhouse Press is an independent, student-run nonprofit press based out of Northern Virginia and established in collaboration with the Fall for the Book festival.

LIBRARY OF CONGRESS CONTROL NUMBER: 2017962318
ISBN-13: 978-1-945233-04-3

Designed and composed by Douglas Luman.

Love Songs for a Lost Continent

"This is the book we needed to read yesterday... a book we will still be reading tomorrow."

POROCHISTA KHAKPOUR

Author of *Sick* and *Sons and Other Flammable Objects*

"Tigers, swans and rampion—Anita Felicelli's Love Songs for a Lost Continent captures the senses with skillful explorations of sexual being and human vulnerability. This collection not only rallies the imagination; it challenges the intellectual self and the diverse self. A beautifully rendered collection, both enchanting and lyrical."

RAE BRYANT

Author of *The Indefinite State of Imaginary Morals*

"This is a wild, startling collection about loss, migration, colonization, and constantly shifting identities. What does it mean to be an outsider, and where does our power really lie? For the characters in Love Songs for a Lost Continent, living and loving in the margins is as precarious as a tightrope walk."

CHAITALI SEN

Author of *The Pathless Sky*

"Love Songs for a Lost Continent defies expectation. You'll think you're being led into a narrative that's comfortably familiar, but instead will find work that pushes boundaries, redefines freedoms both personal and artistic."

SHANTHI SEKARAN

Author of *Lucky Boy* and *The Prayer Room*

"Love Songs for a Lost Continent is an expansive, inventive meditation on the shifting landscape of identity, on how people can be shaped and reshaped by violence and power and love. Anita Felicelli has a singular eye for the moments that transfigure lives, and this tremendous debut collection announces the arrival of a stunning new voice."

LAURA VAN DEN BERG
Author of *The Third Hotel* and *Find Me*

"This is the kind of work that we all need to be reading right now. Filled with heart and heat, these beautiful stories pursue and reinvent ideas of home and self in ways that push our national conversation on identity."

BICH MINH NGUYEN
Author of *Pioneer Girl* and *Stealing Buddha's Dinner*

"These stories probe the limits of love, the fluidity of home, and the pressures and resistance of women in a patriarchal landscape without ever losing humor, engagement, and a quiet elegance and tenderness. They move with assurance through ideas, themes, and landscapes revealing what is new within what might have been expected. A very strong debut."

CHRIS ABANI
Author of *The Secret History of Las Vegas* and *The Face, Cartography of the Void*

"The thirteen sparkling pieces in Anita Felicelli's debut collection grapple with the power of fiction itself: the mythologies handed down to us, the false promises of the American dream, and the stories we don't recognize we're telling ourselves."

KATHARINE NOEL
Author of *Meantime: A Novel*

For Steven

TABLE OF CONTENTS

The only true paradise is paradise lost.

MARCEL PROUST

*I always had a repulsive need
to be something more than human.*

DAVID BOWIE

DECEPTION

Sita's family married her to a Bengal tiger. When her parents had arranged the marriage, she was revolted. To marry a tiger! How loathsome, how base. Was she really so ugly and undesirable that the only interested suitor was a beast?

Nonetheless, reluctant and angry and ashamed, she'd followed him to his home at the edge of the village. But to her surprise, Anand was resolutely romantic, so unlike the boys in her engineering college. He recited poetry, and his pursuit of her was focused and thoughtful. He read the books she recommended, even the British murder mystery novels, discussing why the clues didn't quite add up or marveling at the skillfulness of the author's plotting. They attended outdoor movies every Saturday night, eating popcorn and drinking Thums Up cola at the intermission and sitting in the back, out of sight of the gossipers.

After the tiger was murdered, newspapers across India branded Sita a killer, and all the charm fell away from her memories of those early courtship days. Everyone claimed they knew what had happened. At parties in the neighboring state, raconteurs and conspiracy theorists drunk on cashew feni would put forth detailed hypotheses on why she'd done it and how, describing all manner of bloody horrors. In the village streets, the wallahs gossiped about the latest clues being considered in the police investigation. Grandmothers spent long languid afternoons sipping tea and munching on vada, and although they started with the best of intentions—talking about their children's marital problems and shaking their heads with sighs of ayyo—eventually the conversation would turn to what sort of family Sita must have had, to marry her to a tiger, and what sort of family the dead tiger must have had, to marry him off to a Brahmin girl. Environmental groups called for the death penalty. The shame Sita had forgotten about returned.

* * *

It was a clear Friday morning in March when a neuroscientist loaned his Smriti 3000 fMRI lie-detection machine to the police department in Sita's village. Jacaranda trees in front of the hospital's double doors were blooming, their mauve canopy of blossoms thick and sweet. Beneath the trees, the fallen flowers were nearly reflective, shimmering purple in the light that bleached the gravel road. The Smriti 3000 arrived in two parts: the first was a human-sized computer that needed to be lifted by five heavyset men, and the second was a cylindrical MRI machine with its trail of sensors like red roses on floppy rainbow stems. It was an oracle made of metal, fit for the modern age, and it occupied the hospital room with its cheap Formica-topped desk and black rotary telephone with all the phony confidence and ostentation of a slot machine.

Dr. Kumaraswamy, the neuroscientist who had invented the machine, appeared at the hospital twenty minutes after the machine arrived. He was small and frail with wide grey-brown lips and long narrow nostrils. He walked with an engraved silver walking cane, which he employed liberally to admonish people who irritated him.

"Careful! I say, careful, you bloody moron!" he shouted at the young man trying to follow his directions on how to attach the sensors to the young woman's head.

He spent several hours training all of the hospital technicians and a few police officers on how to record Sita's responses and how to play the interrogation tapes he had compiled to question her.

Senior-ranking police officers watched Dr. Kumaraswamy with a mixture of resentment and admiration. Resentment because he was a doctor trying to usurp their role of ferreting the truth from recalcitrant subjects—and admiration because they believed medicine was the most noble of professions. However cumbersome, however much it jeopardized their jobs, the machine had the potential to ensure that the most elusive and dangerous suspects in India were put away forever or sentenced to death.

Fifty thousand times stronger than the earth's magnetic force, Dr. Kumaraswamy explained. "This is the strongest machine of its kind."

"How does it work?" one of the officers asked.

"It sends radio waves into the suspect's body," the doctor said. "And knocks the protons out of line, then reads the signals released by the protons. See these? The protons in the areas where the oxygenated blood flows produce the strongest signals."

Two police officers and the commissioner hovered around him.

"Are you sure it works?" one of them asked.

"Yes, absolutely," the doctor said.

"You know about the woman we have here?" the commissioner asked. He tapped a shiny black billy club on the table. "Are there any precautions we should take, doctor?"

"None, unless she's pregnant or wearing an intrauterine device," he replied.

"Not a problem, doctor," the commissioner said.

"Then the technician will hook her up. And the computer will tell you if she's lying."

Sita's lawyer arrived to represent her during the interrogation, but he said nothing as wires were fastened to Sita's head. He was a tall man who wore a crisp button-down shirt and spoke with a British accent even when he was speaking Tamil. Although he had been born in Madurai, he'd studied in England from a young age, and he'd returned to India "to do good." He said this without even the slightest hint of wit or amusement.

One of the police officers stood outside the room, his thick arms crossed and his head tilted slightly to listen. The tape played a series of sentences. The machine was humming as it measured the way the young woman's brain responded to them. Bored, the commissioner and the other police officer went downstairs to eat at the cafeteria. The young woman squirmed inside the MRI machine. Bang, bang, bang. The gong-like pulses after each question were so loud they could be heard down the hall.

"Keep still," the technician said.

She wiggled her toes in defiance. The technician took a pamphlet and thwacked her toes with it. She gave one last half-hearted kick and stilled.

A proper voice with a British accent continued to state sentences, each of them short and declarative, together forming a black web of her misdeeds, both real and imagined. The technician paced uneasily back and forth in front of the machine to make sure there were no errors, while the officer and Sita's lawyer took notes. The officer scratched his notes in longhand in a spiral-bound notebook. Sita's lawyer hunted and pecked on his laptop with a bony index finger. Inside the white tunnel of the machine, Sita closed her eyes and tried to remember the city of pink palaces, the rosy homes of kings and their consorts, as the voice told her a tale about her husband's death.

* * *

I bought arsenic from the shop.

The voice on the tape was a polite, confident woman's voice. As it uttered the shaky narrative investigators had pieced together, the machine registered that a quiet territory of Sita's brain was whirring, responding to the words:

I poured arsenic in the batter.

I walked to the bus stop.

I took a bus to Srinivasan's house.

I had planned the murder in the weeks before.

Srinivasan knew about the murder.

We took the rickshaw to the train station.

It was strange how the phrases were worded, as if the proper-sounding voice was meant to be a stand-in for her own husky one. She wasn't quite sure what the Smriti 3000 measured, but she'd gathered from the technician's chitchat with her lawyer that a part of her brain lit up to tell the technician that she had a memory of the sentence being uttered, that it was not an alien thought, but one that comfortably wedged into her mind like the teenage summers spent lounging on the colored sands of Kanyakumari with her brothers or the cheap mystery novels she read. And hearing the sentences, she was persuaded. After all, she had wanted the tiger dead. She'd grown repulsed by him, her contempt born from overfamiliarity.

But during a break, she complained privately to her lawyer that she didn't actually remember what the machine said she remembered. Her lawyer suggested that perhaps she had blacked out the truth. "People don't always know the truth about themselves or what's happened to them." He said this with no hint of emotion, as if it were simply information, not necessarily applicable to her situation. When she raised her eyebrows, he assured her this wasn't what he told the prosecutors. Confusion and loneliness swirled through her.

The technician shepherded her back into the eerie white tunnel of the MRI. The voice and the booming sounds commenced again. She kept her eyes closed.

Outside the Smriti 3000, electrical signals zinged from the colorful wires attached to her shaved scalp and ran to the large computer where they spit out their results. "EXPERIENTIAL KNOWLEDGE" said the screen in big red letters, a proclamation of truth.

I did not care that my husband had died.

The voice stopped.

"What happened?" asked Sita as the technician pulled her from the tunnel. "What does that mean?"

The technician administering the test nodded. He unclipped the sensors from Sita's head and gestured at the truth printed on the screen.

"But it's wrong," she said.

He didn't respond.

The technician gave her a gel to clean the stickiness from her head. It was still horrifying to her to feel the bristles of her hair emerging on her scalp, so similar to Anand's whiskers—prickly, tiny needles spearing her fingertips. Her hair had once been so long, it had extended the full length of her spine, a luxurious cascade of black curls. She hadn't cut it since her schooldays, though she trimmed the ends occasionally. She was ashamed of her vanity now.

Her lawyer shook her hand, and hurried off to his next client. He was absolutely sincere in everything he said, and she knew she was supposed to trust him because he'd studied at Cambridge and came so highly recommended, but all she could feel was dismay that her life was now in the hands of some British man who didn't even know how to make jalebis, who didn't understand it was preposterous to think she could pour rat poison into the batter and not have the finished product taste toxic. Anand would have known straightaway something was wrong. In fact, he probably would have beaten her for making jalebis incorrectly. He'd hit her for less in the past, his claws raking her face. The villagers all knew how he treated her, but they met their knowledge with silence.

* * *

It would have been more bearable if Srinivasan had visited her in jail, if he had wanted to wait for her.

For months before the tiger's death, she'd been seeing Srinivasan during long, lazy afternoons. He was a literature professor at a local college. She met him at a reading by a foreign author one weekend in January. They both had read the book before the reading and brought their copies of the book to be signed, but afterward, during the book signing, he whispered he hadn't been satisfied with the ending, and since she too was dissatisfied, they invented other more exciting endings—the butler was actually a killer! No, the butler had been on holiday and the maid set him up to take the fall.

After the author had signed Sita's copy, Sita was ready to leave, but Srinivasan was waiting for her outside. They strolled through the muddy village streets, keeping their bodies a modest few feet apart, before leaving each other with long looks and promises to meet again the next afternoon. Anand was angry with her for coming home late, but at least he hadn't thrown anything. He lolled on the carpet in front of the television as he watched a game show, growling as the man he hoped would win was eliminated. He rolled over on his back and stretched his limbs, exposing his white furry belly, and then flipped back over again, licking his paws.

It was so satisfying to clean the tiny house during the morning while Srinivasan taught his literature courses. It was so satisfying to leave for a leisurely walk on the beach with her lover—even the word "lover" was thrilling, perhaps partly because of the breathtaking danger and the terrible consequences if the tiger found out, but she did not admit that thought. It was too dark, too disturbing, too complicated.

She and Srinivasan would spend hours wandering between driftwood and wet ribbons of olive-green kelp, dodging the low black cloud of flies that buzzed up from rough sand. Cow dung and cowrie shells. Closer to the water, the sand was packed, icy smooth. They would stand knee-deep in the waves, feeling the fierce rush of it returning to the ocean, the salty white foam like gentle soapsuds around their toes.

Srinivasan wore his straight dark hair so that it fell just above his shoulders. He would tell her stories about his class, advising her on books to read to improve her vocabulary and her familiarity with Anglo literature. He would run a finger around the curve of her cheek, look deeply into her eyes. It was like something out of an American movie where people believed they were soul mates.

His kisses tasted like fresh mint and sweet-bitter fennel seeds, rather than blood and fresh meat. His mother was Punjabi and he was an excellent cook, claiming his proficiency arose from his long-term bachelor status. He would invite her to his house for succulent curries and naan and freshly fried samosas. There was something intoxicating in their connection, consisting as it did almost entirely of delicious food and literature. She'd been taught her whole life that a Tamil woman should be devoted to her husband, should cook and clean and serve him. But in books, in movies, there was romance, and although most people she knew were driven by obligation, her own sense of romance—that it tossed you out on the edge of a cliff, just waiting to fall, that it shook you through and through like a violent earthquake—was vastly more powerful than her sense of duty.

And when he asked her to run away with him to Jaipur, the Pink City, because he'd accepted a job there, she said yes immediately, thinking of fairy tales, thinking of the intricate facades of the palaces she'd seen only in friends' vacation pictures, thinking that all she wanted was to escape her village, escape the people with whom she'd long since stopped identifying.

* * *

"I didn't do it," Sita told her brother. She refused to cry. Crying was for women who were weak, who had done something wrong, who could not control themselves. Or that was what she thought as she tried to maintain a certain measure of control.

She and her older brother, Deepak were standing on opposite sides of a fence that divided the visiting room of the women's prison from the prison itself. The floors were smooth, unstained white-grey concrete that stank of urine. Behind her brother, she saw a vending machine. She imagined putting a few rupees in the machine, the Cadbury chocolate bar she would buy, the way it would melt on her tongue, a soft brown drizzle in the heat.

"Then why did the machine tell the doctors you did?" Her brother wore a pink shirt and his copper-colored skin smelled like Old Spice, a scent he'd bought from a store full of imports. The stench of Anand—mud and fresh grass, the dirty fur, the sweaty skin of a hunter, the metallic taste of blood when he kissed her—never left her mind now, so she stuck her nose between the bars and breathed her brother in. He stepped back, uncertain, and she pulled back, too, eyeing him warily. Why was he so certain about her guilt?

She shook her head. "It told the technician, not the doctors. But I tell you, I'm innocent."

"Come on. They're doctors. And doctors invented the machine," said Deepak. "It's scientific. They can tell if you're lying." Perhaps, like most people, he was giving too much credit to the prevailing notions of the time, that they were right, that they were good, simply because the powerful espoused them.

She knew otherwise. "No, they can't. The machine isn't right. I didn't poison him."

"Okay, well, since there was arsenic in the dosas and you made the dosas—" Deepak looked away.

"They said it was in the jalebi, not the dosas." Sita stepped forward, unsettled, wanting to probe what he knew.

Deepak continued to speak, but most of the conversation seemed trivial to Sita, filled as it was with reminders of a world she probably wouldn't see again. He shared the minutiae of their parents' health troubles. She wanted to tell him to stop, but she didn't know what they would talk about if he didn't elaborate on her mother's hypochondria and her father's bowel troubles. Was there any other common point of reference? He didn't read, didn't watch movies, didn't think about the world. His entire conception of reality grew out of the tiny corner of the world where he'd lived since birth.

Apple pie and sausages. Snow angels and men. Stuff she would probably never want to eat or make, only read about in American books. And yet, and yet—just knowing of exotic things that happened in places other than the village was enough to rattle her sense of reality, make her realize that her life in the village had been more limited than other people's lives elsewhere. Western nonsense, Deepak would have said, if she'd given voice to any of these ideas, if she'd shared what she thought. But East, West—anybody could be free. She knew girls from school who had been free. They'd gone out dancing with boyfriends and planned careers in marketing. When they graduated, they had not gotten married, at least not immediately, but had gone to work in jobs they liked in the city. They shaped their reality, they sculpted it. They didn't wait for the stars and planets to align. The world is changing, she wanted to tell Deepak, but she never did.

Instead she nodded, pretending to listen to the litany of ailments their parents suffered, tuning in again when Deepak began talking about Srinivasan. He said that newspapers reported that her boyfriend had passed the lie-detector test and was living back in Jaipur.

"Why hasn't he written me, at least?"

Deepak shrugged. Sita could tell that he thought she was being shallow, focusing on the wrong things, impractical nonsense again. She could see it on his visage, in the terrible smug curl of his lip as he spoke sentences he intended to be reassuring.

She was supposed to understand that she deserved Srinivasan's scorn—she'd done something so terrible, she would never recover her dignity. She was in prison awaiting trial because she deserved it. She was not supposed to be angry, nice girls didn't get angry. Oh, nobody said, you can't be angry, but it was implied, wasn't it? The way people looked away when she tried to explain how wrong they had it, when her voice rose just a fraction, when she started moving her hands. She didn't know who had murdered Anand, of course, but it wasn't her. She didn't concoct the murder plot her own attorney called "fiendish" as if they were all characters in the black-and-white *Nick and Nora* movie she had seen at a film festival in Chennai last year.

It was only after Deepak left that she had time to wonder why he believed the arsenic was in the dosas, not the jalebi. The machines claimed that she remembered pouring poison into the syrup, and this supposed fact was what the newspapers reported.

* * *

The first thing Sita did when she and Srinivasan arrived in the city of pink palaces was to locate a doctor who would perform abortions with a forged certification. The certification claimed that the abortion was necessary to protect her health, but it was written by a doctor who drew breath only in her imagination: Dr. Venkateshwaran. She didn't tell Srinivasan, of course. She was too afraid of what he would say, what he would think of her. Instead, she snuck out one morning while he was at his new university job.

Morning air. The green, watery smell of monsoon rains as the bright orange rickshaw hurtled toward the clinic. After the procedure, she woke from the anesthesia in tears, not sure why she was crying. The city doctor held something that smelled terrible. "Mam, see here, you were pregnant with a tiger cub," he said with an expression of disgust, showing her the dish, the tiny curled tiger fetus, furless and grey and still covered with viscous amniotic fluid. A tiny tail unfurled beside his body. Unmistakable pointy ears sticking up from the sides of his head. She breathed a sigh of relief that she'd escaped being the mother of this tiny copy of Anand.

"Here, you take it," he said.

"I don't want it," she said. "You throw it out." For more than twenty years, she'd visited the same village doctor. He helped deliver her. She couldn't imagine what he would have said about the tiger fetus, if he'd performed the procedure.

The city doctor forced her to take the dish, and her hands trembled as she took hold of it, but by the time she arrived home, she'd changed her mind about throwing it out. Or perhaps she'd convinced herself she'd changed her mind because she felt strange about throwing it aside, like it meant nothing, when it actually represented her freedom. She was too superstitious to throw it away, and so instead she laid it gently in a large embossed silver jewelry box, as a reminder of what had happened, of what she had done. The box sealed well, sealing away the stench of the aborted fetus.

As much as it saved her, the abortion proved to be her undoing, too, for it was how the police located her. The doctor's nurse saw the news of the tiger's death, the call for information about his murderer. She reported the woman who sought an abortion of a tiger cub at the clinic. As newspapers would report, the police discovered the fetal cub inside a jewelry box.

News of her abortion inflamed not only the villagers, but also the entire country. A woman who would forge a note to secure an abortion of her tiger cub could surely be motivated to kill the tiger that was his father as well, or so they seemed to think.

What Sita couldn't understand was how learning of a possible motive so easily transformed speculation into a firm belief that she had murdered the tiger. How easily the fictions that a closed circle of people told each other could grow wings, take flight as if they were truth.

* * *

After the story of what happened grew fuzzy with time, after the newspapers and the local gossips transformed her story into theirs, it was hard to get any sort of clarity back, to disentangle what she had imagined from what she remembered. She stood on the precipice of reality, but it was not her reality. The memories she understood to be true before Smriti 3000's proper voice had spoken would never be recovered. Instead she had truth as conveyed by the Smriti 3000.

That evening around six, young professionals were arriving home from the city, carrying empty silver tiffin boxes and books for reading on the train. The women she no longer envied, the men who rejected her parents' efforts to marry her off. They were returning to their homes just as she planned to leave hers. No streetlights. Through the window, a faint pink shimmer from the setting sun filtered through the arecas, illuminating potholes and deep gouges on the village road, and she imagined this light was like the light she would see all the time in her new life, in the city of pink palaces.

She made jalebis first. She stood over the cast iron wok, squirting long curling strings of dough into concentric circles in the hot oil. After the jalebi had fried, sucking up the oil, turning a deep gold, she dunked them in sugar syrup. Was there arsenic in the batter? Once the machine told her there was, her mind filled in other information, building off the first lie: the batter was laced with rat poison she had purchased that day. As she dunked the jalebi, she was careful not to lick her fingers as she usually did. She washed her hands thoroughly with the half-dissolved bar of green-blue soap by the sink. Next, she mixed hing, coriander, and mustard seeds into the curd rice. The okra curry was from the day before. She made the lemon sevai last, tossing rice sticks and lemon juice with gusto. As she added chopped coriander leaves, a lizard ran up the wall. She knocked it off and across the cool teal linoleum tiles with a broom, sweeping it out of the house. The night before, she'd prepared the dosa batter, and left it to ferment in a plastic container as she always did. She opened the top of the container and put another cast iron pan on the range. She sniffed the container, noticing it smelled a little different, not bad, just slightly sweet and metallic.

A farewell dinner. Not that Anand knew that it was a farewell, but for her, it had been the most complete way to say goodbye. All of Anand's favorite foods, including one of the primary reasons he had wanted to marry a human wife—the large, just-fried dosas. She liked the sense of closure that preparing the feast provided.

He had been in a good mood for some time and hadn't hit or kicked her in ages. The last fight had involved a lamp flung across the room, smashing against the wall and leaving a red streak from the painted ceramic base. Since that night, everything had stayed quiet for several weeks, yet she was overcome with joy at the thought of her escape.

On the table, she set out stainless steel bowls filled with curd rice, lemon sevai, vada, and okra curry. Fragrant steam rose from the bowls, whitening the air. Anand arrived home at 6:45 as he always did, his fur matted with sweat, lying in shaggy orange and white clumps around his muscular shoulders. His big paws were muddy, flecked with bits of grass from hunting in the nearby forest, and the thick wide nails curling over the edge of his paws were black with grit.

Sita welcomed him with a kiss. She didn't like touching him anymore, but she did not want him to suspect anything. She swallowed the urge to spit in his large eyes. His whiskers worked against her upper lip and cheeks like rasps on alabaster. Places around her mouth were rubbed raw and red now from his kisses. He sauntered into the bedroom to freshen up in the cement shower. She arranged the jalebis on a plate and placed the plate on the table next to a jar of hot onion pickle. Again she washed her hands. She began frying the dosas he liked so much.

When he returned to the kitchen, Anand was discoursing on deforestation, complaining about how his tracking of deer and buffalo had changed as a result of humans. She poured some Kingfisher beer into a bowl and set it out in front of him on the table. Without a word to her, his enormous wide pink tongue lapped it up. When he was finished drinking, he tore into a dosa and slurped from a bright orange pool of molaga podi. She tuned out his lecture. Soon this charade would be over.

She touched her thali, turning the gold pendant first one way with her thumb and then the other, feeling a familiar pang of shame. Just a few months after they married, Anand had begun to snap at her. There would be good days for long stretches and then, without any clear warning, he would snap, "Be quiet or I shall show you my true shape." They were walking by a lake one day when he repeated the words. By now she had come to think of him as an enormous cat, and she laughingly replied, "Fine, show me your true shape."

He growled at her and gnashed his teeth. Sharp and suicide white. His nostrils flaring. Steel blue lake reflected in his bright round eyes. She walked backward for a moment, before spinning and running. He chased her to the base of a jujube tree as she fled up into the branches, coaxing her down several hours later with a slim volume of Irish poetry and a bowl of gulab jamun.

Once she invited him to show his true shape, there was no way to turn it off. He could no longer suppress his true shape, the way he had during their first few weeks of courtship. What she once experienced as a passionate intensity transformed into an energy that was threatening, raging, controlling. He wanted the house to be spotless—no easy feat since he shed long thin orange hairs all over the linoleum floor that collected into hair balls that blew around the room on hot days when she turned on the ceiling fan. He wanted everything in its right place, his music and books scrupulously alphabetized. He was enraged about the politics of the forest, the relentless press of the human population against the trees, and sometimes he took it out on her.

He did peruse the books she suggested, and they still went to the movies. Little luxuries, but at first, somehow, they made up for the larger devastations. For a time, she told herself that his true shape was not so bad.

The first time he hit her with his enormous paw, it was painful because it was surprising, not because the blow had much force. It didn't leave a bruise. There was no proof that what happened had happened and this absence of evidence made it easy to push the hitting, the shoving, out of her consciousness. But her family, for all its faults, had been a gentle one. She'd never been beaten in her life and so she had never developed the vigilance, the anxiety that those who are beaten from an early age grow as an invisible second skin. She soldiered on. By the tenth or twelfth time, her ribs were streaked black and blue. She tasted blood for the first time. He always explained that she didn't seem to understand the first time he told her things. She only responded to extreme messages, to violent measures, and for that he was sorry. When her brothers saw her after one of his beatings, she concocted a story about falling into a statue at the Meenakshi temple, but she could tell they didn't believe her.

On the night in question, she was pregnant, and this seemed like the most extreme message of all. The fetus could be a tiger cub, or it could be a human baby. If the latter, Anand would be unlikely to accept the child. If the former, she would not know what to do. Raise another Anand? The notion was grotesque. Far more likely to be a human, she thought, but she couldn't take the risk that it would be a tiger cub in the image of her husband.

She watched the tiger scoop curry with large pieces of warm dosa. She watched as he lectured her. Licking his paws with abandon as he ate. His shiny black nose sweating as he nearly inhaled his spicy food. She was a good cook. He took so much pleasure in her food that she was almost ashamed, thinking of how absurdly close to freedom she stood, and how he didn't even know. She ate more slowly. Later she would briefly wonder if she was trying to be careful about what she was eating. Was the machine right about her?

Every time Anand picked up a dosa, she discreetly wiped her fingers on the edge of her violet-blue dupatta. She didn't hear a word because she was thinking about escape, about a freedom she'd only ever read about or seen in foreign films, a freedom some of her friends—friends with more liberal parents—enjoyed. She was intoxicated by what she thought it would be like, by the imagined sensation of weightlessness.

When Anand was finished with the curd rice, he reached out for a jalebi, his claws scratching the wooden table. It was covered with gouge marks from his carelessness during meals. He paused for a moment before popping the jalebi into his mouth and said, "You haven't made these for months."

"I had some extra time after my cleaning." She sipped her water.

He handed her a jalebi and said, "Take it. You've been working so hard."

"I don't want to get fat."

She set the jalebi on the edge of the plate.

"You look nice, Ma," said Anand. "You don't want to be a skinny thing, do you?"

She shrugged. There was nothing wrong with being thin, she thought, but of course he liked women with curves and meat. He took another jalebi for himself and bit into it, sighing with pleasure as the sweet liquid gushed across his large tongue. He closed his shining yellow eyes. She was nauseated by the carrot-colored syrup sticking to the brownish-orange fur on his paws. The syrup pooled on the fur at his jowls and glimmered under the overhead fluorescent light, where a few moths were hovering. She placed another jalebi on his plate. He grabbed it and scarfed it down. Another and another. With his disarming weakness for sweets, he ate fifteen or sixteen of them with true pleasure, licking his whole paw after each one. After he consumed everything on the plate, she started clearing the table.

When she was done packing the refrigerator with leftovers, she turned. He clutched his head between his massive paws, digging into his own skull with his sharp claws.

"I don't feel well, Ma," he said. "My stomach pains me."

"Go lie down," she said. "We're out of coffee. I'll just go fetch some at the corner store."

He padded to their bedroom. Usually his tail moved as he walked, but it had been stilled by the torpor that accompanied the poison. She unplugged the telephone. She turned and glanced back at the house, its whitewashed exterior and clunky iron gate, the bright pink and blue kolam she had drawn with rice powder on the doorstep just that morning.

Sita had planned her escape carefully. Anand knew nothing of Srinivasan, but she'd read too many suspense novels to risk his discovery. She rode a bus to the northeast edge of the city to save money, instead of hailing a rickshaw.

As she stepped off the bus at the stop by Srinivasan's house, she breathed in the sweet scent of roses, the warmth of hot dough frying. The shouts of the paan wallah, his teeth stained red and his bare arms blackened by eczema. There were so few of these perfect moments in her life, these interstices between one mundane horror and another.

After the Smriti 3000 did its work, she doubted that this perfect moment had ever existed. It seemed to belong to someone else, someone who was not caught up in a nightmare, someone who had been that most reckless of things—happy. Was it enough to feel this giddy sense of expansion, this blooming, for only a few pure weeks in a whole long lifetime? Perhaps this was still more than her parents—at least the version of her parents plagued by health troubles—had ever known.

* * *

Over the years, she played detective behind prison walls. She developed theories about who had killed her husband, the most plausible of which was that her brothers had done it—had noticed her bruises and believed it was better for her to be a widow— not realizing how painfully close she'd been to escape. At first, haunted by her imaginings of what might have happened, she tried to trick Deepak into revealing more than he already had, but after a few failed attempts at squeezing the truth out of him, she grew resigned.

She would never know or understand what her brothers had done, but no matter. There would be no return to the city of pink palaces. Instead, resignation became a kind of friend, a way to stanch the horrible turmoil that hope stirred inside her blood. Sitting in her tiny prison cell, exiled from her village, she could still remember clearly the stars that night, the white swirl of them like splattered milk, and how she thought for that shining instant as she walked down the street, that the whole universe was now hers.

ELEPHANTS IN THE PINK CITY

In the morning, the Sarma family explored the Jaipur palace hotel grounds. Kai lagged a few paces behind his parents and little sister. As they strolled through the spring gardens past blue iridescent peacocks with fanned-out tails, he daydreamed about what it might be like to be a prince, to have the world at your feet. But as they passed the long gravel drive, his thoughts shifted to consider the mystery at its end—the chaotic streets of the Pink City, a phantasmagoria of forts and street markets and fortune-tellers.

Reading to his family from the guidebook, Gopal explained that the palace, a sedate tan edifice with Islamic filigree and blood-red railings, had been converted to a hotel in 1925. "We got special rates because I'm still an Indian citizen."

"Why?" Hema asked, skipping down the brick path. Prahba had dressed Hema in an electric blue chiffon salwar that matched her own.

"They charge Americans more, but they didn't check your citizenship statuses."

"I'm Indian, too!" Hema said.

"You were born in America. If you come here when you're grown up, you'll have to pay full price," Prabha said.

Hema grabbed her mother's hand, yanking for leverage as she jumped.

"Then again, it's not like you'd even come to India if Mom and Dad didn't make you come, Shrimp," Kai said. He straightened his thrift-store pinstriped suit, which he wore with skull cuff links over a Dead Kennedys T-shirt as a form of protest against the vacation.

"Yes, I would, too!" Hema put her hands on her hips and thrust them forward. "I'll visit India every year all my life, just like Mommy and Daddy."

"Nobody made you come with us, Kai!" Gopal said.

"You didn't give me a choice. You never give me a choice." Kai had come out to his parents during Pillayar Chaturthi. He'd been planning to tell them for some time and resolved to do so while they stood in front of the statue of Ganesha, as a priest spooned vibhuti, sacred ash, into his palm. They returned home from the temple in Livermore in a hot car that smelled like musty marigolds and sugar. He blurted it out, wanting to get it over with. Back home in Palo Alto, Kai had a number of bisexual and gay friends who were out to their parents and had been for years. He hadn't expected his own to take it so badly.

"What? I didn't give you a choice?" Gopal slammed the book shut. "What nonsense! We let you wear that ridiculous outfit, didn't we?"

"Engineering college, no dating boys, skipping the spring break trip, visits to India year after year. Everything in my life has to be your way," Kai said.

"That's enough, you two. We're here to have fun, right?" Prabha pleaded. She adjusted her dupatta, breathing heavily as she huffed up the short flight of steps to the hotel. A month before the trip, Prabha had reminded Gopal that Kai would be graduating high school that summer. She was intent on having one last happy family vacation together and so, instead of spending two weeks shuttling between relatives' houses in Chennai, the Sarmas used their second week to tour Rajasthan and Uttar Pradesh, northern parts of India none of them had ever visited.

Kai sighed loudly in the direction of his mother, veered off the path, and cut across the lawn toward the restaurant.

* * *

It was early for lunch, and the Sarmas were the only people seated at the palace's Pearl Restaurant. On the gaudy gold-papered walls hung gilt-framed mirrors reflecting infinite rows of polished wooden tables and a wide Persian carpet, violet with hot-pink roses. None of them felt quite right under the chandeliers, but Kai was the only one to voice it.

"All this is too fancy. Biriyanis and pilafs and meat." Kai gestured at the placid Renaissance frescoes in oval frames that loomed in the high ceiling. "I just want idlis and sambar."

"We've been away from Chennai a day, you can't be sick of North Indian food yet." Gopal scanned the detailed menu. Kai knew his father was looking at the prices.

"Kai da, you can't spend this whole vacation complaining. What would you like to do today?" Prabha asked.

He frowned. "Nothing. Watch TV maybe."

"But you only turn eighteen once! We should celebrate, so you won't forget."

"We're going to the elephant polo match," Gopal reminded Prabha.

Kai rolled his eyes. The waiter appeared, quietly holding his pen and notepad ready. "You are ready to order, sir?"

Gopal waved a squat hand. "A Kingfisher beer for everyone at the table—except the little one. Do you want a mango lassi, kutty?" he asked Hema. She nodded. The waiter jotted down their orders and smiled with an obsequiousness that made Kai cringe.

Kai ordered only a chicken appetizer.

"That all you want?" Gopal asked. "Get something fancier."

Kai shrugged. "I'd rather have a bucket of KFC, but this'll do."

"You never eat properly," Prabha said. "That's why you're so depressed all the time."

"Not this again."

Prabha's face crinkled, but her tone was conciliatory. "We'll go out again for your birthday when we get back home."

"So, this is an exciting time for you, Kai." Gopal spoke in a cheery voice. "Where are your friends going to college?"

"Mostly UCs."

"And Gavin?"

"How would I know?"

The waiter set down three glasses brimming with amber beer and the mango lassi. Gavin was Kai's best friend, the blue-eyed boy he'd harbored a crush on for three years, the only other boy at his school who bought indie vinyl records and skateboarded at the bowl to The Clash, the boy who'd gone with him to the thrift store to buy the pinstriped suit. The boy who, just last week while they were studying calculus, told Kai that even though he was bi, he just wasn't attracted to *him*. A cute redheaded girl in their Spanish class had already asked Gavin to prom, and he'd said yes.

After the waiter left, Gopal took a sip of his beer. "You're not friends anymore?"

"Nope. You'll be happy to know."

"I didn't want you to stop being friends."

"No, you just told me I couldn't date him, that I couldn't date anyone I find attractive. Which doesn't matter because he doesn't even like me like that."

Hema sipped her mango lassi. Prabha frowned. "Do we have to talk about this in front of your sister? Kai, you know that all this gay business makes us uncomfortable. Let's talk about something pleasant. And how would you know you're gay, anyway?" Gopal continued. "At your age, you don't know."

"Shh." Prabha swatted Gopal's hand lightly.

"Right, you're so concerned about making my birthday special, but let's chat about what college my so-called friends are going to, now that you've forced me to pretend I'm not gay, forego music, and go to some stupid engineering school."

His parents glanced at each other, unsure of how to respond. At that moment, the waiters whisked out silver platters stacked with gleaming metal dishes of meat and rice and vegetables and pulses. Ceramic plates were gently set before them. Trailed by a fragrant vapor of cardamom and anise, the waiters left.

The jubilant hum of Rajasthani being spoken just outside the restaurant doors drifted into the restaurant. Moments later, a group of young men paraded into the dining hall and sat around three tables. One set wore long stiff black coats, their heads wrapped in bright orange pagris. The others wore white polo shirts and shorts.

"Who are they?" Hema asked.

"Those are the elephant polo players and handlers," Gopal said. "For the match this afternoon."

Kai caught the eye of one of the polo-shirted men as he sat down at the table next to them. He was handsome, godlike, very young—perhaps twenty, dark with an aquiline nose and light brown eyes. His tender lips had a dusky mauve cast. He smiled radiantly at Kai.

"Do you like your first beer?" Prabha asked Kai. "Is it going to your head?"

Capsaicin from the chiles that seasoned Kai's chicken had disintegrated on his fingers. He rubbed his nose, setting the edges of his nostrils on fire, and took another sip of the cool froth. "It's not bad."

"I remember my first beer," Prabha said. "We had just come to the States, and we were at a taqueria with your father's colleagues, and as a Brahmin girl, you know, I never touched alcohol, it was as forbidden as meat. But everyone at the table was ordering Tecate or margaritas, so I thought to myself, what the heck? I did, too."

"And I look over five minutes later!" Gopal broke in, laughing, though Kai wasn't yet sure what was so funny. "And she had her head on the table! Completely drunk on one beer!"

Irritated, Kai said, "I hate to break it to you guys, but this is not my first beer." The handsome young man was eating a plate of biriyani with his hand, licking his fingers occasionally and speaking loudly to the other men. He smiled again at Kai when their eyes met, a friendliness that so startled Kai that he could only glare at him and then blush, both ashamed and hopeful that such a moment might reoccur, so he could smile back.

"Where have you had one before?" Prabha asked, her voice reedy and high.

"Just around, on the weekends sometimes."

Gopal and Prabha looked at each other with worried eyes but said nothing.

* * *

An hour after lunch, the Sarmas pushed through a gathering crowd of tourists adorned with large reflective sunglasses and gleaming white sunhats. Over the loudspeaker, a man announced the players in English as elephants lumbered by, tails swishing, their wide backs draped in crimson brocade. The elephants' ancient faces and foreheads were ornamented with elaborate dusty designs in pink, chartreuse, and lavender powders.

Kai located the handsome young man patting the back of a slightly smaller elephant as it loped away from his teammates. Two men rode each elephant—one an expert handler in a formal jacket, the other wielding a polo mallet. At one point, the handsome man's small elephant squatted and took a dump. His handler ministered startling, forceful kicks to the elephant's neck. When violence failed to work, he leaned forward and whispered, stroking the recalcitrant behemoth. Kai lifted his binoculars to take a closer look.

"I want to see," Hema demanded.

"Wait a minute," Kai said.

Hema tried to seize the binoculars, but Kai shrugged her tiny, sticky hands away and re-trained the binoculars, trying to discern from the announcer's comments whether his handler had been introduced yet.

"Give it back to me! Give it back to me. It's not just yours." Hema began to cry, and the spectators sitting in front of them turned to look at her.

"Kai, give it to your sister already! What in bloody hell are you doing?" Gopal snapped. Kai numbly handed the binoculars to his sister. Then the match began.

There were four elephants on each side, black jackets battling red. The smaller two elephants on each team were on the front lines, to attack, while two larger elephants remained behind to defend their goals. A referee sat astride a docile elephant that followed the teams back and forth.

Once the game was in full swing, the handsome man's elephant snapped to attention and charged toward the goal, the handsome man pushing the ball expertly with his stick. Kai jumped up and yelled. A sweaty man in shorts ran after one of the other elephants to scoop up its giant turds. The ball zipped back and forth. The elephants were stomping and trumpeting, their large ears flapping. With comedic timing, one of the red defender's elephants plopped down squarely in the middle of the goal as the handsome man's small elephant approached and scored. The crowd cheered.

Kai leaned over and hissed at Hema, making a menacing face. "I want the binoculars."

"No!"

"Come on! Quit being such a fucking pain in the ass."

"No!" She exhaled with a fake sob. Kai tried to grab the binoculars, but she held them away from him.

"Stop it, Kai," Gopal said, his voice even.

"Stop what? Why do you keep taking her side?"

"I'm not taking her side. She has a hard time seeing because she's small. Fair is fair."

"As long as fair is fair, I'm your son. Not your punching bag."

Prabha rested a soft hand on his shoulder. "Kai, let's talk about this later. When we get back to the room."

"Punching bag? What nonsense!" His father's eyes darkened, an eclipse.

"Ever since I told you that I'm gay, you treat me like dirt." Kai slumped forward, his suit jacket over his narrow shoulders feeling too brash, too big.

"I told you, I don't want to hear about that gay business. We're not going to agree, so let's just drop it."

A little man sauntered up and down the slope between rows of spectators, shouting in a nasal twang as he hawked boiled peanuts in little paper cones. Gopal yawned. "Let's go back to the rooms. I could use a nap."

"I'm going to buy a snack and walk around." Kai stood. "I'll meet you guys back in the room later. Looks like they're pretty much done."

The crowd cheered as the game concluded. The riders dismounted. Kai's player pumped his fist. Kai followed the peanut hawker, bought a cone, and popped peanuts into his mouth one by one as he climbed the steps and trudged along the marble walkway, making his way onto the garden path, and past a swimming pool.

From a distance, he watched the swarm of tourists disperse. He hurried in the other direction, shading his eyes from the sun. There wasn't much time before the tourists who'd come only for the match tried to leave the compound. Two guards in burgundy suits stood at the end of the gate, and they nodded at him and said, "Good evening, sir. Will you need a driver, sir?"

Kai said no, and they opened the gates.

* * *

As the gates closed behind him, Kai reveled in the freedom of not knowing where he was going, of being free from his parents' recitation of facts, their tedious schedules and intricate plans. A mangy three-legged dog limped across the street. Three beggar women with thinning silver hair sat on the side of the road. One of them hobbled toward him and he hurried forward to escape her outstretched arms and upturned palms.

In the late afternoon light, the city glowed rose, luminous, rising out of the deep shadows. As he approached the bazaar, Kai heard the men. He immediately recognized the cadences of their speech though he could not understand what they were saying, the joyful rolling sound of it washing over him. Turning, Kai spotted his player in the crowd.

The player took short strides, a cigarette drooping from his mouth as he searched his pockets for a lighter. He made eye contact with Kai a moment later, and this time Kai smiled.

The player raised his hand in greeting. "So, it's you again. American, no?"

"Yes."

The other men paid him no mind. The player stopped. His eyes bore a sweet, overly sincere intensity. Kai blushed and looked away. Unfazed, the man said, "What are you doing now? You would like to celebrate with us?"

Kai glanced back at the palace gates, now one hundred yards behind him. The group of men strode ahead with arms slung over each other's shoulders, singing and carousing with beer bottles in their hands. "Why not?"

Kai introduced himself. The player said his name was Vikrant. He lit a cigarette and handed it to Kai. "But call me Vik."

"I can say Vikrant," Kai said. He was thinking of how his father mocked his American accent when trying to say Tamil words.

"You are wanting me to call you Kailash, then?"

"No, I'm just Kai."

"Okay then." Vik lit another cigarette. He hooked arms with Kai and ran to catch up with the group. When they stopped running, Kai took a deep drag and coughed.

"You are not smoking cigarettes?" Vik asked. He held out a hand to take the cigarette back.

Kai waved his hand away. "Not many people smoke where I'm from."

Vik walked arm-in-arm with Kai, his warm skin pressed against Kai's skin. Kai tried to suppress his excitement. His father had once explained that men were publicly affectionate with each other in India, and it didn't mean they were gay.

* * *

The deeper they traveled into the heart of the Pink City, the more crowded it became. Businessmen and young women drifted by in faded jeans. Mothers in beaded salwar kameezes with their children hurried past the men. In the bazaar, Vik began speaking in Rajasthani to another man, and released Kai's arm. Disappointed, Kai fell a little behind.

In one stall, a white-haired woman perched on a stool behind a gold birdcage that housed a small green parrot. Tiny pastel strips papered the floor of the cage. Schoolchildren in plaid uniforms were handing the woman rupees and taking slips of paper in exchange. Kai watched for a few minutes. As they left, a little boy knocked over the birdcage. The cage door flew open. The parrot fluttered out and began hopping down the street.

Kai stooped and picked up the parrot. The parrot's heart, big and wild, was beating furiously beneath his bright, fragile feathers. His wings had been clipped. The old woman spoke to Kai quickly, and he shook his head, repeating, "I speak English." His English broke and he fell into an accent. His cousins always mocked him, assuming this was an affectation, but falling into an accent happened every year when he came to India, as if he were remembering something he'd forgotten.

Kai righted the cage and opened his fist. The parrot hopped back into the cage and pecked at the slips, uncovering a rose slip with his beak. Before the woman closed the door, the parrot hopped back to the door and bowed toward Kai. He smiled and took the slip from the parrot's beak. The fortune was written in characters, probably Rajasthani characters, which he could not read. He turned to ask Vik what it said, but Vik and his friends were nowhere to be seen.

He had not paid much attention to the geography of the bazaar. Where had he entered?

As he moved down the street, a group of thin children with scraggly hair jostled him. He stepped on a boy's bare foot. "Sorry, sorry," he apologized. The boy looked at him with a fearful expression before hurrying toward his group. The sun dipped behind the buildings, sending the Pink City into heavy shadow.

"Do you speak English?" he asked a young woman crossing the street. She wore acid-washed jeans under her beaded orange kurtha top.

"Yes."

"Is that the way to the palace hotel?"

"Which one?" she asked. "There are several."

"The closest one." Tears pricked his eyes. He couldn't remember its proper name.

She spun him and pushed him back into the bazaar, telling him to walk that way. He thanked her and hurried blindly in the direction she'd sent him. A man shoved him, and he reeled. A group of chickens blocked his way. Skirting them, he once again spotted the old woman and her parrot. He realized he'd already passed the vendors selling bric-a-brac—sandalwood elephants, miniature ivory gods, larger cowrie shells carved with tableaux, mindless seashell games—many times.

The seashell games reminded him of eating murukku with his father on his grandparents' patio and drinking down the rich cumin flavor with cold buttermilk. The fragrance of his father's Old Spice aftershave as he leaned in to plop cowry shells into an indented wooden game board. There were periods he'd gotten along quite well with his father, often when his father helped him solve puzzles. There had been moments when his father proudly brought him to his office, introduced him to his pale, pocket-protected colleagues, and explained binary code to him. He knew the rift between them had developed long before he'd announced he was gay, but he couldn't pinpoint the moment.

Kai heard someone shouting his name. Still reminiscing about murukku and buttermilk and puzzles, he thought for a moment it was his father come to find him, but when he whipped around, he spotted Vik smoking a cigarette outside a building farther down the street and beckoning him.

"There you are," Vik said. Two blue smoke rings, no trace of worry in his face. "I am thinking you are lost."

"I was. But here I am."

"I will buy you a beer. You drink beer, no? Come."

Inside the warm bar, a ceiling fan was spinning and AC/DC reverberated on the surround system. Polo players and elephant whisperers huddled around tables, drinking beers. A few young women in jeans wove between the groups, laughing.

After ordering their beers, Kai and Vik spoke about their homes, about their fathers, about what they planned to do in the future. Vik had grown up poor in a nearby village and moved to Jaipur only the year before. He worked as a jewelry salesman during the week, and as an elephant polo player on weekends. Kai revealed he wanted to be a musician and go on tour with his band, but his parents wanted him to be an engineer.

Kai searched his pockets, planning to buy the next round. He realized with a start that his wallet, which had only held two 1,000-rupee notes and some change, was gone. He remembered the children who'd rubbed against him. "Oh my god, oh my god," he gasped. "I was pickpocketed."

"This is happening to tourists all the time." Vik went to the bar to order two more beers.

After drinking another beer, Kai ambled into the bathroom. A stench rose from the concrete floor—a foulness so strong it made him woozy. Kai unzipped. It took a few minutes to relax enough to piss in the unfamiliar bathroom. He finished and went to wash his hands.

Vik opened the door and closed it behind him. He stood there for a moment, not smiling. "You like me, no?"

Kai shrugged. He remembered the electricity of Vik's arm touching his arm, the hairs on both arms tickling each other, the sensation of desire. But he knew, too, he might be reading this wrong. There might be signals crossed, there might be disgust.

Then Vik took Kai's face in his warm palms. He held Kai's face for a moment and his eyes shimmered as he swooped in and touched Kai's mouth with his own, before kissing him. Kai felt himself drowning and then saved, as Vik's tongue explored his mouth. Vic's calloused hands slipped under the back of Kai's shirt. He smelled something on Vik, an odd animalic smell, perhaps the elephants. Vik pulled away and unzipped Kai's pinstripe trousers.

"Soft hands," Vik whispered as he turned Kai around. Kai's jaw pressed against the cold concrete wall, and for a moment, he wondered whether this was it and he wanted to giggle, *soft hands, soft hands.*

* * *

After it was over, Vik left to smoke outside, and Kai washed himself in the sink. They returned to the palace hotel in a companionable silence, with Vik's arm slung around Kai's shoulders. All the vendors at the bazaar had cleared out their wares.

"Where you are going now?" Vik asked as they approached the gates through the indigo darkness.

"Agra. Tomorrow we go to the Taj Mahal."

"And when you will be home?"

"Next week."

"I will come to California to visit you someday," Vik declared with great confidence.

For a moment, Kai was pleased, but his joy quickly soured. He hadn't expected to see Vik again. He didn't even want to see him again, but he couldn't say why. His English faltered as he tried to reestablish their connection without the assistance of a beer buzz. Kai imagined his friends' reactions to the funny elephant polo player from Jaipur. Anticipating his father's reaction, he found the prospect of a visit terrifying.

Still, Kai agreed, and Vik handed him a pen. He wrote his name on the back of one of Vik's jewelry shop cards, a tacky affair with mismatched gold retro type.

Vik took hold of his hand. "You will remember me, no?"

Kai nodded. When they kissed, their lips were soft and smoky, tongues blunted by beer, tracing their departure. Kai tried to memorize the smell, so he wouldn't forget: elephants, musky cologne, sweat, coconut oil, metallic hair gel. But in a moment, too quickly, Vik pulled away.

He clapped Kai on the shoulder. "I'll be seeing you!"

At the gate, a guard asked, "Are you Kailash Sarma, sir?" He explained that Kai's parents had called the police for fear that Kai had gotten lost. The gates opened, and Kai looked over his shoulder. Vik was gone.

As he and the guard trudged toward the well-lit lobby, Kai pictured his father's possible reactions, variations on his prior reactions to various misadventures. They would go back to the hotel room, and his father would beat him with a belt, as he had once many years before. They would go back to the hotel room, and his father would start yelling. They would go back to the hotel room, and his father would not talk to him, his deafening silence saying so many things while saying nothing at all.

By the black marble concierge desk of the lobby, two men in olive uniforms were talking to his parents. Hema, clutching her bigheaded baby doll, noticed him first and barreled toward him. "You're okay!" She wrapped her tiny arms around his hips.

"We were so worried," Prabha said, enveloping him in her familiar scent of honey and talcum.

"What happened?" his father asked. Kai couldn't read his face.

"Everything all right, sir?" an officer asked.

"Yes. I thought I'd take a walk in the Pink City, but I got lost and pickpocketed. One of the polo players from this afternoon recognized me from lunch and brought me back."

"But you weren't hurt, were you?" his mother asked.

Kai repeated he was fine, half wanting to admit to his mother—for so long his staunchest ally, even though, of late, she had served as a foe—that something had changed, that his body hurt, that the same thing that hurt also made him feel victorious and confident. He decided not to say a word—perhaps this was the plastic sort of son his parents had wanted all along, a son whose adventures were carefully concealed from them.

Inside their suite, a tray of oranges, figs, lychees, coconut chunks, and mango slices rested on a wood divan carved with marching elephants. "We ordered room service while we were waiting for you, but we saved you some." Hema kicked off her slippers.

"Have some pomegranate seeds." Prabha handed him a silver dish.

Kai eased onto the edge of the master bed with its enormous dream-white canopy, dug into the pile of pomegranate seeds with his fingers, and waited for his father to tear into him for going to the Pink City without them. To his surprise, Gopal patted him on the shoulder, the way he had when he was small. "I love you, Kai."

"I'm sorry I worried you," Kai repeated, oddly touched. His heart came up in his chest, clenching with an unfamiliar ache. He couldn't remember the last time his father had said he loved him.

"Can we go to the magic show on the lawn?" Hema climbed on the bed and began running from one end to the other. The bed rippled with her bounces.

Gopal glanced at his watch. "We might just make it."

Kai's pinstripe suit pants were splashed at the cuffs in some sort of greyish-brown liquid, possibly sewage or mud. He searched his luggage for fresh clothes.

As he changed in the bathroom, he found the rose fortune written in Rajasthani in his pocket. He opened it and looked at the foreign characters. He'd forgotten to ask Vik what his fortune was. Nobody he knew could translate it. After he had changed into fresh clothes, he slipped the rose fortune into a pocket of his suitcase. Already Vik's finely chiseled cheekbones and luminous light-brown eyes were fading from his memory.

That night on the lawn, the Sarma family would sit in the long shadows witnessing fire-eaters and muscular men striding barefoot on hot coals, and the following afternoon, they would ride the train to Agra to see the world's greatest monument to everlasting love. Just one week later, they'd fly in a rickety domestic plane to Chennai to bid teary farewells to Kai's grandparents, before flying via Singapore to SFO, where they would settle back into their modest house, and Kai would finish his senior year of high school, never again speaking to Gavin or skateboarding in the bowl. Although Kai would never hear from Vik all the rest of his life, he would remember as an aphrodisiac the odor of elephants, and he would remember the parrot that plucked and handed him a rose fortune in a language he could not read.

LOVE SONGS FOR A LOST CONTINENT

I might have been a small boy when I first heard about the lost continent of Kumari Kandam, and when the stories came up in a folklore seminar at UC Berkeley many years later, a strange shiver moved through my heart, a moment of nostalgic recognition.

Legend goes that Shiva bequeathed Kumar Kandam to his daughter Pandaia. There in that deep southern paradise, Tamilians fished for pearls and wore dresses fashioned from flowers and foliage and animal skins. The Pandyan kings formed three Tamil sangams, assemblies of poets and scholars, to foster a love of literature, poetry, and knowledge among their subjects. But as everyone knows, bliss never lasts, and utopias are, by their very nature, doomed. The ocean swelled. Whipped into a frenzy by some mysterious force, tsunamis swallowed the sangams with unmatched ferocity. Men continued to die of thirst for Kumari Kandam, but the homeland was submerged, lost forever in the salty black waves.

My father unspooled tales of the lost continent on warm nights. Rattling and keening, trains chugged past our Palo Alto bungalow and the ghostly scent of star jasmine blew into my bedroom window. My mother knew the stories better, and after he started, she would embellish them in her warm husky voice, and so it was her voice, thick with wonder, that followed me into my dreams.

What I didn't realize back then was that the Kumari Kandam legend was about a longing for what was past and glorious for Tamil people. A longing for origins in a vast land that stretched from Tamil Nadu to Madagascar—origins that might never have existed.

* * *

When I was twenty-eight, I was awarded a Fulbright research grant that would take me back to Chennai. To explain the purpose of the grant, I reminded my father and mother of the stories they'd told me.

"Why on earth would we tell you those lowbrow tales of Kumarinatu?" my father asked, scratching his grey beard. "There's no scientific proof for them."

My mother said nothing. She leaned against the back of the scarlet couch and shut her eyes. She'd felt fatigued and unwell for some time, so I thought nothing of her silence.

"Maybe you wanted me to feel a kinship?"

My father swiveled away in his natty grey office chair and gave a short barking laugh. "Looking at you now, how I wish I hadn't."

* * *

"What a thing to say," Komakal said with disapproval when I recounted the discrepancy between my father's account and mine on one of our dates.

With dark amber skin, she was slight and graceful, but she had muscular thighs like the trunks of two palms. The long mass of her hair streamed in a curly, undulating tangle down her back. She pursed her lips and rolled over and away from me. I rose from the hard cot where we'd finished having sex and pulled a stainless steel jug of water I'd boiled from the refrigerator. I poured the water into a tumbler and drank it, then sank down next to Komakal again, running a hand along the supple curve of her hip.

"Yes, but he just wishes I'd become an engineer or doctor. He thinks maybe he sent me off on the wrong path by telling me Tamil myths instead of reading me nonfiction."

"But Tamizh is your mother tongue! Or it should be. Typical Brahmin. He probably thinks Sanskrit is a better language. Ridiculous! But you agree that Tamizh is the most beautiful language in the world, don't you?" Komakal stroked my cheek with her warm hand. Unlike me and the other second-generation kids I knew in the Bay Area, she pronounced the name of our language correctly and spelled it *Tamizh* the way purists do. Not Tamil with an "l," but with the "zh," a sound more like a "rah," a sound with no English equivalent. This was one of many tiny things that endeared her to me.

I didn't know Sanskrit well enough to say, but I wanted to keep looking at her, into the summery midnight of her long-lashed eyes, and I already understood her—she would storm out if she suspected me a traitor to her cause. I nodded.

"It's an ancient language. I don't understand why you wouldn't. And I don't think I would like your father much."

"No, no, he's kind, he's smart. You'll love him." He did have those traits, but I wasn't at all certain she would love him. She'd assessed him correctly. Behind closed doors, my father did occasionally disparage lower-caste people, in spite of marrying my mother, and he did see his family as a kind of chosen people. Worse yet, from Komakal's perspective, he was the son of a long line of bureaucrats. His father was a reasonably well-to-do civil servant for the British who apparently hadn't cared if India would acquire its independence at all.

"I'd rather meet your mother," she said. I'd told her that my mother, a successful engineer, was of a lower caste. Which one was unknown, because her parents had been vigorously anti-caste, and didn't want her to carry any sort of stigma. This satisfied Komakal.

In my mother, she saw a tough and independent woman who had risen from oppression, a kindred spirit.

I met Komakal while she was working at the university library where I spent many anxious hours, not at all sure that my research had value. I was blocked. Superficially, I understood most of what I was hearing and reading, but so much was foreign, all these things to which my parents had never exposed me, but that I was assumed to understand.

On the day I first spoke to Komakal, I'd taped a short, blustery man in a crisp white dress shirt who reminded me of my father. He said he didn't understand why they still taught fabrications like Kumari Kandam in Tamil Nadu. "We should be focused on IT, on becoming a global power for IT," he said, adjusting his gold wire spectacles. "Instead some people stay bogged down in myths, in rewriting the past. Pathetic."

After interviewing him, I'd walked to the library to hunt for memorable passages of text to intersperse with the interview. Eventually, I thought, I might have enough to make a documentary.

Wearing an aquamarine salwar and jeans that set off her dark skin, Komakal was standing on a stepladder shelving linguistics books about Tamil. There was something regal in her bearing, a don't-fuck-with-me look, that had immediately attracted me. I had an excuse to talk to her because several books in that section were about the Tamil nationalists who'd resisted the forceful imposition of Hindi after independence from the British and spurred the Tamil devotion movement—they were among the greatest raconteurs of the Kumari Kandam legend.

From our first conversation, Komakal had been clear about who she was: a Tamil girl from a lower-caste background who hated colonialism, imperialism, and a number of other -isms of which I couldn't keep track. At first, she didn't want to have anything to do with an American man, especially one with a Tamil Brahmin father. She was terrified by the prospect of being sucked into what she perceived as my consumerist Western life. But the way she spoke was somehow deeply familiar. And so, I persisted.

"Did you come to Chennai because you hate it there?" Komakal asked on our first official date: a trip to Karpagambal Mess, a cheap restaurant on a noisy thoroughfare where they served the food on bright green banana leaves.

She was eating a greasy chili uttapam with her fingers, dipping pieces into a plastic cup of orange molaga podi, and her small snub nose glistened with beads of sweat. A dull olive lizard skittered up the stucco wall behind her. An M.S. Subbulakshmi song, with its firm tabla beat and its quavering vocal mountains and valleys, was turned up too loud.

She'd chosen the restaurant, possibly to test me, and since I seemed to be passing this test, I stayed mum about my headache, trying to steal as much happiness as I could from the moment. "No. I mean, I was alienated from my life there. I didn't belong, no matter how much I tried. But I wouldn't say I hate it exactly."

"You felt like an outsider? But you were born there, no?"

"Yeah, but over there, people care about their jobs more than anything else." My older sisters, one a heart surgeon and the other a mergers-and-acquisitions attorney, fit perfectly. "How prestigious the job is, how much you're achieving. There was no time for art or eccentricity or humor—any of the things I care about."

"So, they are materialistic."

I didn't like to think of it that way—she said "materialistic" in a self-satisfied way, like it was a dirty word, but I knew from watching her enjoyment of the beautiful trinkets I'd brought her at the library that she cared about nice things as much as the next person. "No, they were good people. I just didn't fit with them."

"Most of the people I know who move to the States are like you. Upper-caste people from families with money who go to the States and make even more money."

"Is that really how you see me?" I was hurt but tried not to show it. I had only known her for a month and I wasn't sure how vulnerable I should make myself. Of course, she discounted my mother's lower-caste influence. A mother like mine—ambitious, successful, a Silicon Valley workaholic, and yet brought up lower caste in an Indian village seemed about as probable as the yali—a mythic creature carved into the sandstone pillars of South Indian temples in the sixteenth century. The graceful body of a lion, the tusks of an elephant, a sinuous serpent's tail. She didn't fit any familiar narrative.

"There's nothing wrong with it." Komakal shrugged and put the last fragment of uttapam onto her tongue. "It's just who you are." My uneasiness dissipated.

Komakal quickly brought me to her bed. She smelled sweet from coconut oil I'd massaged into her scalp and rubbed along her back, working my hands around her torso to her breasts and pointed nipples. We ran our fingers over and into each other's bodies, whispering against the jangling cacophony of the busy street below.

Around her bedroom were large pieces of driftwood, haunting paintings in which oil colors oozed into each other. Flat black figures of women were stenciled over the blues and greens. On one driftwood canvas, an upside-down woman dove into a dark knot of wood, while on another, a woman huddled in a fetal position as waves of ultramarine and indigo and kelly green washed over her. Komakal painted them in the evenings after work. Time and again in the coming months, I was drawn to them. I couldn't stop staring at their strange beauty, a reflection of their artist. I asked her what they meant, but she had no answer.

* * *

Months later, we took the overnight train on a clandestine trip to Kanyakumari, a beach town at the southern tip of India. Komakal usually went back to her parents' village on the weekends, but she lied and told them she was visiting a friend from university so that we could travel together. Three oceans in varying bands of brackish tourmaline merged around the beach—the Indian Ocean, the Bay of Bengal, and the Arabian Sea. In the distance, an island rose above the waves, home to an imposing black stone statue of the Tamil poet and philosopher Thiruvalluvar, more than a hundred feet tall. Komakal had suggested the trip as part of my research, explaining that the land was considered part of Kumari Kandam, one of the only parts that hadn't been submerged in the floods.

My father's money, a supplement to the grant money, paid for our fourteen-hour train ride from Chennai and for our fifth-floor room in a luxury high-rise hotel with white marble floors and shimmering tangerine curtains that smelled of camphor and otherwise spare accommodations. We pretended we were married in order to stay in a hotel room together.

"I don't know if what you felt was so unusual. Displacement might be the natural state, even a defining state of being Tamizh," Komakal said as we walked along the beach.

"What do you mean?"

She shrugged. "Our people are seafarers. They've moved everywhere around the globe. And really, Tamizh is a marginalized language in greater India, even today, isn't it?"

She phrased it like a question, but she already knew the answer she wanted. My family never talked about any of this. We talked about what we were working on now, about our hopes and future plans, not the past. I wondered if my father would see my new girlfriend as a troublemaker.

"This is why we must keep fighting for ourselves, for our culture and our language."

"I don't know. You seem fine," I said.

"What do you know? You're American!"

"You're right." I didn't want to get into a fight on our otherwise idyllic trip.

She continued, seemingly unable to let it go. "They used to grab at my breasts and laugh. In school. Those Brahmin boys. They assumed that my body was for them."

"I'm sorry."

"Of course, Brahmins don't understand the value of their true mother tongue, the language of the people. They're too busy promoting Sanskrit. You know, my uncle believed so strongly in Tamil, in devotion to Tamil, he set himself on fire. Immolation."

She was proud her uncle had set himself on fire. Doused himself in lighter fluid in the street and lit a match. I imagined the mob, the shock—all for a language, an identity. There was nothing I believed in so strongly, although I wished I did. I was horrified, yet I shuddered with a faint pleasure, thrilled that my girlfriend was from a faraway circumstance, this long line of people who were passionate artists and activists, living in the moment, rather than antiseptic and supportive of an increasingly conservative government. My father would never set himself aflame for any reason, too concerned with accumulating wealth and the security that came with it to ever consider radical politics.

"I think of my uncle all the time," she said. "I see him sometimes in the stars, and when I think about my problems, I think about what he would do."

"Was he depressed?"

Her eyes narrowed. "He was despondent for a reason."

We strolled along the sand for miles, wandering between the long traditional wood boats of the fishermen. The orange orb of the sun hung low over the darkening ocean waves. The sands shifted colors—gold and rose and crimson. My heart stopped. It was spellbinding.

Komakal began telling me the story of Kanya Devi, an avatar of Parvati who was to marry Lord Shiva. When Shiva didn't come to the ceremony on time, Kanya Devi remained a virgin, and the wedding rice that was left uncooked became the stones on the colorful sand of the beach.

After she finished her story, Komakal said in a quiet voice, "You don't love me."

"What I don't understand is how a single couple in Hindu mythology can have so many different stories. We know, of course, that Parvati did marry Shiva."

"You're avoiding my question."

"Of course I love you."

I had never loved any woman in a romantic way. The first of my girlfriends, an outspoken Israeli girl who'd gone to my high school, had been troubled by my refusal to lie and tell her I loved her, especially after we chose to go to the same college. She implied that my depression was an affectation. "And your liberal politics are a fucking sham," she said, tossing her long sandy hair as she dumped me. It took years to recover, but from that, I learned my lesson.

When the second girlfriend, a Stanford medical student and a Tamil Brahmin, second-generation like me, became enraged that I wouldn't tell her I loved her, she began browbeating me. She shook my hand, shouting, "Just say it, just say it!" so many times that one day while we watched a flock of pelicans lift off at Baylands, I blurted it out, feeling the pain of the lie like a gallstone. I knew that I would disappoint her, and sure enough, I cheated on her the following week.

When it came time to say it to the third girlfriend, a Brazilian comparative literature professor who had immigrated to the states during graduate school, I said it preemptively after sex, kissing the tiny star-shaped mole hovering just above her pale pink lip. Then, racked with guilt, I broke up with her, citing intimacy issues.

In that moment with Komakal, I wasn't lying. At least, I believed I loved her. Her emotional intensity was like a fiery corona, drawing me ever deeper into her, but I felt something else, too, a darker sentiment. I couldn't identify what it was in that moment.

"You love me?" She stopped and turned to face me. Behind her, the sun had slipped into a cloud at the horizon, a crescent moon perched pale in the sky, and the beach adopted the numinous blue-silver cast of a holy place.

I faltered—I'd never loved anyone before, how did I know that I loved her? Would she think this meant I also wanted to marry her?—but then I said it again, and it was like I was making her a promise, not just describing my feelings. She told me she loved me, too. Her glowing face reflected the blue-silver light. "I want you to meet my parents. I want you to see the village where I grew up."

"What did you tell them about me?"

"I said you were a new friend from the library," she said.

"Are they going to hate me?"

"They won't like that your father is Brahmin." She spun away for a moment into the long looming shadow of a palm tree. I couldn't see her face. "But tell them about your Kumari Kandam research. They'll like that."

"Do they know that we're dating?"

"They might guess."

That night, she fell asleep quickly and I lay awake in the moonlight, breathing in the wild honeysuckle and camphor. I climbed out of the bed and put on my shirt, massaging the crick in my neck.

The marble floor was ice-cold, and I adjusted the air conditioning. At the teak writing desk, I scribbled notes about Kanya Kumari, what I'd observed, and the myth about Kanya Devi that Komakal had told me. She'd lit a fire inside me. As I looked at my notes—more notes than I'd written during any research session in Chennai so far—I realized that if I stayed with her, I might actually understand the direction of my work and why I was doing it. It was all coming into focus. I stayed there at the desk until close to morning, and then I slouched back to the bed and crawled on top of a shimmery gold throw pillow as if I'd never left, nuzzling her neck and smelling the coconut oil in her curly hair, nostalgic for a time that was already gone, the time before I'd articulated my feelings and committed myself to Komakal.

* * *

I suppose I could have backed out of the dinner with Komakal's family in the village, if only because the work was going so well. Instead I took a southbound train, bearing a box of imported European chocolates. Komakal came to the Nagapattinam train station to greet me, and as soon as she saw the box, she frowned. "Why couldn't you get South Indian sweets?" She tossed the box in a bush by the station that was still damp from the first deluge of the winter monsoons.

"They are not going to hold that against me."

"But I want you to make a good first impression."

"It won't look good that I didn't bring anything."

She considered this and then retrieved the box. We rode her father's motorcycle from the station past a white temple, tremendous and intricately carved, and what seemed like a never-ending stretch of lush green rice paddies to her house. The village was less than a mile from the ocean, and I could smell brine and fish in the warm breeze. I'd never ridden on a motorcycle before, and it felt both emasculating and exciting to be pressed against her thin back, her fragile spine, as she wound through the streets, zooming past a series of blackened roadside hovels and beggars before arriving in the heart of the town at the dilapidated ochre house where her parents and younger brother lived.

As I'd suspected, Komakal had exaggerated her parents' sentiments. I started to wonder if the staunch political beliefs she described in such lacerating terms were purely her own. Her parents seemed to be ordinary middle-class people with the simple hope that their daughter would marry a boy who'd treat her well. Her mother, Agira, accepted the box of sweets with effusive warmth, and she and Komakal went into the kitchen to finish cooking. Her father, Mayavan, brought me into the living room where he was watching a cricket match on an old television with Komakal's fifteen-year-old brother. The house smelled like an amalgam of cumin, red chilies, turmeric, mustard seeds, and sandalwood, a comforting odor that reminded me of my parents' kitchen.

There were, however, certain ways in which Komakal had described her parents perfectly. I thought they would assume I spoke English and address me accordingly, since they knew the language, and that's what Komakal did. At home my parents and older sisters had only ever spoken English, and perhaps this had given me a warped understanding of Indians. But Komakal's family spoke to each other and to me in a tangled black velvet skein of rapid-fire Tamil only occasionally appliqued with English words. I struggled to keep up.

"Komakal tells us that you are here doing research. You plan to be a university professor?" Her father passed me a steel plate of moist idlis, still steaming.

"I'm not sure. In the States, a lot of people don't decide these things so early."

"You are twenty-eight, no?"

I was twenty-nine but wasn't sure I should correct him.

"Appa, he just told you what he's researching. Ask him questions about that," Komakal interrupted. Her mother shushed her, and then, more than a little embarrassed, I voluntarily nattered on about my Kumari Kandam research, and what I was currently doing, recording interviews with everyday people about what they'd been taught in schools and at home about the lost continent.

"Your job is to go around asking people about this?" Mayavan's hand paused over his fish curry. He looked incredulous. "And they pay you?"

"I study folklore because it reveals something larger." I proceeded to quote buzzwords from my application. "I'm writing about colonialism and post-colonialism, and the rebuilding of identity and pride in the face of oppression through oral storytelling."

Mayavan still looked perplexed as he helped himself to the kosumalli, a shredded carrot salad. Komakal's brother said, genuinely surprised and with no trace of malice, "You went to university for *that*?"

I nodded. Agira told him, "But the Fulbright is very prestigious." I felt grateful.

Komakal said, "He's studying the folklore around Tamil devotion, Appa—the folklore around Perippa's movement. He's bringing attention to the language, to us."

"That bloody stupid movement?" Irritation and sorrow for the older brother who had immolated himself flickered across Mayavan's face. From what Komakal told me, and the fervor for Tamil she possessed, I hadn't expected he would feel this way. Komakal's eyes flickered blacker, and she scooped curd rice into her mouth with her fingers. Agira looked down at her plate. Then Mayavan began talking about the match he'd been watching on television and asked if I followed cricket. Flustered because I'd only ever seen *Lagaan*, I told him that I didn't, but that I did watch baseball and weren't they sort of similar? I could tell immediately this was the wrong thing to say, and I wanted to sink into the floor.

Agira brought out a dish of kozhukattai, white steamed dumplings. She sensed my hesitation about eating sweets at all, and misinterpreting, asked if I wanted one of the European sweets I'd brought instead. Embarrassed, I immediately grabbed two soft kozhukattai.

I bit into the brown coconut and jaggery filling. "They're delicious! Is that cardamom?"

"You haven't had these before?" she asked.

I admitted that I hadn't and asked for another. At this she beamed with a radiance that lit up her large, fawn-like eyes.

* * *

Everything had gone reasonably well. Or so I thought. After dinner, I rode to the train station on the back of Komakal's motorcycle and kissed her goodbye and returned to Chennai and the wonderful solitude of my research. I was lit up with the possibilities for my documentary about Kumari Kandam mythology, my mind swirling with realizations about how my parents' different castes might have affected the mythology they'd passed on, and how I might elaborate on these subtle distinctions in my work. I waited a day or two before calling. But Komakal didn't answer my phone calls for a month. She changed her shifts at the library, so it took quite a bit of time and effort to track her down. After several attempts, I found her at the checkout counter, and it took some time to muster up the courage to confront her. "Are you angry with me? I thought it went pretty well, considering."

She didn't look me in the eyes. She stacked books, slamming them on the counter. Other library patrons looked up, startled.

"They don't want me to see you anymore."

"I can't believe that. Your mother liked me. You're always amplifying our differences, instead of seeing how much we have in common."

Komakal sighed and shook her head. She stamped another book with undue force, and said, "What is it you think we have in common?"

I paused, wondering what the right answer might be. "We love art and myths and odd people, and all the stuff most people don't care about anymore."

"She was flattered you liked the kozhukattai. But they don't like that you have no real job."

Dismayed, I asked, "Did you explain, really explain, to your father how hard it is to get a Fulbright?"

"Yes, but you were uncertain about whether you'd go on to become a professor, and you have no solid plans, even though you're almost thirty. He doesn't think you're serious—about anything."

Desperation filled me. Somehow her father had peered into my soul and glimpsed how utterly inadequate I was. In that moment, the love I had for her was an immense black ocean, an ocean in wait, an ocean before a storm moves through it. "Let's get married," I said, seizing her small bony hand in mine and kissing it. "I love you. Why not?"

She looked confused. "What is this nonsense?"

"I'm dead serious."

She scowled and withdrew her hand. "You're using me, isn't it?"

"What do you mean?"

Komakal shook her head. Without answer, she returned to her work and I flagged down a rickshaw to take me back to my apartment.

* * *

My research in Chennai was coming to a close, and my usual anxiety and ambivalence about where I belonged pushed to the surface.

Should I return to California, my birthplace, my home? Would it be better to travel around India as I'd planned before I met Komakal? I'd gathered nearly two hundred hours of interviews, and I slowly reviewed them all on my laptop, editing them into a single file. Video clips of older men and women whom I'd convinced to talk about Kumari Kandam. I tried to translate for purposes of subtitling, but I couldn't think clearly without Komakal as inspiration, and the tedious hours passed without my comprehending a word. I couldn't breathe, the sensation of withdrawal was so horrible, the atoms of my body crying out in protest, my outlook sitting there in a cramped Chennai apartment so bleak.

My father called me in the midst of my despair. I told him my fieldwork was mostly complete. He said, "You should come home. Mom's had a health scare, and you know her. She won't ask you to come herself, but she wants you here." A doctor suspected cancer, he said.

"It might be nothing," my father backpedaled after realizing how he'd frightened me. "You could probably take a few more weeks to travel..." But there would be many chances to sightsee in the future, I thought, so I bought a ticket to return home the following week.

* * *

Just two days before the long flight to San Francisco, Komakal called. "I can't paint anymore," she announced immediately.

"Why not?"

"When you're with me, everything's in Technicolor, but when you're gone, it is in black and white. I went to Marina Beach to collect driftwood, and it all seemed so lonely, so pointless. I came back to bed to take rest, and just lay there for three days."

I didn't reply but dropped the book on Chennai's history I was trying to read. A flicker of hope passed through me. Perhaps everything would work out after all.

"I was just surprised when you asked. But, you know, I think my parents would accept us if we got married."

When Komakal swung by the apartment that night, she noticed my suitcases by the door and made the wrong assumption. She told me that she thought she would be moving into my apartment, and that her roommate might not be comfortable living with both of us at her place.

When I explained, her usually soft face crumpled into jagged lines, and she began sobbing. "I don't want to move to the States."

"But it's my home."

"It was far enough, moving to the city."

I took her hands. "My mother's sick." I told her what my father said, that my mother was too proud to summon me home.

"But when would I see my parents?"

"We can fly them out."

Eventually, she calmed down, and claimed she understood, and so we spent the night reunited. We returned to the hole-in-the-wall restaurant where we'd had our first date and ordered the onion and chili uttapam, sambar vada, and buttermilk we'd ordered the first time around. We meandered down Marina Beach, weaving through a labyrinth of oily dark kelp swarmed with flies, breathing in the ocean air and watching lilac suffuse the twilight sky. We returned to my bed, and resumed our tangle of limbs and tongues, the long slow tussle of sex. We spoke about her parents, and how upset Mayavan had been at dinner. "My uncle was the center of my world as a child. He and my father would take me out on the back of the motorcycle and he'd buy me fancy dresses. He spoiled me," Komakal said. "They agreed on everything. My father worshipped his brother. But after my uncle died, I guess he started to think differently, like maybe it was more important to live."

"It's hard to understand how Tamil could matter so much you'd set fire to yourself. I was taken aback about how casual you were about the suicide," I confessed.

She looked at me uncertainly. For a moment she said nothing, but tears welled in her eyes. "You misunderstood. That wasn't me being casual. Without something that's yours, without Tamizh, without your motherland, you'd be nothing! Absolutely nothing."

I nodded to avoid making her deep sadness worse. But I couldn't help but feel a shift inside, and after that, a tidal guilt, for feeling differently than I'd felt before. Had I built up our earlier romance? Had it been an illusion? Or was it that we'd already broken up once, and I knew we would again?

* * *

When she departed in the morning for work, it was still dark outside, and I was only half-conscious, lost in an alluring limbo of fragments and hallucinations. I kissed her and told her I would write and that I would be back in a month or two. I kind of believed myself. She smiled in agreement, and a wave of nausea hit me looking at the trust in her eyes. A few hours later, I left the key and two suitcases with my landlord and wandered around the campus to get a glimpse of all my old haunts. I ambled by the library, but decided not to go in. I told myself I wanted to avoid a public tearful goodbye with Komakal.

Instead I stopped at a terrace cafe for a fresh lime soda—fizzy and frothy with salt in the first taste, and then the sweetness of the lime. I'd come here so often with Komakal, talking about ideas, making up stories about people we saw. I watched other young people gathered in groups, horsing around—everything filled with the flavor of the past, everything dear.

* * *

For the first few days back, even the sunshine in Palo Alto seemed a little too bright, like it had been manufactured by somebody trying to sell you something, a way of life, an intellectual sleepiness, a corporate complacency. At my parents' house, however, we were on high alert. Doctors had discovered a tumor in my mother's lung, early stage. The days were spent worrying about her, running errands for the family, and trying to reconcile the strong, lively woman I'd always known with the one who wanted to sleep all the time.

"When are you going to meet a girl?" my mother asked, putting down her empty glass of wheatgrass juice. "Maybe you should try online dating."

"Actually, I did meet somebody in Chennai," I told her.

"And?"

"I don't know. Maybe we'll reunite one day."

"You and your sisters! You work too much, like me, I guess. But I want grandchildren." She closed her eyes. "Tell me, what was this girl of yours like?"

"She was intense," I said. My mother grunted for me to continue. "Beautiful. Tamil."

"When are we going to meet her?"

"She's something of an anti-caste activist."

My mother's eyebrows drew together. In spite of her illness, she looked young again with the pearly sheen of afternoon light on her dark brow. "All that doesn't matter here."

"She thinks wherever Indians go, caste goes."

"Only when you're young can you get away with such bold claims!" Her eyes opened, and she paused before she spoke again. "But you know, when we first came here, an Indian woman asked me if I was an Iyer, a Brahmin. It would have been too painful to say no—we had no family in this country, nobody to count on but other Indians—so I just lied."

"You did?"

"But the lie stayed with me. It reminded me of a group of girls who'd thrown rocks at me on the way home from school."

"They did? Why haven't you ever told me that?"

She kept going. "The time someone set my possessions on fire in engineering college, and the warden did nothing. And what did I know of Brahmin customs? So, I stopped going to Indian functions and decided I would just do my work."

"Didn't Dad support you?"

She had a pained expression. "We never talk about such things."

A tremendous sadness washed over me. My mother had been so isolated, and somehow, I'd never even noticed. I ventured, "Mom, that must have been so lonely."

"Nobody talks about such things." She gave a bitter laugh. "Why am I telling you all this? I had my work and that was enough."

She began coughing, and as I fetched a glass of fresh water, I realized how desperately I missed Komakal.

But in the coming days, the feeling faded. I would stroll downtown to listen to the haunting melodies of saxophonists and Andean flautists busking on street corners, hats overflowing with bills and coins flung on the pavement before them. Crowds of different people floated down the streets with their fancy designer bags and brown paper parcels and precocious children in tow. No, I didn't quite fit here, but my life in Chennai still seemed increasingly like somebody else's.

I tried to email Komakal to tell her that I wouldn't be coming back for a while. I typed out a message, saying that I would love to see her in the States and that she should come visit me, and that I would buy her a ticket, but unwelcome thoughts crept in. I imagined her in Palo Alto. Meeting my family and friends over dinner. How backward everyone but my mother would find her. Her earnest, impassioned arguments about caste and feminism. How faint her sense of irony. I imagined my older sisters, their hair immaculate due to flatirons, glancing at each other over their understated rose gold jewelry and shiny designer pumps, and snickering with discomfort. I stared at the screen for a few minutes, shifting words around. After a while, I deleted the email.

A few days later, I wrote a similar letter leaving out the invitation. I wrote in longhand because an email seemed too sterile. Or that's what I told myself—the real reason, I think, was that I hoped longhand would give Komakal time to cool off before responding. I dropped the letter in the international post and returned to my parents' house to continue editing my documentary.

Komakal didn't write back. Not the next week, or the next month, or even the next year. I kept working on my documentary.

Some of the footage included a historian talking about Lemuria, a hypothetical lost land in the Indian Ocean that included California. It was a zoologist's discredited theory, but it was adopted by both occultists in the West and Tamil writers pushing to prove the past existence of Kumari Kandam.

When I showed my thesis advisor what I had so far, he told me about the sighting of a Lemurian, a man from the lost continent living in tunnels deep below the earth. I drove up to Mount Shasta to shoot a video with an elderly woman who ran a roadside market. She claimed that over the years she'd sometimes spotted a strange disheveled loner. He would emerge from the forest, just past the observatory, covered in dirt and leaves, wearing tattered white robes, and babbling in an unintelligible language. "Well, every time it's the same thing," she said, fingering the sapphire pendant hanging from her neck. "He takes one look at civilization and trudges right back into the woods. Skin about your color."

"And you think he's a Lemurian?" I asked.

"Oh, I know he is, honey. There's no doubt in my mind that he is. The lookout's seen him a couple times, too, wandering the woods below the observatory."

I wished I could tell Komakal. I thought she might appreciate this bit of weirdness that connected my home to hers.

And in my parents' backyard, I breathed in the sticky jasmine and hot asphalt, looked up at the green light coming through the star-shaped sycamore leaves, watched a gull circling overhead, listened to the sound of the train chugging along the tracks—suddenly belonging.

* * *

Several years later, when my mother was in remission and my finished documentary had garnered a few prizes at independent film festivals, I did return to Chennai. After a few weeks there,

I called Komakal's mobile phone, but it had been disconnected. Then I called the landline at Komakal's apartment. I wondered if she'd gotten married. I wondered if I could stand it if she was. I could imagine her flared temper, the sound of her yelling. I almost hung up, but I wanted to thank her—without her, I wouldn't have had the inspiration to finish the film.

I waited for four rings. Her roommate answered the phone. When I asked after Komakal, she said Komakal had succumbed to a deep depression and killed herself.

I drew in my breath sharply, and my heart clenched with pain. "When?"

"I don't remember. Maybe three summers ago?"

She anticipated the question I thought was too offensive to ask and told me that Komakal had plunged into the ocean, her pockets filled with stones. She never came out. A group of fishermen swam after her too late. The roommate continued and as she did, I calculated—the suicide had happened a year after my letter.

After a moment, I asked, "What became of Komakal's driftwood paintings?" The roommate told me that her parents had collected them, and she gave me their number. Of course, I would never call.

I took a train to the beach at Kanyakumari and wandered along the coast, noting the statue of the poet, the tourist stands selling cowrie shells carved with elephants and boats and arecas. This is what she would have seen. The sands didn't shift colors until sunset, and then they were pinker, less divine than they'd been while I traipsed across them with Komakal. I collected pebbles along the shore, filling my pockets with them.

The moon rose just before the sun vanished. I'd never truly belonged there—in my motherland—and I hadn't been able to love Komakal the way that she'd wanted, the way I promised I would when she was helping me with my work. I would always be between things and places and people, never all in. Perhaps I was unable to truly love anyone. Still, I stood in the darkening water in my bare feet, as the beach turned silver-blue, trying my hardest to feel what Komakal must have felt as she drifted deeper and deeper into the water. The cold night tides lapped my toes, and then my ankles, and then my shins. I stared up at the blazing stars and imagined myself carried away by fierce floods, a lost continent unto myself.

HEMA AND KATHY

What they did remember—a memory solidified by their families' yearly slapdash recounting at Christmas—was how they met in first grade. While the other kids dashed up the slides and swung, hooting, on the monkey bars, Kathy Yang hunched cross-legged by herself in the tanbark, too afraid to talk to anyone. A few weeks after school started, Hema Sarma sprinted up to her breathless, shouting *Kathy! Kathy!*

"I'm chasing them!" She pointed to the two boys running around the field. She held out her hand. "Come on."

Kathy hated any sort of strenuous physical effort, particularly running, but there was something endearing about Hema's chipmunk cheeks and gap-toothed smile and laughing, mischievous eyes—it was a face that was hard not to love. Kathy didn't know how to say no, so she stood and chased the boys, with no idea of what she would do if she actually caught one.

Hema, always quick, caught a little Japanese-American boy with hair that stuck straight up, and she kissed his cheek with a loud smack. That night, the boy's mother made an angry phone call to Prabha, telling her that her son had come home shaken and to keep her wild daughter under control. Hema and Kathy giggled over this, mocking Prabha's rolling distress, "Vaat is this, Haaaayma? You are chasing boys now? Good girls don't do this, you know."

For years after that, they floated everywhere together, a single organism: HemaandKathy. Their fifth-grade teacher called them peanut butter and jelly. Kathy understood herself to be the peanut butter in this analogy—solid, dependable, quiet, and reserved—and Hema to be the jelly: bold, noisy, imaginative, and dreamy. Their nightly rhythm: checking in by phone, sneaking down the drainpipe for a nightly jaunt because Hema's father didn't want her on the phone, and waving goodnight through their windows. Like clockwork until Hema became a soccer star. Local newspapers dubbed her the Indian Mia Hamm.

* * *

Later, Kathy would reconstruct what had happened that Christmas, trying to piece together whether she'd missed signs that Hema had changed. It was the Sarmas' turn to host dinner. Their house glittered with bushy silver tinsel and paper gold stars, bigger versions of the ones her parents had used to reward her unfailingly good report cards. They'd pulled the usual white plastic tree from the garage and wreathed it in popcorn and felt reindeers.

In the kitchen, Gopal poured mulled cider for Kathy's parents, Nancy and John. Prabha bustled into their pantry, which doubled as a prayer room, ferrying out glass bottles of cardamom and cumin, and white plastic yogurt containers brimming with other comestibles. Gopal and Prabha told Kathy's parents that other Indian parents had told them you must show Ivy League admissions officers your child was both passionate and well-rounded. It wasn't enough to simply have good test scores.

"Can you be both?" John asked. He clutched the bowl of snap pea stir-fry, covered with weeping saran wrap, his contribution to the Christmas potluck. Gopal looked at him blankly.

"Does she really need a private coach?" Nancy asked. She was a professor of chemical engineering at Stanford.

"Well, it's not like they're in the Red Lightnings anymore," Gopal said. He held out a silver tray of pakora. Nancy took one. "Soccer is very competitive these days."

"We just want her to have the best chances," Prabha said.

"Every time we've seen her play, she's been the best on the team. Do you want her to play professionally?" John asked.

"No, no, no," Gopal said. "Definitely not. Hema is going to be a doctor. It's just that we found someone who coaches another of the girls on the varsity team, and we think he's going to be good for Hema's chances at getting recruited." Hema had made it onto the varsity team their freshman year—the first and only freshman ever on the team.

Hema's older brother, Kai, was home for the holidays and he had one ear cocked, eavesdropping on this conversation from the cushions of the living room couch with Hema, Kathy, and Kathy's little sister, Lucy. He turned to Hema. "Hear that? They want to make sure you don't turn out like me. The gay graduate of a liberal arts school nobody knows the name of. To them, success means selling out for the highest price you can get and preferably a designer degree."

Hema shrugged. "Who cares about all that? I just want to be the best."

Kai and Kathy looked at each other and laughed. It was like Hema to skip over any untangling of other people's motives to focus on what she wanted.

After dinner, they drank hot chocolate swimming with peppermint marshmallows and their parents congratulated each other on how well they'd done with Hema and Kathy. Then Nancy and John went home, and Gopal went upstairs to work on his computer.

Prabha flicked on the second half of *Sense and Sensibility* and began cleaning up the detritus of the Christmas feast. Unexpectedly, Kathy teared up as Hugh Grant proposed to Emma Thompson. Furious, she wiped her eyes, hoping nobody had seen.

"Well, that was stupid," Hema said. The credits ran. She blew on her fingernails, which she'd just painted with Pulp Fiction polish. "So boring Elinor gets Hugh Grant? That hardly seems likely."

"Can you do my nails, too?" Lucy asked Hema, extending her bare feet.

"I like Elinor," Kathy said.

"Nobody likes Elinor. She's boring and proper," Kai interjected. He was cooling the chicory coffee made by his mother by pouring it back and forth from a stainless steel tumbler to a smaller dish he called a dabarah.

"But she's not silly the way Marianne is. And look at how badly things turn out for Marianne," Kathy said.

Hema crinkled her nose as she dabbed nail polish on Lucy's toenails. "Okaaaay. Wouldn't you rather just fall madly in love, so in love you actually wanted to be with the person?"

"No way. Elinor has common sense, and that's more important."

Kai laughed and sipped his coffee. "When you're my age, Kathy, I'm pretty sure your answer will be different."

* * *

Hema immediately wanted to please him. Theo was black-haired, handsome in a vulpine way, stocky and muscular, yet agile, and a little older than Kai. He was French and rode the bench for France's soccer team in 1998 when they won the World Cup, then played professionally in London for four years before coming to the United States. He wanted the girls he coached—girls like Hema—to be tough and fierce, to be consummate sportswomen.

Where all the other people in her life wanted her to restrain herself, to be less, he asked her to be more. He wanted her to be as aggressive as he was. He taught her how to commit a foul that a ref wouldn't call, he schooled her in the psychology of the game.

"Get in there," he'd yell from the sidelines at her practices—not in the crazy, anxious way her parents had when they came to her elementary school games, not in the way that let her know how devastated he would be if she weren't the best after all, but with the confidence of someone who knew she had it in her to win. A commanding and encouraging tone in his voice made her want to do better, to scrap until the very end.

"You've got to pass more," Theo said to her one day after her game, handing her a bottle of juice as they walked through the parking lot. "Rely on your midfielders."

"I don't know if I can rely on them," Hema said, still high from the scrimmage, her cleats clipping pavement. "You saw them out there. They just don't care as much as I do."

"Were we watching the same game? I thought they were giving it their all. To function as a team, you have to trust."

He held open the door of his beater, a silver Toyota Camry, and she climbed in. "You want to see a video that illustrates this point I'm making about teamwork?"

* * *

They drove to his tiny studio apartment on El Camino Real. It was three floors up. They entered through a nondescript door with peeling black paint. Inside the single room was a kitchen alcove with the tiniest stove Hema had ever seen, and a couch the pale beige of porridge. Rows of pinkish light sliced through crooked Venetian blinds. Sheets swirled, forming a white rose at one end of the unmade bed. Burgundy pillows, heady with the wintery fragrance of pine trees, were scattered all askew.

They watched his tape, one of the few World Cup games he'd played in. He brewed a pot of Gen Ma Cha tea. He sat beside her, close enough that she could hear him breathing and smell the fragrance of his musky cologne and the popped rice of the green tea, his warm shoulder against hers, and they watched the match like that for hours, as the street lights of Palo Alto began to glow, and night fell around them.

* * *

Practice wound down at twilight. The team and its coach were scattered by the bleachers. The air was heavy with the odor of freshly cut grass. From a distance, Kathy saw the dark silhouette of a man and a girl, their heads huddled together, standing apart from the team, in a world of their own against the streaks of gold and pink at the horizon, and for a moment, she didn't recognize her best friend.

Theo patted Hema on the back. It was a familiar gesture. He shouted something at the whole team like "Go, team, go!" in his French accent and pumped his fist. Kathy would have left without saying anything, but Hema spotted her in the dusk and called her over.

"It's so wonderful to meet Hema's best friend. Hema speaks about you all the time," Theo said.

"Oh, yeah. You too." Kathy shook his hand, and she could feel herself blushing with the awkwardness, his ingratiating formality. She found his accent comical and his manner overweening. He continued to talk, but she had already stopped listening, and eventually she tugged at Hema's arm.

"Isn't he amazing?" Hema asked as they walked away. "He's so wise. I could listen to him talk for hours."

Kathy didn't answer. Hema's rapturous tone reminded her of when they were small and leafing through Hema's stacks of *Tiger Beat*, many of which she'd smuggled out of the library because her father didn't want her reading what he considered trash. They'd compare notes on each issue of the candy-colored magazine, remarking on who was cute, and who wasn't, who seemed like they might be cool in real life, and who they believed were poseurs. Always, their tastes were different.

Prabha shared Kathy's concerns, and this provided Kathy with a small measure of relief. While Kathy was studying in the Sarma living room one Saturday, she overheard Hema talking to Prabha in the kitchen. "Enough!" Prabha said. "You have to think about the future. You have to get a college education, you can't be a soccer star your whole life."

"I could coach," Hema said. "Like Theo."

"Coaching is okay for somebody like Theo."

"What's that supposed to mean?"

"That's not the kind of job we get. You always wanted to be a doctor."

"You always wanted me to be a doctor."

"Sports medicine." Prabha said. "We'll pay for college if you focus on sports medicine."

"Why do you get to paint pictures of flowers nobody wants to buy, but I have to get a job I would hate?"

Hema returned to the living room a few minutes later with a protein bar. Her eyebrows were knit and her smooth cheeks were flushed. "You okay?" Kathy whispered. Hema nodded, but as she settled into the couch, her eyes were closed, a little flame going out inside her.

Kathy said nothing, but blamed Theo. Why had he gotten her hopes up? Hema was smart, like next-level smart, and talented to boot, and he had somehow wormed his own paltry and unambitious expectations into her brain, persuaded her it was enough for her to be just a soccer coach.

* * *

"Do you need an ice pack?" Theo asked. Hema was horribly sunburned, but in heaven. The sweetness of the pain and the tang of the orange juice mixed as they always did in the unbeatable high after she'd scored back-to-back goals.

Hema shook her head, which was propped against the armrest of the porridge-colored couch. He rubbed pink calamine on her legs. Firm but gentle ministrations. She could smell him, the scent of him an intoxicating mixture of freshly cut grass and coconut sunscreen, the smell of endless summer. "I was on auto-pilot for that last goal," she said. "I shot on reflex when she passed to me. It was all those drills we did."

"You were amazing."

At that moment, Hema sat up and looked into Theo's hazel eyes. She kissed him. His lips were warm.

* * *

Summer before their senior year. The air was strangely humid and sultry. Hema waggled up from below her windowsill, wearing an elaborate red dragon mask and khaki army fatigues. Kathy laughed. After an all-nighter preparing her project for an honors science summer camp, she was ready to remove her contact lenses and sleep. But then Hema took off the mask, pulled up the window, and pointed at the ground, a sign that she wanted to take one of their nocturnal walks by the creek. They shimmied down their respective drainpipes and headed wordlessly into Los Altos Hills.

Bay quarter horses grazed in the shadowy dusk. The sounds took on a greater intensity in the darkness with so little to look at—cows lowing, the distant buzz of Foothill Expressway.

"What's going on?" Kathy asked as they neared the creek, their feet making a crackly shur-shur in the grass.

"Do you ever think that our lives here are just unbearably small?" Hema asked. "I can't wait till graduation, till I can just get out of here."

"What's wrong with here?"

"The definition of success is so narrow! There's no space, and everyone is so horribly pleased with themselves. I mean, why even live a life if it's not exciting, if everything is planned?"

Kathy had no answer to this. The creek swished and kerplunked over stones. As they hiked deeper into the hills, the crickets chirruped.

"Hey, you remember how you saved Lucy in that sinkhole by this creek?" Kathy asked.

Hema laughed. "Oh, please, you would have saved her if I hadn't." She bent suddenly and picked up a tiny frog, and held him up to the stars, dark and pulsing. "Look at this adorable guy."

"I really wouldn't have had the presence of mind that you did," Kathy said, stroking the frog's slimy back with her index finger.

"I remember how the tadpoles we caught would turn into frogs and go hopping out of my garage, and my parents would never be the wiser."

Kathy looked away, her throat catching on all the things she wanted to say. Since Hema had started training with Theo, their conversations turned increasingly to the past, and their friendship had dwindled into a series of remembrances—they didn't meet frequently enough to make new memories. Next year, they'd go to separate colleges, and they probably wouldn't do these nighttime hikes anymore. Already, they were too far apart. She said nothing.

Trekking through fronds of sweet fennel, Hema told Kathy that Theo was critical of the way they'd been raised in Palo Alto, how whitewashed and affluent it was—he called it Shallow Alto.

Kathy snorted. "And yet, he's willing to fleece your parents to coach you."

"Well, I mean, he has to live, doesn't he? It's not surprising so many of the girls he coaches have crushes on him."

"Yuck. He's so old." Kathy waited for Hema to agree, but Hema bent down and released the frog back into the creek.

"Run away, little frog," Hema whispered into the darkness.

* * *

Senior year blurred: college applications and elaborately decorated dances and self-important student government meetings. Kathy was startled by the arrival of Valentine's Day. It was as uneventful as every other day, except that a skinny kid in her AP calculus class who was building an app to keep track of homework had handed her a handwritten love letter. She'd glanced through it, mocked a few lines, and tossed it in the trash.

The high school campus was open, which meant most kids would drive off-campus at lunchtime. Kathy usually met Hema for lunch at Hobee's on Friday when they both had a free period just afterward. They ordered their usual hash browns and blueberry coffee cake and smoothies from brightly illustrated menus typed in a quirky, curlicue-laden font.

Hema only shrugged when Kathy told her about the love letter. Usually they would have mocked him together. "He's not really that bad."

"But would you date him?"

"No, but we have different types. Did I tell you I'm trying out for the under-twenty women's team this March? Theo says they're interested."

"He's going behind your parents' backs? What about college?" Kathy asked. She picked at her hash browns drowning in a cool red pool of salsa and sour cream.

"I can always go to college later. I won't always be on a winning streak."

"Did Theo ever go back to college?"

"No, but he wasn't raised like us. He's hot, don't you think?"

"Gross. He's got a weak chin and I think he's losing his hair. He's, what, twenty years older than us?"

"No. Only eleven years. He's twenty-nine years old. When I'm twenty-nine, he'll only be forty, and that's not too wide an age gap."

Kathy made a face. "He's even older than your brother." She pulled the straw out of her smoothie and flecked a purple swirl of smoothie onto Hema's arm. She noticed then that Hema's arm, usually hairy, was smooth, waxed. Hema raised an eyebrow and wiped away the smear with a napkin.

"So? Lots of girls date someone a little older than them. Men mature more slowly than women."

"He had a short soccer career."

"He got injured."

"Unless something's wrong with him, he probably has a girlfriend."

"Well, yes. He was married for a few years," Hema acknowledged. "But it didn't work out. She didn't like how passionate he was about soccer. Can you imagine trying to be married to someone who didn't get the most basic fact about you?"

"I don't get why he's telling you this intimate stuff." Kathy put her fork down.

"He thinks I'm a good listener. What's gotten into you?"

Kathy explained. Hema's patent crush on a man that was so much older was revolting. No good could come of it. But the more Kathy talked, the more adamant Hema was that Kathy just didn't understand him.

"We're dating, you know. I was just trying to figure out how to tell you."

"How long?"

"Since last January." Hema didn't seem to have any idea how strange this was. She had swallowed the secret—it had been swimming inside her for a full year—like she didn't trust Kathy at all.

"Oh my god. You're underage, Hema."

"We're seventeen!"

"We're just kids."

"I'm going to be eighteen in two months."

"He's a predator."

"Stop it. You don't know him."

"I know he's in a position of power over you and he preyed on you."

"Let me get this straight. Basically, you want me to be more like you?" Hema asked. She drew herself up.

Hema's skin was fawn-colored, glowing and moisturized. Her lips were penciled in with some sort of scarlet pigment. Kathy noticed in that moment that she'd started wearing mascara and a wide line of jet-black kohl around her eyes. Just a few years earlier they had made fun of Prabha for drawing kohl so thick around her eyelids, joking that it made her look foreign and slightly ridiculous, like she thought of herself as some sort of Scheherazade. And now Hema was aping her.

"No, I just want you to come back. I want you to be the same person I've known my whole life," Kathy said, trying not to plead.

"Maybe I'm not that person anymore. You're the one who cares about going to an Ivy League school, about making sure everyone knows how smart you are, how successful you are, how important you are. All that model-minority crap. What do I care about any of that? I want to live! I'm going to live!"

"I don't have to listen to this." Kathy threw a wad of cash on the table. She hurried to her car before Hema could see her cry. She'd never heard Hema use that phrase before, model minority, though they'd talked about it in their AP US History class, which was taught by a white man, a former activist who'd studied Buddhism with Himalayan monks in the 1960s. Everyone in the class, most of them white, with a handful who were Chinese American, Indian American, or Japanese American, had scoffed at the term, which they didn't need for their AP exam. Hadn't Hema laughed along with them? Maybe she hadn't, and suddenly Kathy was deeply embarrassed that Hema had taken that term and applied it to her, thinking she was deserving of this cold, sterile, impersonal term, a term that suggested she—Hema's best friend, supposedly—was not an individual, but a tool. She drove back to school, leaving Hema to find her own way back.

* * *

That night was the first they didn't wave goodnight through their windows. The following week, Kathy ate alone on a bench at the edge of the quad at lunchtime. Hema was nowhere to be seen. It was spring, and all the other seniors were planning the class gift, elaborate ways to ask their sweethearts to the prom, and outings to the beach for Senior Cut Day. They were taking it easy, but to keep her growing anxiety at bay, Kathy continued to work as hard as she had before.

She checked her phone every five minutes. No sign of reconciliation—no texts or emails. Hema had other friends, mostly her teammates, and of course she had Theo. Kathy's sister, Lucy, was at high school by then, but she had her own interests—as far as Kathy could tell, they were horror movies, gymnastics, a giggling group of friends, and boys. Kathy only ever had Hema.

She thought of Kai then and wondered what he would say. He had been home for the holidays. He never brought any of his partners home—there was a chill, a subtle testiness between him and his parents that went unremarked. But he was the same old Kai and kind to Kathy.

She searched for him online and called him at work, and after his initial surprise to hear from her, he asked why she'd called.

"Is this a joke? Did Hema put you up to this? My sister can be very persuasive."

"No, this is true."

"I've met that guy once or twice. He seemed nice enough."

"Looks can be deceiving."

Kai still sounded uncertain. "It seemed to me like he cares about Hema and wants the best for her."

"I don't know about that. I think they've had sex, Kai. And he's going to take her to try out for the under-twenty women's team when she turns eighteen."

There was a pause and then Kai's voice was harsh. "I'll take care of it." He hung up before Kathy could say anything else, leaving her stunned by how quick her own betrayal had been. She'd half-expected Kai to tell her to mind her own business, or maybe to say something that would make her understand why Hema would do this.

*　*　*

The next morning, Kathy didn't see Hema as she left her house, pulling a slicker tight around her. It was drizzling, one of those light fantastical California rains, where the sun continues to beam as a fine mist coats everything. Faintly green hills. Gopal's car, usually gone by seven, was still parked in the driveway. A mild acrid odor blew up from the black asphalt and blacker loam.

Kathy stood in the mist and watched through the window for a moment: Hema, Gopal, and Prabha. She could just barely make out Gopal—apoplectic—shouting and pounding his fist on the table. Prabha was crying. Hema stood stock-still, arms crossed, watching her parents.

* * *

When Kathy returned home from school that afternoon with Lucy, Gopal's car was still parked in the driveway, but the living room blinds were drawn.

"Is everything okay with you and Hema?" Lucy asked, jerking her finger at the Sarmas' house.

"I don't think so."

Lucy paused, and then she asked, "Are you ever jealous of her?"

"Why would you say that?" Kathy fumbled around for her key as they walked up the path to their front door.

"I'm jealous of her sometimes."

"Why?"

"She has beauty, brains, talent. Sometimes, when I'm standing next to her, I feel lame and ordinary. It must be worse for you since she's your best friend."

* * *

She didn't come back to school. Kathy learned later from one of Hema's teammates that she'd gone to live with Theo. Gopal and Prabha called the police, but by then the two of them had disappeared.

His apartment on El Camino Real was vacated. Kathy talked the super into letting her into the studio unit and saw that Theo had left behind a couch and a bed. They were stripped of their covers and sheets and pillows. There were a few pots and pans abandoned in the cupboards. Kathy imagined Hema in the tiny kitchen, cooking dinner with Theo, pretending to be an adult, sitting on the counter and swinging her feet, banging them against the cabinets, the way she did at Kathy's house. No pieces of paper in the apartment, no notes, nothing to explain where they'd gone or whether they'd ever be back.

Later, Kathy would hear from her mother that Prabha flew around the country that spring, haunting tryouts in different cities, hoping to find Hema at one of them, hoping to bring her home, even though she was eighteen. But she didn't find her.

Midsummer, Kathy bumped into Kai at the Harvard Square T station. His fingers were entwined with a man's. He looked so different—so happy—and they hugged. "Have you seen her?" Kathy asked, both afraid and hopeful that Hema had kept in touch with her brother, even though she'd cut Kathy off.

"Yes. She's fine. I'm sure she'll contact you eventually." His partner tugged his hand and they had to leave, but Hema never did call.

* * *

Many winters passed. In a blink: Harvard, graduate school in molecular biology, and a prestigious job at a large pharmaceutical company. Kathy passed through the years in a trance, doing what needed to be done, the idea of success—of the ultimate gold star blinking and beckoning her—a light far off in the distance that eventually, one day, with enough hard work, enough adherence to the plan, she would reach out and seize.

One winter, Kathy was promoted to a director position, the youngest director in her company, and she returned to her parents' house for the holidays as she always did, prepared to celebrate. She stepped out of the taxi and into the stark shadows of late afternoon. Rolling her suitcase after her, she noticed a curious emptiness inside her, the flatness like soda after the fizz had gone out. She wasn't even excited about her promotion. She'd imagined it for so long, it was like she'd already gotten it. An unfamiliar car sat in the Sarmas' driveway, and she stared at it.

To her surprise, Hema emerged from the Sarma house. Pregnant, she wore a crimson maternity dress, her hair cropped short. She raised a hand in greeting. "How've you been?" It was as if Hema were returning from a vacation instead of reappearing after years. She had some sort of accent she hadn't possessed as a child. It was like her, when Kathy thought about it later, not to acknowledge what had happened. She'd moved on to adventures Kathy couldn't imagine, while Kathy had stayed on track.

"All right, I guess. Congratulations." Kathy gestured at Hema's belly.

"Oh! Thank you! We're going to raise her in Paris—that's where we've been these past years—but my mother begged me to have her here."

"We?"

"Theo and I."

"You're still together?" Kathy couldn't hide her incredulity.

Hema laughed and held out her hand. There was an enormous ugly diamond on her ring finger, its facets glinting in the dark orange light as the sun slipped toward the horizon. "Twelve years, baby." Kathy could hear in her voice a faint I-told-you-so, or was she imagining this? "Don't look so shocked, Kathy," she said gently. "We were meant to be."

"But you were a star. You had so much talent. You always wanted to play in the Women's World Cup."

A cloud passed over Hema's eyes. "Well, I'm happy anyway."

This was what their epic friendship had come to, this dumb, silent moment on a sidewalk. Kathy wondered what Gopal and Prabha thought—Hema had been their great hope, and in spite of their every effort, she'd followed a completely different path than the one they'd laid out for her. Perhaps Hema was saving face by pretending everything had worked out. After all this time, after losing everyone, after throwing everything away, would she admit she'd made a mistake? There was nothing apologetic in Hema's face, no worry lines, no signs of secret distress, just that look in her eyes, like a light had been turned down. She stood with her hips thrust forward, as if in defiance of what Kathy might be thinking.

Then she cracked a huge smile. "Do you want to feel the baby kick?"

Kathy didn't, but she placed her palm on Hema's hard belly. For a few moments, she didn't feel anything and was about to withdraw her hand, when something rolled against her skin, against her palm. A sharp kick, and then another. A new life. A force even less predictable than Hema. "When are you due?"

"Last week." Hema jerked her head toward the shadowy hills. "I'm trying to get labor going, but this baby just doesn't want to come out." Kathy nodded and started pulling her luggage up the road toward her parents' house and turned into their driveway. At the top of the steps, she paused. This was where she'd glimpsed Hema for the first time as a small child, running with a large bubble wand—bubbles streaming in a long gossamer tunnel behind her before separating into large fragile baubles that burst momentarily, leaving dark wet splats all over the concrete path that led to Kathy's stoop.

She turned and began walking down the steps, putting up her hand to shield her eyes from the intense orange glow of the sun. She wanted to retrace all her steps, to tell Hema how much she'd meant to her, to tell Hema that she made life exciting and new, always, and that she was sorry she'd betrayed her and that she was genuinely happy she was happy, and that somehow, against all odds, Kathy had obviously been wrong about her passion for Theo.

The words stuck in her throat. She couldn't bring herself to call after Hema, who was waddling up the hilly road, heading toward the creek where they'd spent so many long, happy hours together. Holding her hand over her belly, she didn't look back at Kathy, and in a moment, she disappeared around a curve.

SNOW

Dreading the visit, Devi was determined to make herself comfortable. In spite of the swarm of snowflakes eddying around the windows of her third-floor walk-up, she'd tried to duplicate the conditions of her hometown. The girls were working, and so she played Debussy at full volume. The thermostat read seventy-five. After seven years in the States, the cold was still too cold, the snow not much like the white sparkly sugary bees she'd imagined as a child when she'd read about snow in the hardback fairytale book her aunt had brought as a gift from America.

She lounged on the red pleather couch and skimmed a glossy magazine, glancing expectantly at the door every few moments. In one full-page advertisement for matte lipstick that promised to transform her into a brand-new woman, she was confronted with Veronica's wide horsey smile—hideously toothy and self-satisfied. In a fit of pique and hunger, she flung the magazine across the floor with a scowl. At first, it felt good, letting out all her disdain and anger in this tiny gesture, a gesture that was more than what she usually allowed herself. But the release passed too quickly, and soon she was back to worrying. She told herself she'd have the foundation commercial soon. She'd get her first check from that assignment and repay her roommates for her share of the heat and sundry expenses.

Footsteps outside the door. She picked up the magazine and placed it on top of the glass coffee table and took a deep breath.

The first knock was soft, tentative. Pause. Another knock. Devi unlocked the front door and smiled so wide it hurt. "Susannah! How was your flight?"

"Devyani!" Susannah was shorter than Devi, with glowing skin, so dark it was almost black, and features like a little girl's—big eyes, curly hair, a space between her front teeth, and a soft wide nose. With her irregular, mussed ringlets, Susannah looked to Devi like the unkempt villager who cleaned her parents' house in Chennai.

Unsure of whether to hug her cousin and mostly not wanting to touch her, Devi waved her inside. "I go by Devi now. It's easier."

Susannah stomped on the welcome mat, and her leather combat boots exhaled a puff of snow. "For Americans you mean? Should I take off my shoes?" she asked.

"Probably best."

Susannah squatted in the middle of the room and tugged at her boots with a despairing expression. After she finally yanked them off, she deserted them in a pile by the door and looked around the room before settling precariously on the edge of the couch. The warm, overripe scent of summertime rose petals trailed after her. Sighing, Devi picked up the boots with two fingers, holding them out in front of her, and dropped them on the silver wire shoe rack. She towed Susannah's suitcase into the corner and asked after Susannah's parents in California and their restaurant, Madras Magic. She paced back and forth, trying to think of something to say.

The cousins made stilted small talk. After a few minutes, Susannah wiped sweat from her brow. "You're making me nervous. And this place is hot as hell."

"I just have a lot of energy." Devi dropped onto an armrest, regretting the coke she'd snorted before Susannah arrived. Her heel started jiggling. "So, you're only here for a weekend. That's not really long enough for me to show you all of Manhattan or even more than the highlights."

"Oh, I've seen everything. I've been here before."

"Really? Your mom didn't tell me that."

"Many times. I just didn't want to inconvenience you by staying longer."

"I suppose you haven't eaten yet?"

"My head's still in the Bay Area, but it is dinnertime, isn't it? I could eat."

"We're going to a lovely, upscale restaurant with some of the other girls from the agency—my roommates."

"Excellent."

Susannah sounded far too relaxed, and so Devi gave her what she thought was a meaningful look and gestured at the bathroom. "Is that what you're going to wear?"

"Oh, you think I'll show them up in this?"

Devi frowned. "Maybe you ought to put something nicer on?"

Susannah rolled her eyes.

The train was delayed by thirty minutes, so they ambled down Avenue B to East Fourteenth Street. The icy journey through Alphabet City seemed unduly long to both of them, a light snow drifting about their faces, neither turning to look the other in the eyes. All the news of the past several years had been brought properly current in the apartment, and the forty-eight hours that remained loomed dangerously long and unscripted ahead of them. Devi adjusted her stocking cap. "Did you tour the law school when you got here? Did you like it?"

"Not really. The students seemed stuck-up." Susannah clapped her mittened palms together.

"Isn't it one of the best law schools in the country?" Devi was perplexed.

"That doesn't mean they have to be so snobby."

"You know, I don't see you as a lawyer."

Devi expected some pushback, but instead Susannah beamed, as if she'd been paid a compliment, and brushed wet snowflakes from her cheeks and eyelashes. "Me neither. But constructing arguments for everything is the only thing I'm reasonably good at, I guess."

"You? You're kind of touchy-feely for a lawyer, aren't you?"

"Sure, but I need to make money and if people will pay you to make really good syllogisms for money, why not? Or maybe it's the whole immigrant thing. You know what I mean? You never feel like you can just relax."

Devi didn't think of her cousin as an immigrant—Susannah's family had moved to the States when Susannah was a baby, making her incontrovertibly American—but Devi also wondered whether her anxiety about this visit had been misplaced. Devi remembered Susannah from when Susannah had visited a little more than six years before: a scowling teenager with magenta streaks in her hair and a chip on her shoulder. When her aunt had phoned to arrange Susannah's stay in New York, Devi had feared a visit full of interminable stretches of sullen defensiveness and perhaps moments of recrimination for perceived wrongdoings. This older Susannah was confident, not easily ruffled, and deadly calm. But people didn't change. Not really. Somewhere under the fragile shell of her cousin's inexplicably good manners, the real Susannah, the true Susannah was squirming with impatience, waiting to be reborn.

Devi stuffed her hands in her pockets, fingering her subway tokens and spare change. Susannah wasn't pretty—not by a long shot, even with her frizz smoothed down with cheap metallic-smelling drugstore gel—nor even especially intelligent—after all, she had gone to a public school for her undergraduate degree. But at least now she could converse without losing her temper or referencing the lyrics to atrocious goth music.

Inside the dimly lit restaurant, they met five models, three of them Devi's roommates. They were sipping fruity, sparkling bellinis and devouring date bread and poached persimmon salads and olive oil panna cottas, all of their dishes raw and vegan except the bellinis, and they cackled as they talked rather heatedly about a Milan Kundera novel.

Devi cleared her throat and introduced Susannah. "The girls," Devi said, gesturing at the women. One of them, wearing a borrowed dress, was a runway model who routinely booked prestigious gigs, but often didn't have enough money for rent. The others maintained a steady stream of commercial catalog work. Devi unwrapped her coat and hung it on the back of a chair, running a hand down her gold dress to smooth down scale-like sequins.

Susannah wore a black shapeless dress made of some kind of rough cotton, and Devi noted she didn't even have the grace to be embarrassed or humbled in the face of so much beauty. Instead she plopped down and dug into a raw lemon panna cotta with gusto. The models continued to debate a bowler hat in one of Kundera's novels.

Veronica leaned over and whispered in a pitying tone, "Someone invited Jake. That's not a problem, is it?"

Devi shrugged, trying to hide her discomfort. Jake was her agent, and the son of the agency's owner. They'd dated briefly, and the memory of spending an entire paycheck on diamond-studded Tiffany's cufflinks a few months earlier in the mistaken belief that they were exclusive, and so she could spoil him, still made her blush.

"Who's Jake?" Susannah asked. Her voice was casual, the familiarity of somebody who was making herself comfortable in an unfamiliar situation, instead of waiting to be invited. It was brazen, and it annoyed Devi that she didn't understand the proper hierarchy, or where she belonged on it.

"No one," Devi said.

Veronica asked Susannah where she was from, and how she and Devi were related. Devi was sure that Veronica noticed how different Susannah was from the rest of them, how lumpish, but if she did, she did not advertise her disdain. Devi supposed Veronica was too kind for that, and she applauded her own taste in friends.

Moments later, a Persian waitress came and took their entrée orders. Devi ordered another small plate salad.

"That all you're going to eat?" Susannah said. "I ordered three dishes. You can definitely share."

"I don't want to pork up."

"You know, I can totally see a family resemblance." Veronica cocked her head to one side and adjusted her pale blonde ballerina bun.

Susannah laughed. "Really?"

"We don't look at all alike." Devi tried to hide her distress. "I mean, not at all."

"It's in her bone structure. And that gorgeous skin. She has so much potential, especially now that the agency is looking for more diverse models," Veronica continued. "But I could also see her as an edgy model, instead of a commercial one. Have you ever considered modeling?"

"Never," Susannah said.

"It's incredibly hard, of course, but lucrative if you're on the commercial side. I paid all my college loans within a year. Devi, what was your major at Yale? French?"

"Italian."

"Same difference, right?" Veronica made a face. In her bright laughter, the celebratory clinking of champagne glasses. "No money in it! You ought to move to New York, Susannah."

"She's going to law school."

"Oh no! You can't! That's so boring." Veronica seized a Kalamata olive and began nibbling its purple flesh, working her way around the pit. "We'll see what Jake thinks when he gets here."

By the time Jake arrived an hour later, the women were drunk. Jake was tall with rakish dark hair and a weak chin, not especially handsome, but made so to Devi through his impeccable tailored suit and crimson silk tie and the intricate gold timepiece on his wrist.

Devi excused herself as he slipped into a chair the waitress placed on the other side of Veronica and hurried to the bathroom.

The bathroom was sterile and beige, reeking of lemon. Inside one of the stalls, she knelt before the toilet and stuck her finger down her throat. It took some finger dancing, but in a moment, she vomited up the poached persimmons and two or three peach bellinis. Immediately her body felt lighter, unburdened. She was about to flush the toilet when she heard someone come into the bathroom and paused.

Two people were making out. Lips smacking. Piggy grunts. Heavy breathing. She peered through the crack between the door of the stall and the metal frame. Jake was pulling Veronica's ruby red slip dress down and sucking on one of her tiny white breasts, murmuring something—repeating *sweet little whore*—as his trousers collapsed around his knees. He thrust into her hard, knocking her head against the cold beige tiles on the wall. She didn't flinch. Devi wanted to sob. She'd slept with Jake, too, before she knew that everyone did. So, this was what that looked like.

Presently, Jake pulled up his pants and Veronica pulled the spaghetti straps of her glittering dress onto her shoulders. Jake splashed some cold water on his face, slapped Veronica's ass, and strode out of the bathroom. Veronica ran a pale mauve wand around her mouth and smacked her lips.

When they were both gone, Devi waited a beat before emerging from the stall. She set her compact on the aluminum counter beneath the mirror and pulled a plastic packet from her purse. She dumped some powder onto the mirror of her gold compact and rolled up a dollar bill. Snorted. Trembled with the calm, clear pleasure.

At that moment, Susannah came into the bathroom. "You do coke?"

Startled, Devi knocked the compact with the remaining coke onto the floor. A pale cloud floated up from the floor, disappeared like dust motes under the fluorescent lights.

"No!" Devi stifled the urge to get on her hands and knees and snort the powder right off the tiny floor tiles. She stuffed the dollar bill and compact into her minaudière—she could just imagine this bit of information circulating through the grapevine of aunts, a source of tut-tutting, whispers about where her mother had gone wrong, whispers that it was the influence of America, that drugs were an American vice, what a shame. She fastened the clasp of her bag and rubbed her nose.

Susannah shrugged and opened the door of a stall. "I don't care if you do, or anything, you know. No judgment."

"Who are you to judge me, anyway?" Devi asked, before she understood Susannah was trying to convey indifference. Unable to swallow her words, she spun and stalked out of the bathroom.

After dinner, Jake hailed a cab. He and Veronica were draped over each other in the front seat, and Bianca, Angie, Devi, and Susannah squeezed across the vinyl back seats, their lean thighs squished against each other like packaged sausages. Two of the models remained on the sidewalk, lit cigarettes, and motioned them onward. The cab rolled forward into traffic. It flashed across town, eventually stopping at Jake's request in front of a club with a queue that snaked around the front of the building and turned into a narrow alleyway full of dumpsters and the stink of raw sewage.

"Are you all right?" Susannah whispered. "We could just go home."

Devi ignored her. Jake and Veronica nonchalantly bypassed the line, and the rest followed them inside and through the crowd to the backlit bar. Inside, Devi drank a gin and tonic and danced for a few minutes before snagging a corner booth where she could observe the others grinding against each other.

In spite of her ballet training, Devi was uncomfortable at popular clubs—uncomfortable with the floppiness of bodies, the gross, unseemly way complete strangers wrapped around each other, crushing their parts together. She'd gone to a well-respected convent school before coming to the States, and the incongruity of her life before, and her life in New York, made her feel as if she were an innocent strolling through an awful, surreal Fellini film, viewing a parade of deplorable freaks.

Susannah danced by herself in the middle of a throng of strangers. Surprisingly, she was a decent dancer. The last time

Devi had seen Susannah was when she was sixteen years old and had just arrived at the San Francisco International Airport from Chennai to stay with her aunt in the suburbs of Fremont for three days before flying to New Haven for college. Susannah had been gangly and awkward. In spite of the skylights, the house was always shadowy, reeking of sandalwood smoke from the incense Susannah's Catholic father burned all weekend and every evening. Noisy, too, but not with sounds of civil conversation, like her house in Chennai, but with the maddening, discordant sounds of NPR and the Beatles and Siouxsie and the Banshees—each of the three people in that family listened to something entirely different. Evidently, they didn't want to talk to each other, and who could blame them. Every once in a while one of them would try to drown the others out by turning up the volume just a tad until the whole house vibrated.

Although Susannah was just a year younger than Devi, she had still been in high school then. They'd taken BART to the city, and because neither of them was in possession of more than their train fares, they window-shopped in Union Square and strolled around the Civic Center. Gaudy baubles and skyscrapers and plate glass windows and pigeons—the new world was startling. Devi noted the clean austerity, and even though San Francisco was not the largest of cities, she immediately saw her own life had been small and disorderly by comparison.

What she remembered most clearly from the visit, however, was overhearing Susannah complaining to her mother that Devi did not know how to use the toilet and had peed on the back of the toilet seat. Susannah's overworked and proper mother admonished her that the splashed liquid wasn't pee, but water, and that using cups of water to wash as people did in Chennai was far more hygienic than using toilet paper. The memory still made Devi burn with shame.

Exhausted, the dancers came to the booth where Devi was sucking a stiff lemon wedge from the rim of her third G&T. Veronica slid in next to Devi, her face flushed. "I was just telling Jake that he should have Sue come in to do head shots."

"You should," Jake said.

"You're so lucky that you know Devi," Angie said, sticking her blue gum-wrapped tongue out for a second, like a blonde Kali.

"I don't want to be a model," Susannah said.

"There's a lot of money in it," Jake said. "And I do have a client that wants someone with your skin tone."

"She's awfully dark to be pretty in a conventional sense." Devi looked down at her glass. It was empty except for ice cubes. She slithered down on the vinyl booth and crawled under the table, past all the legs. She wondered if she should ask Jake directly about the foundation gig in front of the others. The following day was when she was supposed to find out, but surely, he already knew.

As she emerged on the other side of table and stood up, Veronica was saying, "Oh, I would just love to have such beautiful skin. I can't tell you the number of tanning accidents I've suffered."

"If you think it'll pay well, I'm game," Susannah said to Jake. She looked at Devi pointedly. Devi shrugged as if she didn't care. She trudged to the bar to order another drink.

* * *

The next morning, the cousins woke early. Veronica, Bianca, and Angie were still sleeping. No snow, but the sky was overcast, the light watery and thin. "I can never sleep after drinking that much," Susannah said as Devi stumbled into the kitchen, rubbing sleep from her eyes, her tongue furry. Susannah was frying eggs on the stovetop and drinking a glass of almond milk. The odor of hot eggs and paprika made Devi want to throw up. She scooped espresso grinds into the machine.

After she'd pulled her shot, Devi said, "So, you're the guest. What did you want to do today? I was thinking blowouts. I need to get my hair done this weekend."

"My other cousin Lucy Marie wants to meet us. I thought we'd see some art—I've never been to the Frick."

"Your other cousin? Does she live here?"

"She just moved here with her husband."

Devi wrinkled her nose. Susannah's cousins on her father's side were Catholic villagers, untouchables who had converted to avoid the caste system. Everyone in Devi's Brahmin family knew the match was inappropriate, and that the scandal was why Susannah's parents had left India when she was born, not to return for ten years. "They aren't the type of people who go to art museums."

"What's that supposed to mean?"

"Those kinds of people are not cultured, are they?" She frowned. Her thoughts weren't coming out right. How to say this? "They're not like us."

Susannah raised her eyebrows and said nothing for a moment as she scraped the eggs onto a plate. She clattered around, opening drawers. Devi handed her a fork from the dishwasher. "They'll go. They're my cousins, they're family—they'll want to see me while I'm in New York. And after that, Jake asked me to come in to do some head shots."

Devi frowned. Family. Okay. That was probably a dig that meant she should join Susannah at the museum.

*　*　*

Susannah's other cousins waited in front of the Frick, the sloped snow hardening into long dazzling white slides across the steps below them. They were a dark, stout couple, well groomed, and evidently a bit older, wearing thick green and purple overcoats and hats and wool scarves. Lucy Marie wore a tiny gold cross around her neck. Susannah hugged them and called Lucy Marie "akka" because they were cousin-sisters, even though she didn't call Devi that, and as far as Devi knew, she didn't even know Tamil. Devi shook their hands quickly in greeting and stuffed her hands back in her pockets. "So wonderful to see you again! Do you like art?"

"Yeah," Lucy Marie said. Her husband, Paraag, nodded.

Devi smiled. Lying, of course. They probably hadn't been to a single art museum since coming to Manhattan. "Which artists do you like?"

The couple looked at each other. "Van Gogh?" Paraag volunteered. "Monet?"

"Oh, for Impressionists, we should have gone to the MOMA." Devi looked at Susannah trying to convey *I told you so*, but Susannah showed no signs of comprehending her expression, so Devi led them into the building, gabbing the whole way about how dull the Frick collection was compared to the Met or the Guggenheim.

As they drifted through the collection, Devi was astonished by how much time Susannah took, reading each placard and scrutinizing every painting as if she were trying to determine whether it was a forgery. Devi had completed a room before Susannah was finished with two paintings. Lucy Marie and Paraag followed her, whispering to each other.

In the next room, Devi asked, "Do you really like these?"

Susannah frowned, taken aback. "Yes."

"But not really, you don't. They're kind of boring, right?" Paintings were the sort of thing people pretended to like to appear cultured, to indicate their higher position in the social strata.

"Art history was one of my majors."

Devi hadn't known that. "But what do you see in them? There's nothing there."

"There's a there there," Susannah said, and snickered to herself before scrutinizing the next painting. Mystifying.

They pressed onward. Devi touched her smartphone repeatedly to determine whether Jake had called her about the foundation assignment. No emails. No texts.

Frustrated, she excused herself. Once inside the cool, reassuring quarters of the bathroom, she snorted a line of coke and reviewed her Twitter timeline and emails. Still no email from Jake, though he had time to tweet all morning.

After the museum, they lunched at a Gujarati buffet. Devi listened in silence and pretended to eat as the others caught up on gossip about other cousins Devi did not know. Finally she interrupted Lucy Marie's monologue about her sister's friend's wedding. "Isn't this the best food? These are the best ladyfingers I've ever had. What do you think, Paraag?"

"Perhaps a little pricey?" Paraag fastidiously wiped his thin lips.

"Oh, you can't afford this? I thought you said you were an engineer? Well, that's okay, lunch on me!" Devi said. "I'm waiting for confirmation that I'll be the new face of a very chic brand of foundation, so it should be no problem."

"He didn't say he couldn't afford it." Susannah's eyebrows knitted together.

"Isn't that what you meant?" Devi asked Paraag.

"No, no. That's very kind of you, but I can get lunch."

"Yes, we can buy our own lunch." Lucy Marie glared at Devi, who pretended not to notice as she turned her head to spit more rice into her napkin.

Once they'd finished the sticky gulab jamuns, Devi and Susannah bid the couple goodbye, and hailed a cab. At the agency, a photographer led Susannah to another room to do her makeup. Meanwhile, Devi found Jake's office. He was working on his computer. Pleasantries were exchanged, dragged on a bit longer than they should have, and finally she came to the point. "I didn't get an email from you about that account."

"I thought it best we do that conversation in person," Jake said. "You know how I hate drafting those assignment emails."

Bad news. Devi wished she could run outside and pretend she hadn't confronted him, but instead she used as brave a voice as she could muster. "Give it to me."

"The advertising firm wanted to go a different direction. With somebody who looks more ... dramatically ethnic."

Devi nodded vigorously, so he wouldn't notice tears welling in her eyes.

"You haven't worked in some months now, and my father thinks that, well, perhaps you ought to look for a new line of work. You're starting to show the signs of aging."

"I'm not even twenty-three yet. What signs?"

Jake looked around as if he wanted to escape, but then with an air of resignation, he propped his legs up on the table and looked into her eyes. "You're getting crow's feet, for one, which makes getting advertising work for makeup rather difficult. On top of that, you've developed some chub, a spare tire, like so many Indian models seem to do. And your hips—you just don't have the elongated look that's called for. I tried to pitch you to some of our editorial clients, but you're too conventionally pretty for that sort of work. Your look isn't unusual enough. I'm sorry if this stings, but you'd rather I be honest with you than waste your time, right?"

"I think I'd rather you waste my time."

Jake chortled as if she were joking.

"Maybe you don't understand, my visa depends on this."

"That's the thing. Your visa is up for renewal this summer. We won't be renewing. We can't sponsor you if you're not getting work."

Devi began pacing the office. She tried to keep the hysterical edge out of her voice. "What? You're joking. What am I supposed to do? What will happen to me?"

"Your family's still in India, aren't they?"

She decided to change tacks and approached Jake, placing her hand on his crotch and massaging. She whispered in his ear. "I can't go back. You don't want me to go back, do you?"

He grunted. She unzipped his jeans and stuck her hand in his boxers, running her hand over him, trying to do what he'd liked before. She kissed his neck and ducked down to take him in her mouth.

After he was finished, she looked up and asked, "Change your mind?"

"Oh, honey." He pulled his pants back up with a sigh. She stood. "You're very good, I'll give you that."

"Going back would be failure."

"Come on, it can't be that bad. You have a humanities degree, don't you, hon? You can get some secretarial work."

Afterward, Devi left the building and went to the cafe next door. She ordered a cup of coffee with cream and two sugars, realizing that it no longer mattered, if it had ever mattered, if she added cream and sugar to everything now. As she rode the elevator up to the agency to wait for Susannah, she sipped her too-sweet coffee and thought of the tropical heat of Chennai and her parent's cramped yellow stucco house on a quiet street. The tiny back room where she'd practiced going en pointe, where she'd rehearsed for the part of Clara, the parts of Odette and Odile. Her mother frying dosas and bringing her filter coffee topped with foam during breaks, how much her mother adored her. She thought of the financial sacrifices her parents had made so she could go to an Ivy League college and live in the States, so she could be a star.

It had been her dream since childhood, seeing the creased faded blue aerogrammes that came from the States from her three aunts who had moved there. Devi's mother would write detailed missives back to Susannah's mom and the other aunts in the States boasting of Devi's long list of accomplishments—that she'd been a finalist for Miss India, that she'd won a national essay-writing competition, that the British ballet company believed she was the best ballet dancer in all of India, that she'd been admitted to Yale and would live in a place that looked like a stone castle on the brochures, Saybrook College. But now this blow—there was no way to save face except perhaps to get some boring office job with an enormous corporation. She resolved to contact the alumni foundation for leads.

In the lobby, Susannah was grinning and shaking Jake's hand. "We'll be in touch with the details, but plan on extending your stay in Manhattan," he said. Devi tried to make eye contact with him, but he pivoted and disappeared down the hall.

As the cousins boarded the elevator, Devi asked what had happened. Her stomach rose into her throat as the elevator sank. Susannah's eyes were glowing, and she demurred, but Devi pressed for details.

They were walking out of the burnished steel elevator when Susannah said, "They took some preliminary headshots, and there's already some interest in a makeup company that does foundation. I never thought something like this could happen to me."

"Me neither. You know, at the convent school there was a little black Dalit girl and I remember the others used to chase her down the street screaming kaka kaka. I never wanted to play in the sun for fear of that." Devi laughed bitterly and continued, "America is so different. Here people try to tan."

Susannah didn't say anything for a moment. She looked hesitant like she was weighing her options, and then making up her mind, she said, "I'm going to go stay with Lucy Marie for a few days."

"What? You can stay with us. I don't mind. I don't mind at all. Why would you go stay with her? They live in Queens, no? You definitely don't want to stay in Queens."

"Come on." Now Susannah sounded bored.

"Come on what?"

"You know why."

"You're offended?"

Susannah didn't answer.

"I'm sorry. I was just pointing out one of those interesting cultural differences."

They trekked back toward the apartment in the silent dusting of snow. Devi led Susannah through Greenwich Village and stopped in front of an unmarked red door. "Just give me a moment."

Susannah followed her into the crowded speakeasy. Its fading, dark pine communal benches were lined with patrons and the lingering smell of old smoke. Large black-and-white portraits and the dust jackets of famous books lined the walls, lending the bar the magical weight of history Devi had expected to find everywhere in New York, too. Behind the bartender was a mirrored ledge that made the room seem more spacious.

"Devi!" John, the bartender, was a friend of Veronica's. He wiped the inside of a highball glass with a limp rag. "What can I get you? On the house."

"Lemon drop?"

As he busied himself pouring the vodka and triple sec, she leaned across the bar and whispered. "Actually, I was hoping to pick up some coke."

The bartender blushed. His eyes darted around, looking at the other patrons in their pressed button-down shirts and jeans. He cut a lemon clean in half. "I don't know why you'd think I have any. Will you and your friend settle for a drink instead?" He smiled at Susannah.

Fury swelled in Devi. Why should Susannah of all people get a free drink? She'd robbed Devi of her opportunity. "Veronica told me she buys from you."

"I don't need anything, thanks," Susannah replied. She touched Devi's arm. Devi flinched, letting a jangle of dark emotions— resentment, rage, bitterness, and frustration—consume her. Rage like the whitest light. So incandescent, she gave in to it.

"Veronica doesn't know what she's talking about." John placed the lemon drop in front of her, mopping up some cloudy liquid that had sloshed onto the bar. He crossed his arms, as if daring her.

"Yeah, right. Well that's just great. I know you're lying." She could hear herself talking, as if from afar, as if watching a ship from the shore. She wanted to jump up and down and shriek.

"Look, you got a drink on the house. I've got other customers."

"No, you don't. Come back here! I want my coke!" Devi shouted, as John turned to walk to the other end of the bar. She stomped her foot, and then she stomped again. She started to cleave in two.

He returned to hiss at her. "I'm going to have to ask you to leave."

"Devi, let's go." Susannah tugged her arm.

Devi slapped her hand away hard. "Let go of me." It was all too much. Why didn't anybody want to help her? Devi grabbed the cocktail glass and flung it at John's head. He ducked. The glass smashed against the mirror and the row of bottles behind him. Incandescent shards, a cloud of sugar, a cloud of sparkles, a cloud of white sand descended on the bar. Everything glittered in the light as if with fairy dust. As Devi stepped backward to escape the beautiful wreck, somebody slammed against her shoulder. She stumbled in her high heels, lost her balance and fell face-first toward the bar, starry with glimmering glass splinters. The last thing she felt as her forehead slammed the elegant dark wood was a piercing pain, as if a cold tooth had sunk deep into her eyeball.

*   *   *

As Devi slid forward into consciousness, she could hear the whir of a machine, and when she ran her hands over her arms, she could feel an array of thin wires. She opened her eyes reluctantly. From one eye, she could see the hospital room in which she was confined. Susannah was reading in a wooden chair in front of the window, and glanced up with a wary expression, like she was expecting a tantrum. It was snowing again, spectacular white fireworks in the grey twilight outside the glass. From the other eye, darkness.

Devi touched her face and felt something hard and secure taped around her right eye, pressing her cheek. "I'm confused."

"Some of the mirror must have gotten into your eye."

Images came to her, glancing images from before her blackout— her shameful screaming at the bartender, the glee she'd felt whipping the cocktail glass at him, the pain in her eye. She hoped she was wrong about what she remembered. Surely someone else had done those things. "That's why I'm wearing a bandage?"

"Are you anorexic?"

"No."

"They asked some questions. I think they think you are. You haven't eaten a full meal since I've been here."

"I diet. All models diet."

"I don't diet," Veronica said. She was standing at the door, sipping from a waxed paper cup of coffee. "I keep myself fit with Pilates. You do have a dreadful coke habit, dear."

Devi fingered the taped edges of the eye bandage, wondering what would happen if she ripped it off.

"Leave that alone," Susannah ordered.

The doctor arrived with a flock of nurses. They said she would need to stay overnight. Susannah and Veronica said they would return in the morning and left.

"How long will I be a cyclops?" Devi pointed at the bandage.

"Your eye needs a chance to heal."

"What are we talking about? A week? A month?"

The doctor waited and shook his head. "It might be better to have that conversation later, when you've had a little more chance to recover."

"I'd rather know."

The doctor said, "We're pretty sure you're going to experience blindness in one eye."

Devi took several deep breaths as he shifted in and out of focus. "Can you fix it or not?"

"We plan to have an eye surgeon, a specialist, take a look at it. But right now, I'll be honest with you, the forecast isn't good."

"Surgery's probably expensive?" She had no insurance, nobody who could afford to loan her the money. She thought of her parents struggling to pay even a portion of her college tuition and felt nauseous.

The doctor looked pitying. "If it can make a difference."

* * *

She slept in fits and starts. When she woke, the snow lay so thick outside the window that the glass appeared to be another opaque white wall. No outside light could seep into the room. She lay awake, brooding over her lost career, over how ugly her life looked. She dug into her memories but couldn't think of who or what to blame for what had happened, except perhaps herself, but the thought of how wildly she'd behaved made her stomach roil in shame, and she didn't want to stay with that memory. She kept her good eye closed against the fluorescent hospital lights, trying to forget the humiliating sound of the cocktail glass smashing, the shower of glass splinters.

Later that morning, Susannah returned, bearing a black plastic box with a clear lid. She opened the box to reveal golden brown vadas from a South Indian restaurant nearby. "I snuck these in. I thought they might remind you of home." She looked pleased with herself.

"Where's Veronica?" Devi asked.

Susannah shrugged and glanced away. "She said she had something she needed to get done, and she would be by later."

Devi knew she would not, especially not after she talked to John the bartender and found out what had happened. She ran a finger along the starched hospital sheets and eyed the fritters. All that oil. Reflexively she calculated how many calories might be in them.

"Do you remember visiting us in India when we were ten and eleven?" Devi said as she bit into a vada, even though she could tell it was still too hot. The trace of steam released the scent of curry leaves—home.

"Yes."

Dark brown bits of vada dropped on the hospital bedsheets. "We all thought you were so weird. You wore green eye shadow! And you thought our pizza and soda tasted bad, as if yours was so much better. You got sick all the time." It felt good to confess this, to see the look of consternation and pain as Susannah's eyebrows knitted together, to see someone else just as confused as she was.

"I don't remember all that. I thought we had so much fun together. We brought you a Hans Christian Anderson book. You introduced me to Enid Blyton and the Five. I never had any cousins, or anybody to play with, and you guys all had each other."

Devi continued to stuff vada into her mouth, shocked at how comforting it was to eat this spicy, salty comfort food without worrying about the pounds the vadas might pack around her hips, the puffy bloat they might trigger. Who cared? "We all imagined you had this decadent life in America, that you had all these fancy things, and ate bonbons and took bubble baths. You were just so strange, and yet for some reason, you looked down on us."

Susannah crinkled her nose as if the dissonance of what Devi was saying was too much to understand. "Actually, we were poor for the whole decade before we came to visit. It was so lonely here. We had nobody and nothing. Everything was just a constant struggle of trying to figure out what different things meant, what the correct pronunciation was for words so as not to get laughed at, how America worked."

Devi considered this disturbing thought—poor—for a moment. Snowflakes flew past the window, whirligigs of white. Poor seemed such a bald-faced lie. Of course, if you lived in America, it meant you were richer than those who lived in Chennai, and Susannah's parents had built an enormous, successful restaurant chain. Her voice was accusing. "All your mom's letters for years were about expanding the restaurant. About the awards she got, about being featured in food magazines." You couldn't be considered truly poor with all that wealth. Susannah did not have a clue. People didn't change, Devi reminded herself, remembering that awful disagreeable girl with the ugly, decadent magenta hair.

The chair creaked as Susannah leaned forward. Utterly baffled, hair in two messy braids, wearing shapeless overalls, tiny cheap zirconium studs in her ears, the rose-and-metal scent of her hair gel floating about her face, clasping her cheeks between her palms and wanting to understand. "I don't get it. You had everything when I visited. You had a huge family, and grandparents, and aunts and uncles and cousins. You all belonged to each other."

Devi could feel the iciness around her heart begin to thaw. As she stared at her cousin, she began trembling with a dark, terrible guilt. Perhaps she'd been looking at everything the wrong way if there was nobody else, nobody besides dumpy old Susannah, to visit her in the hospital.

"Are you still going to stay with Lucy Marie? You can stay with me, you know. I'm sorry for how I acted. I was just on edge from not eating, and the coke."

"Yes, I know. I understand." As if she suddenly knew who Devi was and didn't care anymore, Susannah sank back in the chair and fussed with her satchel. Her desire to understand Devi had faded into something else. "But I've already moved my stuff to Lucy Marie's."

Devi picked at the edge of her bandage. Sharp pain. "Do you want to move it back though? Please, I should make it up to you."

"She invited me there. She actually likes having me around."

"But I need you here."

"It's snowing again." Susannah gestured at the window as if this were an answer.

Devi was reluctant to let Susannah go. Would she rat her out to the family? Would she forgive her?

Susannah wore a stoic expression, like she'd already made up her mind, and there was nothing Devi could do to change it. She reached over and hugged Devi with stiff arms, holding herself as far away from the hospital bed as possible. Devi tried to hold her there a little longer to emphasize how truly sorry she was, but Susannah extricated herself without meeting Devi's gaze again.

After her cousin left, Devi began composing a letter to her mother in her head, explaining what had happened. It was more peaceful in the hospital bed wearing an IV than at the walk-up trying to figure out what to eat or not eat for dinner or deciding whether or not she had enough money to go out. She felt utterly calm and cared for. She wondered, what if she told her mother the truth? What if she explained how horrible her life here was, how there was no recovering from the person she'd transformed into in Manhattan? But her mother wouldn't understand this idea of reinvention—she didn't understand how rapidly you could change in America, how quickly your fortune could shift, how Devi had turned into somebody else here, and then turned into somebody else again, somebody else who'd failed—a reality that would have been unthinkable six years ago when she'd shone with so much promise. Back at home, where everyone on the block knew each other's business, people didn't reinvent themselves just for fun, the way they did in the States. They were defined from birth by the stars, and her mother would expect her to be the same glittering figure as that gifted teenager who'd boarded a plane at Chennai International Airport.

Instead, Devi would start the letter by explaining how well Susannah's visit had gone and segue into a spare account of this horrible freak accident that had partially blinded her. The bar would become a hole-in-the-wall restaurant, no, some middling restaurant that Susannah with her poor taste wanted to try. Someone else, a drunken troll perhaps, would stamp his foot and fling a hurricane glass. She would tell her mother how important it was for her to be around family right now, how she needed to start over. She consumed the last vada with a voracity she hadn't experienced since childhood, feeling the pain and contentment of her stomach expanding. Perhaps she would want to throw it up later, but she continued chewing, letting the glassy false comfort, the illusion of home grow, until she was satiated, and there was nothing true left.

ONCE UPON
THE GREAT RED ISLAND

When we first arrive on the great red island, Leon spends a few nights in the bustling capital, Tana. He has plans to meet with a handful of Indian and Chinese vanilla dealers. "This could get boring. Here—get a little sightseeing in, why don't you?" He holds out ten crisp bills.

I stare at the wad of cash without moving, feeling a little queasy. We'd planned to visit the rainforests east of the city together, but the lodge is going to be far more expensive than I can afford on my meager savings. Blushing, I wonder what my girlfriends back home would think of Leon's largesse. My parents taught me to spend frugally, to refuse even tiny indulgences, to worry incessantly about the invisible encroaching poverty they'd always felt as Tamil immigrants. Occasionally, after college, I'd rebel by spending a sum for luxurious beauty that would have shocked them, succumbing to the allure of an obscenely priced tasting menu, and then stewing in despair when the credit card bill arrived. But looking at the slat of sunshine from the hotel window grazing Leon's relaxed jaw and sincere grey eyes as he hands me the money, I swallow my pride. I can't afford this escape without him. I take the money from his warm dry fingers, and he squeezes my shoulder. I travel ahead in a cream Renault 4 that smells like cheap cigarette smoke and vanilla.

* * *

I spend my days hiking in a hazy eastern rainforest preserve with a group of tourists led by Solomon, a seasonal nature guide for the lodge. He alerts us to hot pink frogs, brilliant purple orchids, chameleons stock-still but for their long, darting tongues. There's so much beauty, such vastness here! It shocks me. I didn't know being alive could feel like this, like there's something so much larger at work. How far from civilization we are. Fewer people, less stuff, no expectations. There won't be any suffocating office conflicts to wrestle with, no relentless water cooler chatter. It will be just me and Leon in paradise. How light I feel imagining our future.

"It is taboo to hunt the Babakoto," Solomon notes, pointing at an indri crouched overhead. "One of the legends says that villagers used to send a honey hunter to venture among the rosewood trees. He would examine bee droppings on the leaves and watch the wild bees as they swarmed by, a dark swarm against the glowing red of the sun. They needed to determine where the swarm had settled to know where the honey flowed. When the honey hunter found a dark hole in the tree where the swarm lived, he would light a piece of dried sisal and draw the bees out of the tree with smoke. Slowly, he coaxed all the bees, including the queen bee, from their hollow and when they were out, he would gather the honeycomb.

"Early one morning, the honey hunter brought his son with him to gather honeycomb. The villagers awaited his return, but as night fell, he was still missing. The next morning, an elder organized a rescue party. They followed the large footprints of the man and the light footprints of his child into the muddy woods. Suddenly, the footprints stopped. The villagers looked around. One of them pointed at the sky. Far above, two indris were leaping. Branch to branch, branch to branch they went. The villagers watched the two as they escaped into the forest. They believed these indris were the man and his son, transformed, and singing a sad song. Nobody knew why they'd changed. Nobody knew why they were singing. But they named the indri 'Babakoto,' meaning 'Father Koto.' Listen to them."

We all stop and listen. The indris' haunting, dissonant howl is an aching, an echoing, from all directions at once. In that lamentation is everything.

An hour later, our group happens upon a baby indri. He's crumpled, lying in a clearing with a long red gash on one black limb. A feline creature with a cruel head like a mongoose's leaps down from the branch above. He circles the baby.

Solomon holds up a hand, whispering, "It is a young fossa. Careful."

Without thinking, I grab a stick. I poke at the fossa, urging him away from the indri. The fossa bats back. He's mean, cunning. I shake the stick, infuriated by his gall. Finally, he saunters off with an infuriating confidence. I scoop up the indri, and everyone gathers around me to pet him as he trembles in my arms. He smells like leaves. So soft, so helpless.

"It's a baby," Solomon said. "But in our country it is illegal to keep Babakoto."

"If I don't take it, the fossa will come back and kill it." I know right away we belong together. It's something about the way he snuggles into me, curving his body to fit mine, like he is simply an extension of me.

"And so it goes. This is the way of things here."

"But, if it's taboo to hunt the indri, surely there's no harm in saving the indri from being hunted by another creature? Otherwise what's the point?"

"That's different."

I carry the indri back to the lodge. Inside my room, I fashion a bandage out of a rough towel. Perched on the edge of the bathroom sink, the indri stares at me, his eyes gleaming like two flashlights, silent and completely trusting.

Later, Solomon knocks on my door. He's rounding me up for the nocturnal nature walk. "What do you think I should feed him?" I ask. At first Solomon resists my plaintive entreaties, protesting that what I'm doing is illegal, but three hours later, he returns with a poultice and gauze to dress the wound. I've worn him down perhaps. Or he's just plain kind, more likely. Around dawn, he appears again. "Come, Tarini. I'll show you what he can eat."

We wander the rainforest, listening to the haunting daybreak sounds of the other indri. I've wrapped a sheet around my shoulder, and the rescued indri wiggles, settling into the sling. "How come he's not howling or singing or whatever?" I ask.

"He's just a baby. His song will come when he grows up." Solomon snaps leaves from a bush. "You want young leaves. Like these red ones, see?"

A moment later, the right name for the indri drifts into my mind: Howl.

When Leon joins us a day later, we learn Solomon's wife lives some miles east in the region known for vanilla cultivation. Our relationship with Solomon seems fated.

"If you'll help us find a place, we'll hire you as a consultant. As our private guide." Leon turns from Solomon to me with his usual smug need to explain how things really are. "Locals will be more comfortable with us if he's on board."

I suppress a giggle, not wanting to upset someone who takes himself so seriously. From the start, I've secretly suspected Leon is in over his head, buoyed by a confidence I envy. But don't get me wrong. Mixed in with my doubt is the hot, fierce desire to be proven wrong: I desperately want him to be right that I'm overly pessimistic, a downer, and that this will be our happily ever after.

Solomon brings us to his village, returning to the thatched house he shares with his wife while we bunk at the Ivolo Hotel. Wounds healed, Howl accompanies us on our quest for the right farm. While we're alone together, I wait for his song, trying to coax it along by imitating the strange sound I remember. He cocks his head and looks at me funny. I make all sorts of strange sounds, but my familiar can't find his voice.

* * *

After weeks of searching, Solomon finds us a farm mysteriously abandoned by a French vanilla baron. We fall in love. The village president requests a hefty sum for it, but even in the dim light, it is noticeable that Leon doesn't flinch. This is both thrilling and disturbing. Maybe he doesn't really know what he's doing. Maybe my parents and friends were right for thinking I was crazy to follow someone so cocksure, so unwilling to acknowledge doubt in any situation. I've never made a deal, never bargained, because I'm always anxious that someone will call me out, call me on being an outsider.

The village president shakes his head like he knows we won't make it here and pities us for our delusion. And there's Leon, puffing himself up like a little boy, making himself confident enough for the both of us. I feel shame like an anvil on my chest. Why should Leon have to bear all of the discomfort by himself? Leon's got an energy that makes me feel all sparky inside, hopeful, like anything, even our crazy vanilla farm idea, is possible. So, I stifle my fears and latch onto his reassuring appearance of knowing. I nod along and try to look more certain. Back home, he was way more successful than me. Maybe he understands something about life that I don't. We conclude the deal at twilight.

Solomon drives our Renault 4 up the long winding road to the dark farm. He holds two lanterns in either hand like luminous scales of justice. Outside, the night philharmonic is in full force—a susurrus of leaves, the yowl of wildcats, ghostly whistling, and the occasional bright chirp.

Inside, the air is dank, musty, subtly sweet. We light candles around the villa. We light the wick of a kerosene lamp by the straw-filled plank bed. Howl darts around the room, nosing furniture, seemingly delighted by everything he sees. Dried ylang ylang flowers slump over the windowsill in the big room—limp yellow claws tinged with chartreuse. I run a finger over the rosewood dining table and draw up a velvety coating of dust and silt. In the corner are erotic ebony carvings somebody left behind. I choose a shapely woman bent at the waist, bowing to an upside-down world, and place her in the center of the table, arranging ylang ylang around her like I'm setting up an altar. There is promise here. This villa could be a home.

"You are sure you will be all right here?" Solomon asks me. He doesn't look at Leon.

"Yes, of course. Thank you."

After Solomon leaves, we flop onto the bed. Leon starts reading a vanilla cultivation book out loud, his booming voice misplaced—outsized for this villa. I stroke Howl's silky head.

"We're hand pollinating? Won't that be a little … intense?" Perhaps I should have asked more questions in San Francisco, but Leon's color-coded spreadsheets and profit charts had seemed well conceived. Knowing nothing about where we were going, I was impressed with their financial detail and foresight.

Leon's French father, Clement, had always wanted to return to farming, the vocation of his father and his grandfather before him. He'd died earlier that year, leaving Leon devastated, with no living family, but with a sizable inheritance and the half-baked notion that he should adopt his father's dreams as his own. I'd met Clement just once, after Alzheimer's had already ripped apart his memories and cognition, but I doubt that this sort of adventure on an island in the Indian Ocean is what he had in mind.

And we've come to an impoverished country, a country Clement's father helped colonize. When I consider how little we truly know about the country, I feel afraid for us. Leon assumes his vast sums of money will make the adjustment easy-peasy, just as it made our dating smooth and unhampered in San Francisco. A dollar goes so much farther in a Betsimisaraka village. But it's not just about having the money to do this, I want to tell him, it's not just about vanilla markets, or your past experience as a hedge fund manager. It's about the villagers' perceptions of us, about our ability to become a part of society here, to blend and belong. Knowing he'll dismiss this as sociocultural mumbo jumbo, knowing he won't give me any credit for knowing more than he does how hard it is to be completely new to a country, I stay quiet, fingering the rough blanket.

"It's going to be awesome." Leon's voice booms. He slams the book shut. "We just need to hire some people in the village to do the pollinating."

I tuck Howl into a basket stuffed with blankets in the corner, even though he'll likely leave his post soon to skitter around the floor. He murmurs in protest but settles. "When do you think the flowers will bloom?"

"I think we should be able to pollinate the flowers in a few months after we've retrained the vines." He keeps smoothing his hair back, a recognizable gesture of irritation.

"Are the vines supposed to be crazy and overgrown and black like that?"

"They're supposed to coil around the support branches. But in this case, they've run wild for years, so ... I don't have all the answers yet, you know! Man! Sometimes you can be such a killjoy."

I blow out the candles and turn down the wick. Thin wisps of smoke. The scent of melted wax curls toward my face in the blue moonlight. We reach for each other. His ocean cologne has worn off. His hard shoulder smells like wax and kerosene. A fruity musk. Or is that Howl? We're in a place of beauty, but there's also a danger—stepping off a precipice into the terrifying unknown—and my heart quickens, flutters up in my chest.

In my dream that night, I part my lips to speak. I'm standing outside my own body at some distance, watching my lips move, soundless. Nothing. Nada. After several false starts, I start singing the haunting, baroque melody of the indri. I realize at some point I am in a dream, and that if I stop singing, I will wake up, terrified that I may never sleep again. Tentatively at first, and then with verve, I keep on singing until morning. When I wake, Howl is lying in a pool of silence at my feet. I breathe heavily, exhausted by the intensity of my dream.

* * *

I imagine we'll take a few days to relax, but Leon's itching to retrain the vanilla vines. He pays five young, poor Betsimisaraka boys from the village: Louis-Paul, Pierre, Josef, Radama, and Antso. I'm sure they should be in school. According to Solomon, they need the jobs.

On sunny days, they bend sturdy vines over branches of the tutor trees, training vines around lateral branches, and burying them in soil to stop them from growing hundreds of feet. The morning passes quickly. Over lunches of zebu meat and rice and vegetable soup, I try to teach the kids English. I miss conversation. "Trop dur!" Too hard, they cry. The ebony figurine watches us from her upside-down vantage.

"English could be useful someday, if you do business with Europeans, or even if you're just dealing with tourists like Solomon does," I tell them. I'm not sure these boys in their frayed hand-me-downs will ever go to school, much less take jobs that require them to speak English, but it makes me feel better to believe I'm helping them, that I'm useful somehow.

Sometimes Leon spends lunch cursing over the slow dial-up Internet connection. Other times, he helps me with the English language lessons. "Try again," he says when the boys trip over the words. "English is so damn illogical." He smiles at me, his eyes reassuring and knowing.

There are no bookstores or libraries nearby, so I special-order books from overseas. The boys don't care much for English lessons, but they love story time. They crowd around, all sharp elbows and ribs and murmurs, as I read with Howl on my lap. We try to translate certain phrases to French. I'd always wanted to learn French as a child, but my dad refused to let me take it as a second language. He believed it was an elite language. "I want you to fight for the masses, for justice. You're in California, so you'll learn Spanish." He'd hoped to grow me into a Gandhi, a Che Guevara, a Martin Luther King Jr., one of these icons for justice, you know, who cared about fair conditions for the common people. But unsure of just what to say and whether I was even allowed to say anything, and always more attuned to beauty rather than fairness, I'd not turned into a fighter at all. Dad never really recovered from the disappointment.

After we decided to move to Madagascar, I'd taken a crash course in French, but learned only enough to get by at the market. And so, I read kids' books that feature foodstuffs—*The Hungry Caterpillar* and *Bread and Jam for Frances*. Most of the food is entirely alien to the kids. After the third or so book, the boys fall asleep on either side of me, their warm breath tickling my shoulders, as I move them onto the ground. They wake later to train vines.

* * *

Nights in Madagascar are warm. We drink *betsa betsa*, rum made from fermented sugar cane, and steep herbs and bitter orange peel in jugs of liquor. We circle around memories of our lost San Francisco lives like planets around the sun. I miss the quietude of public libraries. Leon misses the buzz of televisions in the bullpen at the busy hedge fund where he worked and his community garden. Sometimes, soaked in rum, we confess transgressions and cry over personal tragedies, momentarily forgetting the unbearable dark cramped rooms of the villa, the claustrophobia, that oily kerosene smell. We have drunken sex, most of it vanilla, Leon jokes.

"It's odd that such a lush fragrance is code for boring. We could go a little wilder," I say. But we never do.

* * *

When Leon leaves for Brickaville to network, I hike through the woods in my red rain boots, splashing through puddles. I study the leaves overhead for the yellow eyes of lemurs. Rarely do we spot one, and if we do, it's never another endangered indri. Howl leaps out of my arms the moment we step outside. He races across the boughs overhead. Sometimes, in spite of my unsteady footing, I follow Howl up a tree. I imagine what it would be like to be him in such a green paradise, to be far away from humans, free from their foibles, their perpetually defective and harmful systems. He waits for me before jumping to another branch, and soon I climb down again.

On one particularly long ramble, I spy a conspiracy of brown lemurs gamboling in a clearing. They pause, and Howl joins them, touching noses with a friendly lemur. I watch for a few moments, wondering if I should leave, whether I should allow them to bond properly, but then another, bigger lemur cuffs Howl in the face, and I can tell it hurts. He bounds back to me. I cradle him and even though I know it's ridiculous, I reprimand the entire conspiracy at the top of my lungs. The other lemurs slink away, disappearing among the gangly rosewoods.

Occasionally Solomon drops by to help gather leaves. As we walk through the woods, he says, "Howl could do this for himself, Tarini. The indri should be living out here." He says it offhandedly, but I can tell from the intensity of his gaze that it's a rebuke.

I nod, as if to agree, and play a little game of telling Howl to leave. I know full well Howl has no interest in leaving me. We are a team. "Go on, go!" I shout for Solomon's benefit. I can tell from Solomon's expression that he doesn't buy it but will put up with my charade. Howl jumps into my arms, whimpering. I hug him tight. "See?"

As the first year passes, Solomon and I grow closer, but he never warms up to Leon. I hear whispers when we walk around town: vazaha.

I confront Solomon on one of our forest strolls, and he admits that the older villagers are afraid of Leon because he reminds them of the French colonizers. The younger ones are simply following the elders' cues. I feel for the villagers. I remember the stories my dad used to tell me about the British. Any of these villagers could be my family. They look startlingly like my great-grandparents, who had fought for independence. I'm surprised to realize that I feel more for them than I do for Leon. It's like San Francisco, and all the things I had growing up have receded. I can barely remember that other person, that San Francisco self, that city person who talked about disruption. A pall settles over our nightly drunken bonding. I am trying not to think about Leon as if he were a blurry, distant stranger, rather than my boyfriend.

* * *

Once a week, we trek into the village to buy groceries. Sometimes we run into Solomon at the market. "Have you hired your guards yet?" I'm buying a sack of rice and Solomon is examining loquats.

"No. But we don't even have harvestable vanilla pods yet."

Solomon shakes his head. "It is risky, what you are doing. You have a big farm. Many things could go wrong. There are kalamoro. There might be gangs."

I did read about kalamoro in a guidebook. They're wild, supernatural, hirsute imps who supposedly live in the mountains. But I hadn't read about gangs. It seems ludicrous to anticipate violence. There's too much gorgeousness. This red land seems more suited to a fantastic reinvention of what the world could be like than a place of theft and bloodshed. But Solomon's round face is creased in fear for us. I bite my lip.

Leon appears, and drops a bumpy breadfruit the size of a football into my woven knapsack.

"It is not so safe. Kalamoro have been seen in these parts before, and you are almost two kilometers from the village. Until you are settled and you hire guards, you should not stay out there alone."

"Guards?" Leon asks. "To protect us against make-believe creatures? No. I'm not going that far. We appreciate all your help, Solomon. But we can take it from here." He pats Solomon on the back, the condescending way he'd pat a valet back home. Solomon flinches, and takes a step away.

As we take a shortcut up the hill, I push a little bit. "I wonder if Solomon is right."

"About?"

"The need for guards. I mean, he's from here. He's lived here his whole life. He knows more than we do."

"Those are just superstitions. Surely you don't believe in kalamoro." Leon brushes his hair back a few times and climbs with longer strides. I have to run to keep up, and I feel slightly humiliated, as if I'm not worth slowing down for. "Solomon is just your typical Malagasy. So much in this culture is stigmatized—fady this and fady that. I read about all this in my grandfather's journal years after he died." His breathing is ragged, and he talks fast.

I'm silent for a moment, wondering how to respond. "You never did tell me what happened with your grandfather. Why'd he leave this country?"

"It was the late fifties and the natives were insisting on independence. My grandparents sold their plantation to the locals and returned to France and became traders. It still makes me so sad, how they were driven off their property, their farm! For no good reason. What's got you jumpy?"

"I don't know. I just have a bad feeling about not listening to people who presumably know what they're talking about." I feel embarrassed for him, that he truly believes what he's told himself about his ancestors. And why is he willing to spend so much to buy a farm, but unwilling to pay guards? I have questions like this every day, but I rarely voice them, anticipating how quickly Leon will shut me down. It's just that he's got some blind spots, some weaknesses, I tell myself. It's not that he's a bad person.

"Trust me, we're going to be fine. I know it can get a little lonely with just you and me and that lemur, but don't give in to your irrational fears. We're going to make it. Just hang in there, okay?" He slings an arm over my shoulder as we arrive, hearts pounding, at a grove of peeling cinnamon trees on the top of the hill.

A rumor circulates through the region's arteries of gossip and speculation: a white couple has moved into a house near the palm-lined village square with its bleached cobblestone walkways and thin, sputtering stone fountain. Solomon picks up this rumor from Tanjona, a bartender at La Tropique, while trying to secure intelligence for Leon on when vanilla dealers will pass through the village. One day I see a couple sipping sodas on a bench by the empty marketplace building, a neglected relic of French colonialism. I introduce myself.

Alicia is tall and platinum blonde with toast-brown eyes and a pointy nose, sharp at the end like a beak. Brian is balding and wears glasses but is handsome in spite of his cheap ugly clothes, like a dime-store Gregory Peck. They're from Michigan and Pennsylvania, respectively. Alicia was a high school drama teacher before joining the Peace Corps. "We met here in Madagascar while working for the Peace Corps," Alicia says. "Both of us were completely enchanted."

"With Madagascar and each other," Brian adds. Perhaps the sincerity and syrupiness would have been off-putting in San Francisco, but here, it feels utterly charming.

They tell me about an initiative they've been working on, teaching the community sustainable farming techniques. "After our time was up, we decided we wanted to stay in this beautiful place and continue the work informally," Alicia finishes.

"We have a little farm. You should come for dinner." I'm thrilled at the way these words roll off my tongue, to be speaking in fluent English with someone besides Leon.

* * *

"How did you two meet?" Alicia asks that night over a bowl of noodles in broth. She pours herself another lowball glass of rum. Leon recounts how we met, arguing over who should get the last nopales at the farmer's market. Leon had won, of course.

Two years ago, his aggressiveness was a sexy contrast to my ex-boyfriends, all of them slackers who found me too intense simply because I kept a calendar. He asked me out, and it seemed clear he'd been pretending to crave nopales in his breakfast tacos just so he could talk to me. I was flattered. For him, fight was flirtation. Determined to impress me, he whisked me to Gary Danko, a restaurant so expensive the cheese came around in a separate course on a silver cart, and I'd made him the breakfast tacos the following morning.

"She was exotic *and* domestic. A perfect combination."

I've never heard him articulate this before, and it's at that moment I realize he still doesn't see me. I'm neither exotic nor domestic, and the description makes me think of a mail-order bride. We live alone together, but when he looks at me, he sees somebody else, an idea of me, but not the flesh-and-blood me.

Aren't we all just ideas to each other, though? Just ghosts walking around looking through each other at what we want to see? I don't know. But Alicia and Brian nod as if they understand. I try to smile to be polite. "He was so generous in the beginning."

"You don't think I'm generous now?"

"No, you're still generous. But we had a love-hate relationship at the start."

"You hated me? I didn't know that."

"No, no, I didn't hate you exactly, but we disagreed on a lot of things." I turn to Alicia. "We still do. I mean, he's a Republican. He's the one percent—a total robber baron capitalist."

"Well they've proven communism doesn't work." Leon laughs, a little too loudly. There's a slight wheeze in his voice. "It's not good enough to just complain about something that's worked well for a lot of people. What exactly do you propose?"

"A lot of people? Really?" I expound on social democracy in Europe, but trail away, feeling inadequate and dumb with all of them staring at me so skeptically. Why did I bring up politics, something Leon and I will never see eye to eye on? Perhaps this is exactly what I should bring up now that we're so far from home. Perhaps I can make him see me, instead of his shadowy idea of me.

"It's true the Grand Old Party's lost its way. I'm embarrassed every time I hear a Republican politician speak these days," Leon concedes unexpectedly. Rescue. Instead of relief, however, I feel distressed. He doesn't believe I had a good argument to make. Again, I fake a smile for appearance's sake, but I'm so angry, I've gone blind. There's a rage in me I didn't know was there before we came here.

"Opposites attract!" Alicia's voice is chirpy.

After Alicia and Brian leave, I let Howl sleep on the bed in defiance of Leon's distaste for him. "I've been thinking, shouldn't you release him back into the wild?" Leon blows out the candles. "He's making this place stink. Remember what Solomon said about them being illegal as pets?"

"He's bonded to me now."

"You mean you're bonded to him. I think you care about him more than you care about me."

"He's my familiar," I whisper. I pretend to be asleep until Leon starts snoring. His aggressiveness seems more pronounced here, lying on this bed with Howl. I listen to the buzzing and scritching of predators, of the wild, just beyond the walls.

"You can't make a big deal about any loss on the stock market," Leon used to say at the start of our relationship. He was trying to explain to me what he did for a living. "Or you'd be yo-yoing up and down constantly." But this is just what he does now that we are in Madagascar—makes a big deal about everything. What seemed at first like a kind of liberation terrifies me now. He's always up, focused on the future, on the next big thing. Where can you go if you haven't accurately assessed where you've already been? While his imagination is expansive and ebullient and fearless, mine, by contrast, is constipated, perpetually frozen, always already anticipating regret.

* * *

After a few shared meals, Leon uses his indefatigable charm to recruit Alicia and Brian to work on the farm. Soon we are spending all our time together and the delight that motivated my initial invitation dissolves into annoyance. While Leon is grateful to have more working bodies, I no longer have time to read or sit with my own thoughts. Every moment is swallowed up by this new group—interpreting their needs and desires and thoughts and spitting out what version of myself might work for them. I might as well be back in San Francisco, fielding the usual civilizational pressures. The coffee dates, the efforts to get mentorship, the casually racist remarks and the self-righteous gaslighting when you confront it, getting cornered by groping drunk tech bros at office parties or the boss over the copy machine. Even my pleasure in tutoring the little boys, something I assumed I could count on for years to come, has been cut short. Because Alicia knows Malagasy and speaks French fluently, she is better equipped to teach them English. Now they snuggle around Alicia at lunch reading the storybooks I special-ordered for them. Even worse, Howl takes a shine to Brian, occupying his lap for entire evenings.

I resent these interlopers, resent having to feign being busy in the kitchen so they won't guess that I'm upset. Before, the boys saw me as an ally. Before, I was the only person to whom Howl would cozy up. Although the villagers perceived Leon as *vazaha* and kept their distance from him accordingly, they'd liked me. Now, when I go to the market, I'm stuck with Leon, Alicia, and Brian, and there are almost no opportunities to strike up new friendships or even keep up my good relationship with Solomon.

I mention my anxieties to Leon that night, but he replies, "I don't know what you're so worked up about. It makes sense." He lounges in bed, snacking on the lychees that grow nearby, peeling off their red bumpy skins with his dirty fingernails, and popping translucent white fruit into his mouth. "People want to be with people who are like them because it's more comfortable. It's easier. You don't have to learn any new social customs or standards. Besides, you can still make friends with the locals. Who's stopping you?"

"Nobody," I admit. "But we spend all our time with this one American couple. It's unhealthy. It's incestuous. It's like how my parents only hung out with other South Indians when we first moved to the States. I thought we'd be going to the local balls and getting to know our other neighbors. For me, the whole point of coming here was to start over, to get, I don't know, psychologically further away from where we were. You just want to create a mini-America in a different location."

"Well, your parents worked with other types at their offices, didn't they? Why wouldn't they want something comfortable in their off hours? And why would you want to go to the balls? Those are for Malagasy people, not expats like us."

"I don't see why you should expect to be comfortable if you uproot your whole life. Assimilation is uncomfortable."

"For fuck' sakes, what are you on about now?"

Looking at Leon's sneer, I decide to stop talking. I've never felt these social customs that bind Leon, Alicia, and Brian—this small-talk way of relating warmly, but only politely—are truly mine. They're merely an elaborate ruse I've performed my whole life, while simultaneously living a wholly different way with my parents and relatives, one full of loud, animated conversations about the news, pop culture, books, conversations marked by generous hyperbole and sharp honesty verging into offense, and what Leon would consider an excess of political passion. This idea that I belong with Leon, Alicia, and Brian, continuing a charade of polite remove, now seems laughable.

I doodle on a piece of paper with an iridescent purple pen. An indri in an inky rainforest peeping out from behind a tree, its mouth scratched over a million times with pen. Little music notes float out.

"Why do you forever insist on your difference?" Leon is smoothing his hair back, defensive again, but instead of retreating, going on the offense to settle the score. "You're not special. You're just as American and bougie as the rest of us."

I say nothing. After all, how he sees me is exactly how I've presented myself from the first, and maybe it's sort of true. But it's only now—at the farthest point from California—that I understand I've been working a fraud upon my companions. Even in this lonely place, I feel closer to everything I see here than the people I grew up among.

*   *   *

That winter, Alicia starts working on a dramatic adaptation of Agatha Christie's *And Then There Were None*. "I just finished drafting it. I'm not sure it's any good."

I remember my mother, an enthusiastic reader of murder mysteries, giving me a leather-bound copy of five Christie novels when I was ten, and this particular novel was among them.

"She's being modest. I read it," Brian says, lifting a forkful of pork dripping with ginger sauce. "It's absolutely wonderful."

I eye them suspiciously. Alicia and Brian relate to each other in a peculiar way, like they've taken a course on being a couple and are modeling perfection for Leon and me. We have been squabbling more and more, bitterly like brother and sister. I imagine that if we were to scan Alicia and Brian's necks we would find regulating chips.

I'm giggling to myself when Leon says, "Well, what's to keep us from putting the play on? We'll gather the natives and do it in the square." He finds a pad of paper and begins scribbling ideas onto it with the bug-eyed mania I recognize. It's the same expression he wore in the weeks before we came to Tana. Brian and Alicia chime in with suggestions.

"Aren't there ten horrible humans in this story? A butler, a doctor, a judge." I tally the characters I remember on my fingers. "I don't think we can find enough fluent English speakers to play all the parts."

"Of course there are enough of us." Leon sticks the pencil behind his ear. "We'll go ask Solomon to round up some actors."

"Solomon can't make English speakers appear out of thin air. And I don't know how interested the villagers are going to be in Agatha Christie." It's hard to disguise my irritation with Leon now. He stands for everything I've been trying to escape.

"The thing you'll learn about Tarini is that she likes to fancy herself as somehow closer to the natives than we are." Leon holds his palms out as if to say, what can you do?

"Well, maybe she is. She probably has a family history related to imperialism somehow." Brian stacks Alicia's and Leon's dishes on his own and turns to me. "Don't you?"

I'm simultaneously startled, uncomfortable, and relieved. A laugh escapes. I nod.

Leon looks confused. "What are you talking about? She's not African."

To explain himself, Brian says, "Well, but she's Indian. I traveled through Tamil Nadu and Karnataka and Andhra Pradesh after college. The psychological mindset of the colonized is different. Isn't it?" He stacks dirty dishes in the sink and turns to me.

Righteousness burns through my body, a fire in my fingertips, and at first, I'm not sure why, because I kind of agree with him. But on the other hand, I've been proven right—I'm an outsider among them, they do see me differently, even though they pretend we're exactly the same. "My grandparents organized and fought against the British, but weirdly they were Anglophiles, too. Their attitude was like Stockholm syndrome on a continental scale. Is that what you mean?" I immediately regret the metaphor. It seems a total betrayal of my family who loves me, and also unnecessarily hostile to Brian. Most of the time, I can't find words to articulate my anger, but lately they've been gushing out.

"Sorry, maybe I didn't phrase that right?" Brian laughs good-naturedly. Leon scowls at me, a look that warns me not to rock the boat, not to give these two people he likes so much cause to leave us here alone.

Alicia's forehead furrows in concern. "So, you're against Agatha Christie?"

"Not at all." The version of the novel Mom gave me was structured around the ten little Indians nursery rhyme. Before it used "Indians," it had used the n-word, and later editions I'd picked up simply referred to soldiers. The ten little Indians of the novel were lily-white Brits who had committed transgressions that escaped adjudication in court, and this was why they were invited to Indian Island—to be subject to a rough justice. A line floats up in my mind: *One little Indian nothing to be done/He went and hanged himself and then there were none.*

"Great, so it's settled." Leon looks relieved. "We'll find some natives to join us."

* * *

The vanilla orchids bloom in November. Buds unfurl from their stems, curls of little white-yellow petals emerging waxy from the greenish buds, caterpillars crawling out of chrysalises. After my morning jog, the village boys—now numbering ten—show up to do the work of hand pollinating. The blossoms must be pollinated within twelve hours of blooming, or no pods will develop.

It's a delicate balance, Leon says, since we can only hand pollinate a few blossoms on each stem or risk disease. Using beveled bamboo picks, I move the rostellum, the membrane between the anther and the stigma inside the flower, and smush the lascivious yellow pollen into the stigmas.

You push and push. You hope they connect.

* * *

Of course, the pieces of the play do not come together quite as quickly as Leon imagines they will. It's too challenging to find fluent English speakers, so the president of the village suggests we translate the play and mount it in French instead.

I'm still not as fluent in French as the others are. "It's okay. I'm not much of an actor anyway. I can be responsible for costumes or set design."

Dismayed, Alicia adjusts the saffron kerchief tied around her head. "I want you to be part of things. I hope you don't feel excluded."

I smile to try to make her feel better. "Really, I can't act to save my life."

"You can direct," Brian says.

"But I was planning to direct," Leon says.

"He'd be much better," I say. Alicia and Brian glance at each other. I've got an idea about what they think of my relationship.

While Alicia translates the play into French, I sketch a design for the set, and draw elaborate costumes. Leon gives me money to order cloth in bulk from abroad, and they come from Coimbatore, from my parents, in white and jewel tones.

"I wish I could sew," Alicia says one afternoon while Leon is away in Brickaville. "Did someone teach you?"

I say my mother taught me to use a sewing machine in middle school. I describe how I'd had to sew my prom dress because there was no money to pay for a real one.

"You and your mom are tight?"

"Not right now." There's an awkward pause, but I say it anyway. "She wasn't such a big fan of me coming here, giving up my job, my independence."

"Neither were our parents," Alicia gestures at Brian, who is reading on the divan. "Mine were hoping I would have two point five kids and settle down in the suburbs. But I love it here so much."

Brian glances up. "Mine want me to be happy, but I think they thought I'd be doing something more lucrative with an engineering degree."

"Tell me about it," I say. "My dad grew up in a village with too many siblings, and his mother was constantly strapped for money to feed all the kids. He made me start working at age fifteen, hoping to make sure I wasn't ever dependent on a man. He was so disappointed in me for choosing to do this."

For a moment, I'm scared I revealed too much and embarrassed them with yet another shameful fact about myself, yet another stupid faux pas—I reveal myself, which is to say I blunder so frequently out here. But Alicia says her Midwestern mother is one of ten siblings and talks about how easy it is to get lost in a large family and to feel like you want to do things differently in your own family. "Yet somehow things turn out the same." Brian chimes in with a story about the Irish potato famine, and how the stress of poverty can pass from generation to generation, even after the threat of starvation subsides. Maybe it's epigenetics, I suggest, and they nod, like maybe they agree with me, and we chat for a minute about how confusing it is to tease out what's caused by nurture or nature. Soon, Alicia resumes her typing, and Brian goes back to his book and the afternoon disappears in the now companionable sound of hunting and pecking, the sewing machine's whir.

* * *

One morning, Solomon and I are roaming the woods to gather Howl's food when I make an offhand, disloyal remark about Leon. I know I've started to make these remarks a little too often, but I can't help myself. I feel guilty, but increasingly, I also feel justified in my distaste for Leon, even if he's the only reason I'm here. "He doesn't really understand why the villagers might see him a certain way."

"What do you mean?"

"Well, he doesn't give much thought to colonialism."

Solomon kicks a pebble. "Do you?"

"Me? I think about it all the time." My cheeks get hot, and I gather a handful of leaves so he won't see.

"But you are American in many ways."

"Not at all. Nobody else thinks so. Why do you say that?"

Anger streaks across Solomon's face. "Like with your lemur. You took it as a pet, even though I told you it's illegal. This is not how Malagasy people behave. This is an American thing to do, isn't it?"

"But he was hurt," I protest. "He would have died! I was saving him."

"You ignore the traditions of the local people in favor of what you think should be done—I tell you it is bad for that indri, for our way of life, but you insist that your way is the only right way. This is what imperialists do … and I care for this job, but you and Leon are barely paying those boys anything. Oh, they appreciate the pay, I'm sure! But you can't say you are different than Leon when you are making money from our land and barely putting it back."

Solomon sees me as an outsider, as an enemy, as a cog in the very wheel I'd come here to escape. I don't know how to respond to his accusations and fall silent in shame and anger. Am I going to give up Howl? No; I've resolved to keep him. So anything I say will be inadequate to fix this new ugliness in our relationship. And who is Solomon to tell me about Howl, anyway? He's the only creature I feel close to. I cross my arms. "I don't feel powerful enough to be what you say I am."

"How you feel about it doesn't change what is."

Some part of me believes he is right. The rosewoods loom overhead, impossibly tall. The wild forest shudders.

* * *

Within a few weeks, the vanilla pods, dark green and oblong, tremble on the vines. "You've got to brand the pods," Brian insists. He demonstrates by pricking a pod with a piece of bamboo, creating a kind of Braille on its surface. "There was a village a few miles away where they didn't bother, and bandits came by. They depleted the crop."

"We're in the middle of nowhere," Leon says. "We should focus on expansion, not protecting ourselves against some imaginary threat." I sigh and look at him pointedly, but he ignores me.

* * *

One night, Leon clears his throat, shuts his book on curing techniques, and turns to me. "We aren't much like each other, are we?"

"What do you mean?"

"I mean, we see our lives here in completely different ways."

Taken aback, I let my book drop.

Leon continues, "Even back in San Francisco, we knew it would be a big risk coming here together. Starting this whole new life."

"It was an adventure." For a moment, I think he's about to dump me, and I'm surprised to realize the thought worries me. But I look up, and there's a certain gentleness, a summer in his eyes.

"Of course, but it's frightening for you, too, isn't it? To depend on someone like me so completely? I'm more money-minded. And I can be kind of self-involved and egotistical and pigheaded. Or what was it you called me? A robber baron! Well, I'm sorry for that."

I wonder if Alicia and Brian have revealed something of our conversations, but Leon takes my hands in his with the earnestness of someone who wants to truly understand me. Where this insight has sprung from doesn't matter, at least not in this moment.

"I would do it again." I fall into him.

As our breath mingles, I feel myself sinking into his recognition, the sweet, shimmering mirage of being seen, of being exciting, of going back to the way I'd felt those first few elaborate dates in San Francisco, before I'd started to feel inadequate and ashamed, before I'd started to feel like a ghost, an idea.

* * *

One July at daybreak, we erect my set design in the old colonial marketplace building. The village president is thrilled the building is finally being put to use. The players, a mix of teenagers and adults, arrive in a haze of excitement. They try on their final costumes, squeezing into tight mid-century British attire.

As the drama begins, Howl is sitting on my lap. Solomon plays the most critical role, the part of the judge. When Howl watches the scene where the group finds the judge dead—executed by an unknown murderer, dressed up in judicial robes—he bounds onstage. Squeaking, he seizes Solomon's face between his black paws. Solomon extricates himself and tries to resume his death stare, but Howl jumps on his head, steals his silver-grey wig, and dashes around the stage. The audience whoops and laughs. The atmosphere of menacing gloom is ruined. I suppress a laugh.

Leon storms onstage. "Tarini! Grab that fucking lemur!" His voice shakes with rage as he continues. I chase Howl. The laughter grows deafening. Finally, the lemur pivots, wig in mouth, and leaps into my outstretched arms.

"Désolé a propos de ça," Leon says to the audience. He whispers to me, "Get him out of here."

Afterward, the actors and the audience join around a long table at a wealthy villager's house to eat. Leon sits down across from me with his plate of food, leaning forward with an accusation. "Why'd you have to bring him? You couldn't leave him home even for a few hours, could you?"

"I didn't want to leave him alone there in the house for so long."

"You wanted this to fail. You were against the play from the start."

"You guys worked so hard. Why would I want it to fail?"

"I want that lemur gone." Leon wags a finger at Howl, who shrinks back against my breasts.

"It wasn't so bad." Alicia slides into the seat next to me. "He's a wild animal, it was natural for him to be confused."

"Are you kidding me? It was your script—you should be more upset than anyone."

Alicia shrugs. "It was meant to be fun."

Leon shakes his head.

* * *

The following sunrise, I'm jogging hard to forget the mayhem of the day before, when I notice something is different. The vines are naked, shorn of ripened pods. At first, I think I must be wrong, but as I run between the dim rows, the rising sun illuminates the empty vines. I race back to the house, anxious and disbelieving.

When I tell Leon, my voice tentative, open to the possibility I've hallucinated this loss, he streaks out of the villa. Not sure what to do, I fetch bath water from the well. From a distance, I can hear his cries of anguish. I take my bath in the barrel and try not to panic.

The kids show up at their usual time, but I tell them they should go.

As they turn to shuffle out, Leon storms into the villa. "Do you know who did this?"

"No sir," they answer.

"You must know. Was it Solomon?"

"They don't know." Dread blossoms inside me. "Look at their faces. They worked as hard as we did. They were looking forward to a bonus from the sale. And Solomon is our friend."

Leon grabs the ebony figurine of a woman and throws her across the room, where she smashes into a ceramic vase. Shattered pieces of the vase fly everywhere, but the figurine remains hard and intact and unyielding. Howl jumps into my arms.

The boys flee.

"Solomon knew, the boys knew, we had no guard," Leon says. "We hadn't finished marking the beans. They resent us, you know. They really do."

I'm surprised Leon has considered their feelings at all. "I promise you, they don't."

"What the fuck? Are you defending him? It's outrageous! I've lost everything, and your only concern is them."

"Maybe we deserved it. We should have gotten guards, like he said."

Leon looks at me with so much hot contempt in his eyes, I feel I might burn. "We? We? What have you contributed? You're a freeloader. Practically a squatter. Come to think of it … were you in on this too? Did you steal from me?"

"No." In spite of everything, I'm shattered.

"I want you gone. Get the fuck out." Leon stomps out of the villa.

Hours pass. I see Leon wandering among the ravaged vines, shouting and distraught, a madman. He paid significant sums for the farm, but the financial loss is less significant than the loss of time—years of work gone, our lush and voluptuous dreams ripped from the vines without a single return. Finally, he walks to the car in a determined huff, his body leaning forward, pushing against some invisible wind.

I hunch forward on the divan, my nose against the glass of the window. I strain to see the car as it heads down the hill. It isn't wise for Leon to talk to Solomon in this state—I'm sure this is where he's going. My whole body is shaking, and I can't seem to stop it. Perhaps I should chase him, perhaps I should say something, but there's nothing more I can say, is there? Perhaps I'll pack my bags and find a way to Tana alone. I'll hitchhike.

An hour later as I'm stuffing clothes into my suitcase, heavy with disappointment, I smell something acrid. The air is smoky. I check the stove, but it is off. I walk outside to look beyond the escarpment at the plumes of black smoke. I jog toward the precipice. Shading my eyes from the sun, I squint over the vista I love. All this time, its titanic beauty has made everything seem possible, and in this moment, it's no different. What should have been impossible has happened.

The village is burning. Long red houses with fine white trim set ablaze. From such great heights, it is horrifyingly gorgeous, how the orange flames caress the painted wood, and the smoke swirls into the sky, nearly obscuring the tremendous clouds.

I sprint to the road with Howl. Past rice paddies. Past two men peeling cinnamon from trees. I veer downhill to the shortcut. I'm not sure what to do, but something has cracked open inside me. I must do something. Halfway downhill—my nostrils flaring, my lungs expanding—I can smell everything in the rainforest with preternatural acuity. Wild apples, acacias, lichen, black-scarred clearings for farming rice. My nostrils flare. I brush a hand across my face—the softest fur. Climb higher, farther from the red soil leeching into creek water, ever closer to the scorching white noon light.

Howl and I follow running blood through shadows. Yaw around a rosewood, tear to the end of one bough before swerving onto the next, and the next, driving ever higher, ever closer to the village, nearly flying. As we swing through branches, approaching the gyre of smoke and flame, an aria stirs within my ribcage.

Watching flames destroy the land I love, it is Howl, my familiar, my double, my twin, who starts to sing for the first time. The sound escaping his body is magnificent and otherworldly, telling of ghosts and cities and sirens—an unyielding green scream.

THE LOGIC OF SOMEDAY

By her twenties, Susannah had come to believe that pain was a kind of currency. Everyone had something they always wanted to do someday, and most people were willing to pay for their dreams with pain. Once she realized this truth, she saw it everywhere, even in the places she'd least expect.

When she'd been shunned by both the white and the Tamil Brahmin kids in her class, the elementary school librarian, an elderly black woman wearing chunky jewelry and a heady violet perfume, had given her The Velveteen Rabbit, and it had quickly become her favorite book. She believed it was about how love made you real. But twenty years later, when she read the book to her babysitting charge, she realized that the stuffed rabbit became real not so much because of the power of a small boy's love, but because, after he endured the pain of being taunted by real rabbits and the small boy abandoned him, a fairy recognized he deserved to be real. So it was the pain perhaps, and not love, that served as a catalyst.

For Drew, the dream was to become a successful marijuana farmer, and it was only late in their relationship that she understood he would sacrifice everything to it.

* * *

It was 2004, and they'd been together for three years. The grow room had a wild smell, a forbidding swirl of marijuana, fresh paint, and animal droppings. Drew was down on his hands and knees tending to the girls in their white buckets, slowly clipping their sticky leaves with great concentration.

"Done yet?"

"No. This needs to be done right and doing things right takes time." He wiped sweat from his freckled brow. A dealer Drew had met just days before wanted to pick up a dozen dime bags that night.

"You're using a shit ton of energy with these lights."

"Don't use some environmental excuse to nag me."

"They're waiting for us. They don't like when we're late." Trying not to beg, Susannah added, "Come on! It's a free meal."

"Look, I already told you I would go, so I'll go. But I gotta get this done first." He continued to clip silently. His chestnut brown hair and tiny hoop earrings gleamed. The halide light bounced hot and white off the dimpled silver foil tacked against the wall.

Forty minutes later, Susannah hurried into the dimly lit Thai restaurant, alone and irritated. Her parents were already sitting at a table for four, and they didn't remark on Drew's absence at first. But when they finished ordering, pink linen napkins drooping on their laps like injured birds, her father said, "So Drew couldn't make it, huh?"

"No, he was busy with a project."

"Isn't he unemployed?"

"Yes. But he has projects."

Her father raised his eyebrows.

"I don't know why you can't understand that," she said.

"We'd like to talk to you."

"We're worried." Her mother fidgeted with her napkin and adjusted her batik tunic.

"How serious is this relationship?" her father asked, the dark orange-pink slivers of his papaya salad hovering near his mouth.

"Serious," she said, meeting his gaze.

"Like marriage-serious?" Above them by the wall, a giant gold Buddha loomed over their conversation.

"Who knows," Susannah said. The waiter set tom kha and pad thai noodles on the table. She shoveled the noodles into her mouth—hot and sweet. They felt like slippery worms on her tongue. Her parents disapproved so strongly that there was no room to question her relationship with Drew at all.

"Because he doesn't act like it." Her father's elbows were on the tablecloth and his fingers were clenching and unclenching. Her heart tightened in response to his worry. They had married outside their castes and against their own parents' wishes, but they thought they were entitled to an opinion about her life anyway. In her purse, at that moment, there was a wedding photo of them that she had taken from their photo album when she went to college and carried around like a sentimental fool to remind herself how lucky she was that they had defied tradition. A bare-bones ceremony, her mother wearing an ordinary sari—as if it were any old day—almost no guests, none of the usual family support and pomp that attended Indian weddings. "He doesn't act like it's serious, and if someone isn't serious, you really should move on."

"And he smokes," her mother said, dabbing white soup from her lips with a napkin. She was referring to cigarettes, not marijuana—drugs of any kind would have been a whole other issue. "He's not very smart, is he? He didn't go to college. He doesn't care about his health. You can't have a family with someone like that."

"I'm not any better than him."

Toward the end of the meal, Susannah's father announced in a more cheerful tone, "I've been watching *The Bachelor*."

Susannah snorted. The reality show where one relentlessly boring white man was pursued by a bevy of shiny, hopeful girls that usually included at least one sociopath. Her father continued. "And it seems to me that American men are not looking for a commitment with girls who just hang all over them. I mean, it's disgusting, the way these American girls just throw themselves on this one guy. I just don't want you to be like those girls."

"You're offering me dating tips from *The Bachelor*?" Susannah sneered.

You can act according to the script for Tamil culture or the script for American culture, her dad would often claim, but you can't pick and choose what you like from each script.

"Well, yes. Dating in America is so different from what we had in India, you know, and these reality shows are giving me an idea of how it works."

"They edit reality shows, you know, they're not real." Susannah stabbed at her tofu. Her parents never talked about it, but they had been brought up in segregated realities, and so they had completely different ideas about what Tamil culture was, what India was, maybe even what happiness was, and she'd grown up not quite sure which parent's version of reality she should trust. She wished she could honestly tell her father he didn't understand American social rules at all, and that's why he didn't understand her decisions, but she wasn't sure she would go that far. She was a bit of a freak regardless of what cultural standards were being used.

A few minutes later, Susannah's mom volunteered, "We could put up a matrimonial ad for someone here. Or even someone from India. The other day I heard from Anjali's mom. Remember how I told you she couldn't find anyone? Her parents put out an ad and found a suitable match with an engineer from Bangalore. Do you want us to do that?" She did not say outright that nobody would want Susannah, with her dark brown skin and flat nose and fuzzy, curly hair, if she waited much longer, but this was what Susannah heard. She was only twenty-six, and none of her friends were married, but to her Tamil mother, she was reaching the end of her shelf life.

Susannah considered asking what Tamil man would answer an ad that told the truth. After all, her mother had lost her Brahmin status and, for many years, her ties to her family, just for marrying her father. But her mother's chocolate brown eyes looked bright and wounded, as always, and Susannah couldn't bear to see them look even more devastated. Instead she said, "Anjali is one of those nasty girls who told me I wasn't really Indian when we were in school together because you gave me a white name. I can't believe you still talk to her mother."

"You never told me she said that. What ignorance! There's no such thing as a white name."

"Of course I told you! You just blocked it out, the way you always do."

"What do you mean?"

"What do I mean? That's what you do, what you've always done. Deny and avoid everything you don't like. Racism, bigotry, misogyny. Just pretend it doesn't exist. Maybe it'll go away!" Anger, hot and throbbing just beneath her skin. It was a relief to finally say it, even though she knew her mother, never one for introspection, had no idea how to respond.

Her parents glanced at each other and frowned but said nothing.

When her father left for the bathroom, her mother murmured in a soft voice, "I just don't want you to be *alone* your whole life."

"What do you want from me? I'm not alone."

"Life is so hard. Marrying someone who is looking in the same direction makes it easier. You and Drew are so different."

Susannah wanted to ask how well her mother had known her dad in the three months before they married, and whether she would do it again, knowing the isolation that would come from being just the three of them alone in a foreign country. "Mom, come on, you don't even know him."

When she returned to the warehouse, it was almost midnight. Drew and Aristotle were watching Adult Swim at a tilt, sitting on the couch with a missing leg. A pungent spliff still fumed in the ashtray, a brilliant orange gleam on a balsa coffee table stippled with ash and cluttered with spare car parts and the metal guts of a half-built computer.

Susannah slumped on the armrest of the couch and stared at the screen. The thought of dumping Drew made her heart feel small and cramped—wasn't true love supposed to transcend all that? Her parents had been so in love once, they flouted all convention and escaped to another continent to start a new life. Perhaps it hadn't worked out so well, perhaps they were no longer in love, staying together only because that was what you did, but at least they had their original happiness, their hope, to look back at.

* * *

Sometimes you find someone hot because they trigger a secret, rarely traversed corner of your psyche, because they induce a strong click of recognition inside you. Other times you lust after them only because they aren't who you expect them to be. Drew was neither of these. Aristotle was both.

Aristotle was muscular and black with a voice like molten gold. "I'm a cinephile. I want to make films," he said one evening early in his acquaintance with Susannah, when Drew was out delivering marijuana to a buyer.

"What's your favorite movie?"

"Hard to say," he said. "There are so many."

Susannah smiled and turned back to her book, ready to dismiss him as just another pretty face.

"*In a Lonely Place* and *Bridge Over the River Kwai*. It's a tie."

"You serious?" A jab of delight.

"You thought I'd answer with some Spike Lee title? Or maybe—"

"Not at all. But that decade for film is my favorite, too. For the quietly glamorous films, more than the grim ones."

"Quietly glamorous like what?"

Susannah was taken aback again. Drew rarely asked her questions about herself, and they usually watched the movies he wanted to watch, full of pointless irreverence and fart jokes.

"*Roman Holiday*," she said. They compared notes about film until Drew returned a few hours later, needing Susannah to help him trim leaves for another delivery.

The following week, Drew's parents, who were retirees, invited them to dinner with some of their friends. They drove an hour and a half to their mansion in the hills and ate under heat lamps on the patio at a reclaimed redwood table overlooking a Benedictine monastery. Drew's mother had dyed her grey hair platinum blonde and introduced Susannah to her friends as Drew's friend, not his girlfriend. Drew did not correct her. Susannah smiled politely and shook hands.

Drew's parents asked how he was doing, and he lied without even blinking, claiming he was doing some freelance work for an animation company. "How's that extra bedroom for another renter coming?" his father asked. He passed her a glass of Two Buck Chuck—a two-dollar Pinot Noir. Drew had told her that they saved their special reserve wines for romantic evenings alone, the opposite of Susannah's parents, who only ever brought out their best for guests. "Can I get my tools back?" Drew had borrowed tools from his father to build the grow room and developed an elaborate cover story. "It's all done," Drew said. "It looks fantastic. I'll show you pictures sometime."

"You look so handsome these days, Drew. Just like a younger version of your dad," said one of the friends. She pushed her purple designer glasses back up on her attenuated nose. "And handy, too! I bet Susannah appreciates that. It's getting so expensive in the Bay Area to hire folks to help around the house."

Susannah smiled and nodded.

"Drew's friend just graduated law school," Drew's mother said.

"Oh, are you planning to be a corporate lawyer?" another woman wearing garish pink lipstick and culottes asked Susannah.

"No, environmental. Plaintiff's side."

"Oh. Isn't that interesting," said the woman, conveying with her tone that it was not interesting at all. She began eating the arugula salad that Drew's mother put in front of her.

"I keep trying to get her to interview with blue-chip firms so I can retire and we can be fabulously wealthy," Drew said. "But she's a do-gooder."

"Well, I think that's wonderful. Just so long as you're not planning to work for the Southern Poverty Law Center or some kooky liberal organization like that," said Drew's father. Drew's mother started to reminisce about the good old days when you could get a colored girl to clean your house for dirt cheap. Colored girl. Although she was Indian, Susannah wondered if Drew's parents saw her as the colored girl with whom their son was "friends." She seethed. Why did Drew let them see her that way?

On the ride home, they listened to rap music, not speaking. An intense heat wave had arrived in Oakland, and the moment they walked into the warehouse, Drew turned on an industrial-strength fan. Susannah went into the kitchen. She didn't want to clean it again. It took Drew three or four days to bother loading his dishwasher, and in the meantime, he stacked the dishes high inside the sink and then barricaded the edges with five more towers.

"I can't do this, I can't do this. I hate the stink. I hate everything about this! Can't you just cut back? Just a little?" She threw a metal spoon into the careful pagoda of dishes. A cup at the top slid off and all the other cups followed, landing with a clatter. She palmed sweat from her forehead.

Drew said something, and they yelled back and forth, not able to understand each other over the wind from the fan, until Drew turned it down. "No. I mean, come on, Susannah. You knew this was me going in." He stepped back toward the refrigerator.

"Well, you weren't growing back then. You weren't dealing."

"What do you want? I got a medical card."

"It's just for personal use."

"The po-po aren't coming into this warehouse and they wouldn't care even if they did. My best doesn't seem to be good enough for you."

"Maybe we should break up."

"Is that what you want?" He grabbed a Red Bull from the refrigerator.

"Why don't you see yourself, like really see yourself?" Susannah crossed her arms. "You're an addict. All your friends are addicts."

"Pot isn't addictive."

"The worst part is you think all this is normal."

"Well, it's not like I ever told you I was normal. If you'll remember, I warned you I was just the opposite."

"You can't start your day without it, not an hour passes without you smoking it. How can you not see how depressing that is?"

"Everybody loves a wake-and-bake stoner."

"I don't know about that."

"If it's so depressing, why be with me?"

"Because I love you." Just as the words left her lips, she realized they weren't quite true, and maybe never had been. He never probed who she was, he never criticized her, and so they were perfectly comfortable together—but had he ever really seen her?

"Listen, the world is cruel. It's a fucked-up place," Drew said. "I need something to make it less terrible, so what? That's America, baby." Silence. A hiss after he cracked the aluminum tab back to open his drink.

Susannah took a deep breath, trying not to say too bluntly the angry things she was really thinking. "You're always saying it's fucked up. But really, your parents are filthy rich and you're talented. This world was designed for people like you."

"Well, I told you about my *issues* from the beginning."

"I should have believed you." Susannah stomped into the warehouse bathroom, locked the door and sat down in the tub. He didn't follow.

Drew had once promised their relationship would be entertaining. It was during their fourth date, a night of chicken tikka masala and a Kabuki-influenced theater performance about a green bird. He had passed her Indian food test by agreeing to eat some form of it, even though he would have preferred steak. Back then, contrasted with all the Federalist Society joiners in her

1L class, she found him refreshingly anti-corporate and sweet and odd, and so she didn't quibble that chicken tikka masala wasn't truly Indian, but a British bastardization of Punjabi cuisine.

They were walking up Euclid Avenue to Susannah's apartment when she asked Drew what his tragic flaw was. The wind picked up long ochre and sienna-colored leaves as they climbed the steep hill, passing them forward like batons.

"Tragic flaw? What do you mean?" he asked, lighting a cigarette and holding it out to her. She shook her head. He took a drag.

"Everyone has one. Like Hamlet might say that his flaw was being indecisive. Romeo might say he fell in love too fast. Frasier might say his was being pretentious. Or maybe the characters wouldn't say, but other people, professors, would. You know what I mean."

"Jesus. Does anyone watch *Frasier* anymore?"

"Don't keep me in suspense."

"I just want to say the right thing."

"There's no right answer."

"Well, I mean it's not like I have no flaws." He had big bones and stood there like a fairytale giant, a hulk, a shelter, with the wind blowing his wispy chestnut hair back. Enormous and unapologetic.

"Ha, I hope not!" Susannah tapped her black leather boot on the pavement. "You'd be boring if you had no flaws."

"My flaw is... I'm always trying to make girls laugh."

"Not exactly what I had in mind. I was thinking something sad." She started walking down Scenic Avenue toward her apartment and he followed.

"Oh, trust me. I want it so much, it is sad. Though I'm sure all the shrinks my mom dragged me to would come up with other stuff."

"What flaws would they say?"

"Oh, god, it's what they've already said, which is everything," he said. "ADHD. Oppositional defiant disorder. Bipolar disorder. Narcissistic personality disorder. Conduct disorder. Since I was five, my mom had them watching me in a little room to figure out what was wrong with me, observing how I played. They all had different diagnoses. You name it, I've been diagnosed with it."

"You're kidding." Viewed through the lens of diagnosis, Drew's calmness seemed peculiar, rather than organic, something to fear rather than trust as Susannah had been doing.

"No, she thought something was wrong with me. Really all I wanted was her attention."

Susannah laughed to be amiable.

"I was on a boatload of pills until I was eighteen. Then I refused to take them. But pot is nature's medicine. It keeps me feeling normal." He wasn't curious what Susannah's tragic flaw was and she didn't know what she would have answered.

In her kitchen, she had uncorked a bottle of sparkling wine. The cork narrowly missed Drew's head as it sailed toward the blue and pink chalk messages on the blackboard her roommates had stolen from TGI Fridays. She poured the bubbly into two garage sale beer steins. Drew handed her a black-market Vicodin and she washed it down. Meanwhile he busied himself at the kitchen table, shaking a trail of pot into the center third of a rolling paper and arranging the flecks with thick, freckled fingers.

Susannah wondered how his parents could put him in a room to be observed when he was five—however much her parents annoyed her, she could never imagine them trusting someone else to tell them who she was—and a wave of tenderness washed over her as she imagined Drew as a little boy, slowly becoming aware that people were watching him from the other side of the glass as he played, the paranoia he might have felt.

He had finished rolling the spliff and clinked his glass against hers. "To our relationship. I can promise it will be entertaining."

* * *

When Aristotle came home, the heavy metal door to the warehouse slammed behind him, and Susannah climbed out of the bathtub and listened at the door. He and Drew began talking and Aristotle admitted he'd lost his job. "So I was late to work. Again," he said, his sheepishness plain in his voice. "But I also think they were looking for an excuse to fire me."

"I'm sorry, man," Drew said. Someone turned on the television— another cartoon with its sounds of wascally wabbits falling off cliffs and a popgun going off like fireworks.

Susannah washed her face in the sink, thinking about the matrimonial ad her mother could place. To draw interest from any of the Indians in America she'd ever met, it should say something like "Fair Brahmin woman with wheatish skin seeks handsome young doctor." But those were lies. She was not fair. She was not a Brahmin. You were supposed to take your father's caste, and so she could say Christian or Dalit, to attract other Dalits, but that, too, didn't seem quite right. After all, she'd grown up mostly among Brahmin immigrants like her mother, eating TamBrahm food, reading Amar Chitra Katha comic books, and learning Hindu mythology. She was an outcaste, a misfit by all the standards.

When she emerged from the bathroom, Aristotle and Drew stopped talking. Drew looked down at his book. Aristotle was extremely handsome, distractingly so when he looked at Susannah. Even his gaze unnerved her. She slipped into the bedroom to continue eavesdropping in peace, but neither of them said anything notable. Eventually Drew came to bed, and they fucked, the kind of clawing and sweating and writhing that led to an intense orgasm on his part and a faked one on hers. After a fight like that, their relationship was too fragile not to do it. As usual, Drew was out of condoms and he pulled out before coming.

* * *

"We're going to be late," Susannah said. She stood by the front door, winding a scarf around her neck.

"Let me just finish rolling my joint." Seeing Susannah's irritation, Drew said, "What? You know I can't sit through the whole movie without it." As she waited for him to finish rolling, and knowing they would be late to the movie, she could not stop thinking about her parents. Every time she thought of their worried faces and juxtaposed them with the entitled yuppie obliviousness of Drew's parents, the more anxious she grew.

But as they hurried to the movie theater, a homeless Latino man asked for change, and Drew paused to hand him a twenty. "Need change?" the man asked.

"Nah, man, keep it," Drew said. She squeezed his hand as they continued toward the theater.

When they returned from the movie, Drew had to drop a bag off with a customer. Susannah was supposed to be studying for the bar exam, but instead she started cleaning the warehouse. She was going through her purse, throwing away receipts and old business cards, when she noticed Aristotle watching her from the couch. "What's gotten into you?"

Susannah shook her head. "I'm sick of this."

"The mess? It does get pretty filthy around here. I'm sorry."

"It's not your fault. Who lives like this? Who would put up with this extravagantly unsuccessful pot farm? He's too much."

"I don't know. Even people who are fucked up are loved by someone."

"I know that."

"My mother put up with my dad's affair for thirty years. He's had a mistress for thirty years. Can you imagine? But she's still putting up with him. Are your parents still married?"

Susannah nodded.

"An arranged marriage?"

"No, they married outside their castes, outside their religions. It was what they call a love match." Both families had been equally unhappy with the marriage, which was seen as shameful, impure, and wrong. Her mother's clan disdained her father and his family for being untouchables, and they didn't much care for her either. Her father's Dalit Catholic family was suspicious of her mother's fair-skinned Brahmin family. Brahmins didn't allow Dalit in their homes, didn't allow a Dalit to touch their food or even the pots they cooked with—it was the intense, unyielding upper caste abuse of Dalits that had motivated their escape to Catholicism. She learned over the years that being Dalit was so stigmatized even among the Indians in the Bay Area that it might ruin her mother's restaurant, marketed around authentic Brahmin home cooking and traditions, if they told people the truth. For a moment Susannah thought she would elaborate to Aristotle, but she didn't want to share something she'd never even shared with Drew.

"I thought all Indian people got arranged marriages. Were they rebels?"

"Rebels? I guess so." Susannah had never considered her parents this way, as strangers worthy of admiration. She blushed. Something about the hungry way he was looking at her from under his long lashes made her feel like he was drinking her down.

* * *

At the start of their relationship, the perpetual haze of smoke had been novel and romantic, a respite from student life. Susannah didn't know Drew dreamed of having a hydroponic marijuana farm. She'd lug legal textbooks to his apartment and after she studied, they got high, had sex, crashed, and woke up to the hypnotic drum of the winter rain steaming up the windows, the grinding pulse of dance music on Drew's alarm clock.

"Do you think I'm pretty?" Susannah had asked Drew one night. They'd been dating for about a year and were lying in bed spooning in the dark. The neighbor downstairs had been pounding on the ceiling of her apartment with a broom handle to tell them to shut up while they were fucking, and now they could hear her storming around in her own bedroom.

"Yes, you're the most beautiful girlfriend I've ever had," Drew said. He pulled her tightly toward him, hugging her like he could make her real.

Susannah laughed. She was the girl who wore thick Coke-bottle spectacles until she went to college. She probably should have gotten orthodontia as a little girl, but her parents had spent the income from her dad's engineering job to open her mother's restaurant in Fremont, and later expanded it into a chain.

"Don't get me wrong, you don't look like any other Indian person I've met, but weird is a good thing. Your eyes! You have the most beautiful strange eyes. And of course, you're the smartest girlfriend I've had, too."

The smart part seemed rather obvious, but the weight of Drew appraising her face this way was stunning. Her parents, relatives, and friends had always found her lacking. Just before law school, she'd been chosen to be a model for makeup by a New York company because, supposedly, she was ugly-beautiful. But after a few screen tests, the company had dropped her. She was not beautiful, period. Drew's tiny compliment was so heavy that it carried her away from all the friends who told her he was a slacker who wouldn't amount to anything, that he was nothing but a stone gathering moss and force as it rolled downhill, pulling her down with him.

"Someday I'm going to take you around the world," she said, imagining the kinds of adventures they could have once she had a decently paying law firm job.

He sat up and reached for his glass pipe on the coffee table. "Amsterdam?"

"I was thinking more like Morocco or Chile or Iceland. Oh, I know, the Galapagos," she said, thinking of places her friends and family had never been. "Some place strange and special. Like our relationship."

"I'd settle for Amsterdam. It'd be easy to find weed there."

* * *

After the bar exam, Susannah discovered Drew had hemorrhaged all his money that summer investing in his farm. She'd just started a job as a first-year associate at an environmental law firm in downtown Oakland and she assumed he'd take up a sys admin job again or go back to school. In her elaborate daydreams, they would move in together, get married and have children. Her parents would have to get used to him, if he were their son-in-law.

But next month, the water company shut off water to the warehouse. Not wanting the girls to die, Drew took a crowbar to the sidewalk and pried up the concrete lid of the water tank. He cranked the water back on. And then the electricity was shut off. They lit the warehouse with white candle tapers. Soon the place smelled like hot wax and looked funereal.

Aristotle complained, but he hadn't paid rent. Without halide lights, the girls wilted. Drew took them one by one to the backyard to suck down some of the faint autumn sunlight. He lined them up on the cold backyard deck beside the chain-link fence, but there wasn't enough sunlight. They couldn't be revived.

When the East Bay Municipal District realized Drew had tampered with the faucet, they fined him. He could not pay the fine or the overdue electricity bill, so Susannah wrote him a check for a grand. "I'll pay you back soon," he'd said.

One night, when Drew had fallen asleep on the couch, a twinge passed through her abdomen. She ran cold fingers under her T-shirt and across her stomach. It was starting to bulge with a hardness she'd never felt there before. She hadn't gotten her period since summer. After a few minutes of panic, her first thought was of Drew's family, about the possibility of having a baby whose grandmother still referred to colored girls. And then she thought about her own mother, and how she'd never truly broken with her conservative family members who were bigots, simply because they were family. Her mother had never said fuck off, and would never say that, even from an ocean away. She would be kind. But her mother's choice to keep the peace, even after her family had rejected her, even after they repeatedly rejected Susannah, had always made Susannah feel like she wasn't good enough. It had secretly made her feel like maybe those bigots in her family had a point, like maybe they knew something about her she didn't. These thoughts were still running through her head many days later, after three over-the-counter pregnancy sticks confirmed Susannah's suspicion.

The following week, she and Aristotle were sitting up late on the couch watching old movies. Drew was at a friend's house mooching off the friend's weed, since he no longer had any of his own. Aristotle was drinking from a bottle of Cabernet someone had given him as a gift. He offered Susannah some, but she declined, claiming to be on antibiotics.

Sitting a foot away, Aristotle was wearing a Pistons basketball jersey, which set off his dark coppery skin. His cologne was musky and dark, but sweet like decaying apples and good sex. She watched him out of the corner of her eye as Bogie kissed Ingrid Bergman.

"How's your job search going?" she asked.

He shook his head. "It's not."

"Maybe you should apply to film school?"

"Yeah, I'm thinking 'bout it." He waved a hand dismissively and leaned toward Susannah.

They kissed, a gentle kiss, a sweet deep kiss that tasted like wine and orange Tic Tacs but felt like coming home. But then their noses knocked against each other. His warm hands were running up her arms, and suddenly they were too close, too familiar, too alike, and all she could think about were those damn Tic Tacs. She couldn't breathe. She pulled away.

Aristotle hovered in front of her face for a second, like he was about to confront her. Maybe he'd ask why she'd reacted like that, maybe he'd ask what this thing between them was. Instead he took a big swig of wine and leaned back. She looked at her hands and wondered what to say.

He said, "I think this is cheap, what the screenwriter did here. Why doesn't Ilsa just refuse to go? She doesn't love that guy. It's a stupid twist."

"She knows deep down that her future is with Laszlo, maybe. They've got a higher purpose."

"Isn't love the highest purpose?" Aristotle said. He looked right at her with his large clear eyes. For a split second, she saw recognition there. "Staying with Rick would be worth the consequences, wouldn't it?"

"There's no purpose to pain." She was too attracted to Aristotle not to push him away. "Suffering is a constant, but it's completely meaningless."

"It all means something someday," Aristotle said.

"Someday never comes."

To her surprise, Aristotle laughed. "Damn! You're so cynical."

He slurred the word "cynical," and she realized he was drunk. She started to feel queasy. "What do you mean?"

"Well, you'd think you were really put upon from the way you talk. Indian girls! You're such princesses."

"What do you mean?"

Aristotle leaned back and whistled. "Let me guess. You probably have a rich family and you've lived all your life totally sheltered in the suburbs wishing you were white. Your parents paid for college and law school. You went to law school partly to please them, but also because you have no passions. Your parents probably hate black people." He hadn't actually liked her, Susannah realized with a pang of despair, as he chugged more wine.

"My family doesn't hate black people." Trying not to cry from disappointment, she kept her eyes trained to the television screen. Rick said, "Louis, I think this is the start of a beautiful friendship." The two moseyed through the deep grey fog toward the glimmering lights, and the music swelled.

A week later, Susannah still hadn't told Drew about the baby. She simply wore bigger and bigger suit jackets buttoned over her belly to work. Drew didn't notice—he was worried that Aristotle hadn't paid rent for three months.

"He's not even trying to pay me. I mean he just smokes all my pot and hangs out all day," complained Drew. He swiveled away from his workspace on a rolling office chair.

"That's exactly what you do," Susannah reminded him. Ever since Aristotle had told her what he thought of her, she'd burned with the desire to prove him wrong. Last week, Aristotle had cooked dinner with ingredients she'd purchased, including gravy so decadent you wanted to swim in it. During dinner, Susannah dropped little facts about her life, facts about how poor she'd grown up, about how ostracized she'd been, facts to show Aristotle he was wrong about her, but he displayed no surprise or interest. He seemed to have forgotten all about their kiss.

"That's different. It's *my* place."

Susannah didn't say what she was thinking, that Drew's parents were "loaning" him money to pay the rent on the warehouse, not knowing he'd maxed out his credit cards on equipment and plants for the grow operation. From their conversations, she'd gathered Aristotle didn't have a family who could afford to bail him out of trouble. "Mm-hmm."

"I'm gonna lock him out." Drew picked up an X-Men comic.

"You can't do that under California law."

"What's he gonna do? Call the cops?"

"Aristotle's not a bad guy, you know."

"Why are you on his side?"

"I just don't want you doing something illegal."

"I'm not running a halfway house here or something," said Drew. "My parents think I should kick him out."

"They think you should break the law?"

"Well, they won't give me the money to start the eviction process properly, so in effect."

Late that afternoon, Drew changed the locks on the front door.

They were fixing dinner when they heard the clank of the metal door being kicked. "You fucking piece of shit. Let me in! I live here. I need my shit, man! Let me in!"

"Not by the hair of my chinny chin chin," she whispered offhandedly, still bitter about what Aristotle had said about her. When Drew laughed, shame flooded her.

The odor of fresh basil stained the cold kitchen air. Sesame oil sizzled in the wok. A few minutes later: a sharp cracking, a breaking.

"Oh fuck, the lock." Drew ran for the front door. At first, Susannah continued stirring the broccoli with a slotted spoon, but since she couldn't quite make out their words, she stopped and tried to listen. They shouted obscenities, mostly fuck-yous, at each other.

Tussling.

Clanging against the concrete floor.

Susannah dialed 911 on her mobile phone.

"Help! There's a fight here." She told the police dispatcher the address.

Just as she entered the front hallway, Aristotle wrested himself from Drew's headlock and leaned back. He was wearing the same rumpled red flannel button-down he'd been wearing a couple of days before. He was holding an empty bottle over his head. Before Susannah could say anything, he slammed it down on Drew's skull. Drew kneeled like a supplicant before losing consciousness and slumping to the floor. A thin stream of blood trickled down his forehead.

"Shit, man. I'm sorry. I didn't mean to do that…" Aristotle crouched for a split second to look at Drew, then jumped up and ran out the front door. Susannah kneeled beside Drew in confusion.

Moments later, two OPD officers knocked. Susannah answered the door. "Who called?" they asked. Drew was blinking and regaining consciousness. She didn't answer at first, but after a few minutes of questioning, told the police about Aristotle. They ran back into the night to find him as the screaming whine of sirens approached. She slipped outside for a minute to wave emergency responders into the warehouse. The air smelled like plastic burning, as it often did when the neighbors were smoking crack. Down the wide empty street lined with warehouses, she saw Aristotle being handcuffed.

His face gleamed by moonlight. Even from twenty feet away his eyes looked big, his life slipping away from him into trouble, some dark alternate history. There were a lot of things Susannah wanted to call after him—she was his lawyer, he shouldn't answer any questions, he should remember it was self-defense—but she was trembling so hard with fear and doubt that she said nothing. As the responders came up to the door with a stretcher, she motioned them inside. Not a single officer commented about the stench of pot or the lit spliff in an ashtray in the kitchen. Nobody even asked to see a medical card. Drew had been right—nobody cared a whit about his stupid infractions.

As she watched the responders tend to Drew, carefully transferring him to a stretcher and wheeling it out the door, she realized what her tragic flaw was. She was a coward. She would choose to be alone and aloof, but comfortable and uninjured, over justice, over a real connection, even over love. But, of course, she would have lied if anybody asked her.

* * *

When Drew returned from the hospital after midnight, Susannah made instant ramen, and set a bowl in front of him. "I'm pregnant." She handed him a spoon.

"What? You are? But I pulled out every time." He looked at her stomach. "How much are abortions?"

"I'm going to keep it."

He pleaded with her, pointing out that he wasn't ready to be a father. It didn't cross his mind that his opinion was not important to her—that she was telling him simply as a matter of course. He said he hoped he would be ready someday and she would still be around then. "Just look at me," he said, trying to be funny, pointing at the stitches on his head. "I can't even take care of myself."

The more he talked about his inability to function in the world or care for someone else—things Susannah already knew—the more distant she felt. She would not be like her mother. She would not raise her child to think that holding onto blood family was more important than everything else. Another thought blossomed in her mind. All her life, she'd only known one story about love: you sacrificed everything else for it. Perhaps this was what her parents had been afraid of, that after gorging on this one story of theirs she would mistake pain and adversity and sacrifice for love. She burst into tears and went into their bedroom to pack and type a resignation email to her boss, leaving Drew baffled and shaking his head.

She would not see Drew for many years after that, and then only in passing at a burger joint in Berkeley—his brown hair had grown into a ponytail and he was with a skinny blonde woman who was dressed in a long purple skirt and Renaissance Faire peasant top. The baby was at kindergarten, so there was no reason to speak. Susannah nodded to Drew, and kept walking by, like they were only acquaintances.

* * *

When Susannah arrived at the original location of her parents' chain restaurant and market, Madras Magic, with her old blue suitcase and a hatchback full of odds and ends, they were working, as they always were. They said they didn't want her to have the baby either, one of the few things about which they agreed. All around the store, they'd strung tiny colored lights. Red and gold and green blinked on and off, as her parents talked at her, first yelling, and then, when that didn't work, appealing to her sense of logic. And then, when all else failed, simply stating what they thought should be obvious to her.

"You're ruining your life!" Her mother was kneeling in the snack aisle, stocking big plastic bags of murukku and sev on the lowest rack.

"I don't care. I'm committed to doing this, and it's the happiest thing that has ever happened to me."

"You should have an abortion." Her father came out from behind the cash register with his stainless steel cup of filter coffee. "Is it the money? We'll pay for it. You're simply not thinking this through. How are you going to raise a baby as a single mother at a law firm?"

"It's not the money. And it's too late for an abortion."

"Susannah, you don't understand how hard it is for those women. You don't know how expensive childcare is in the Bay Area. And taking care of a baby is hard, harder than being a lawyer. And *paavum!* A baby growing up without a father! It shouldn't be! This isn't the life we want for you." Her mother jumped up with an indignant expression.

Susannah wanted to say that all she wanted was someone in the world who was like her, who loved her, who needed her, who belonged with her. And after all, even if she was going about it from a different direction, a painful direction, wasn't creating her own family so she wouldn't go through life alone just what her mother had wished for her? Instead she said nothing.

Susannah's mother walked to the other side of the store where a metal statue of Saraswathi, the goddess of wisdom, sat cross-legged, wreathed in fresh marigolds. She kneeled before the statue, lit sandalwood incense, and began to pray. Susannah's father returned to the front of the store, shaking his head and drinking his coffee.

There was no precedent for what she was doing—had any Tamil girl in all of America's history had a baby out of wedlock? Doubtful, but then again, they probably wouldn't tell the story of it. There hadn't been a precedent for her parents either, and in spite of their faces, heavy with many disappointments, it had turned out all right for them. She might never travel the world, nor be a famous environmental lawyer, nor force her parents to understand her, but once upon a time, long, long ago, they'd flown across a vast ocean just so they could live by their own rules. This was not the life anyone would have envisioned for her, but in the end, she was only doing what her parents had done, making up the rules that would lead to her future. There was nobody she belonged to, until one day there was.

EVERYWHERE, SIGNS

The answer for me back then was yes—most numbers vibrated. They vibrated in Pittsburgh, they vibrated in Chennai, and the belief that I was deeply connected to everything in the world by numbers was infinitely comforting to me. My toes quivered when Miss Wabash—despised by the other fifth graders for her strictness—teased out these reverberations in purple chalk during the math hour. Amma, noticing how much I loved numbers, had asked Miss Wabash to give me extra math worksheets, even though it was not computation that thrilled me, but the numbers themselves—the accounting of all that was domestic or wild, safe or dangerous, a kind of language that remained stable no matter the city. I faithfully tallied the number of fruit jelly candies Amma bought at the greengrocer, the number of perforated ceiling tiles in my father's office, the number of thrushes sipping from the birdbath by my classroom, the number of former friends who called me a terrorist in the months after 9/11.

The trouble began during our annual three-week winter trip to Chennai in 2001, just a few days before we returned home.

The prospect of returning to Pittsburgh filled me with dread, even though this time my grandfather was coming to live with us because his heart condition had worsened. We were staying at his small, sparely furnished two-bedroom flat with its orange and white tile floors and pit toilet. Thatha was a retired mathematics professor and the beige walls were lined with overflowing bookshelves. It was a Friday with no cosmic significance according to the numerology book I'd convinced my mother to buy that morning. Yet it remained seared in my memory because for many years afterward, my mind worried over how easily everything could have gone differently. If only they had.

After lunch, I'd read the frontispiece of the numerology book: an optimistic promise that inside were answers about why there was so much chaos in the world. I finished calculating my family's karmic numbers according to the instructions, and then I'd laid out all of Thatha's heart pills on the dresser and counted them. Sixty-one. When I was done counting, I gathered the pills and rearranged them in their five respective bottles. I wandered out to the narrow cul-de-sac in front of my grandfather's stucco split-level. On the porch, my grandfather was smoking a cigar while my mother scolded him for not taking care of his health in a blend of Tamil and English. "You're doing this to yourself," she said. Thatha rubbed his swollen legs under his veshti. I didn't like how shrill Amma's voice became when she spoke to Thatha and tried to hurry past them with my book in hand.

"Put that rubbish book away," my grandfather called after me. He continued chastising my mother for buying the book as I walked into the cul-de-sac, but I pretended I didn't hear him.

Pot-bellied clouds, the grey of gunshot, rolled overhead, signaling an impending monsoon. Up the street, near the busy intersection, six idle young men chewing betel leaves hovered on the sidewalk and cattle lumbered alongside nimble yellow rickshaws and bulky motorcyclists and honking cars. In the other direction, three housewives squatted in front of their houses drawing elaborate kolam with white, pink and green chalk. Twelve neighborhood kids chased each other screaming and laughing, and for a moment, I wished I were among them. My old friends from the convent school had returned to the classroom after Christmas, so I'd tried to play with the neighborhood kids, but my accent had changed in the three years since we'd moved to the States, and they'd mocked me. It was not as painful as my life in Pittsburgh, where the kids teased me about the veil of downy hairs on my upper lip and arms and shunned me because my mother packed me lunches of rice and sambar in a steel tiffin every day. Some of the girls had told me sambar was the grossest thing they had ever smelled or seen someone eat. Often, one of the boys would grab the tiffin tin and throw it away, leaving me to fish through the trash for the tin so I wouldn't have to explain to my mother why I'd come home without it.

Next door were our family friends, the Kumaraswamys, with whom we'd been friends before we moved to Pittsburgh. Through the crisscrossed black metal bars of their front gate, I saw Latha Kumaraswamy sitting with her toddler in the dimly lit room, listening to the Rolling Stones' *Sympathy for the Devil*.

I called through a diamond-shaped opening.

Latha unlatched the heavy gate and tugged it open. "What do you need, Hagar kutty?"

I asked for her birthdate, explaining about the numerology book, its practical magic, and how much it seemed to explain. She sniffed. "We don't believe in that kind of superstitious nonsense," she said, but invited me in for tea.

In the sitting area, an army of porcelain animal figurines looked out from the curiosity cabinet. Anju placed a doll's cup in front of me. "Paal venama?" I nodded and she poured milk into the cup.

Latha said, "Tell me about America, Hagar." As I talked, she smiled, not in the condescending way adults did when they thought they'd made headway with a recalcitrant youngster, but as if she were genuinely interested. "And do you like your school?"

I nodded, but what I really wanted to say was that I desperately missed my old friends, and I missed my grandfather. Latha continued asking questions—there was something exciting about being asked questions by a grown-up, as if I were an expert on America. "And the other children are nice to you?"

I hesitated a moment, and then I answered yes, as I knew my parents would want me to answer. In truth, just before our trip, Bobby Jamison had ambushed me in the cafeteria. He grabbed me by the shoulders and shoved me up against the concrete wall so that the back of my head banged against it and my teeth rattled. His freckles loomed so close to my face, I could smell the tuna fish on his hot breath and the gathering sweat under the brim of his backward baseball cap. He pinned my wrists over my head, and squeezed them with such force he left painful, moon-shaped violet bruises. Beyond him, I saw the lunch lady, her hair wrapped in a net, watching from ten feet away. She did nothing. "Go back to Iraq," he yelled. I told him I was Indian. He spit at me, and let go of my wrists, and strode away without a backward glance. Afterward, I went to the girls' bathroom, curled up in the corner, and counted the tiny powder blue tiles on the floor until I could no longer see the beige grout between them, until they blurred into a sea. Miss Wabash rolled her eyes when I told her about the attack and said nobody likes a tattletale and boys would be boys.

The worst of it, though, was not the bruises, but what had happened with Anne. Last year, Anne and I had slept over at each other's houses, French braided each other's hair, and played on the same handball team at lunch, and even on 9/11 when we learned of the nightmarish crashes of the airplanes, one of them in nearby Shanksville, we huddled together and whispered over our matching mauve ballerina lunchboxes. One day we were trading Fruit Roll-Up flavors, and the next, silence. When my mother called out of concern, Anne's mother said Anne couldn't come to playdates at our house anymore. My mother's lips tensed after she told me, like she was keeping herself from saying something else, and when I asked her why, she shook her head.

"Are you getting good grades?" Latha asked.

"Yes."

The commotion from the neighborhood children playing outside subsided as Latha's cook arrived to prepare dinner. Clanging pots, red chilies frying. The warm, comforting golden smell of ghee and cumin, the sound of mustard seeds sizzling. Latha would soon tell me it was time to return home. That's when it happened.

I dug my teeth into my lower lip, and said, "The teacher, she puts me in a garbage can."

"What?" Latha swung Anju onto her hip. "What are you talking about?"

"She makes me come inside during the lunch hour every week and forces me to stand inside a garbage can."

"What? In America? Truly?" Latha's eyes narrowed. "Are you making up a story? Hagar, it's wrong to make up stories."

"No, auntie, it's true! She thinks I'm a terrorist." I added, "I'm not a liar."

Latha slipped her feet into her black chappals. "Come, I'm going to walk you home." In that moment, I remembered the scolding my father had given me for being so sullen before we boarded the plane. *This is India, not the States, so smile and be pleasant,* my father had said, and what had I done instead? Made up an awful story. I was mindfully backpedaling, trying to come up with some way in which what I said was true.

"You don't have to walk me." I'd lit a match and given it to someone else to hold. What surprised me in that moment was that there were no signs I would lie, nor any that Latha would respond so strongly. It was December 27th. An odd number. A seven. It should have been a lovely day, like all odd days were, and it almost had been. I dragged my feet as we returned to my grandfather's house in the darkness and drizzle. Rain clouds obliterated the moon. The narrow street smelled like running mud and leaves. Above the neighbors' houses, a pair of lanky palms shivered against strong gusts of wind.

"I want to talk to your mother," said Latha when we reached Thatha's gate. She forced her mouth into a smile, but the corners of her eyes stayed in place.

Inside, Amma sent me into the bedroom. Standing with an ear to the closed door, I could hear them firing back and forth in Tamil, my mother's voice rising both in pitch and volume compared to Latha's hushed replies. Amma opened the door unexpectedly, knocking me back. Latha was gone. "You told her your teacher puts you in a garbage can? What is this?"

"Amma, she did. She hates me." Even after I'd done all her extra math problems correctly and quickly, Miss Wabash had said offhandedly that I was probably not going to be good enough at advanced mathematics to be a mathematician, and this statement alarmed me. In my convent school in Chennai, I had been at the top of the first and second standards. Most of what Miss Wabash taught in our Pittsburgh classroom, I'd learned from my grandfather before starting school, but every time I raised my hand, she said, *Oh my god, enough! Let somebody else answer.*

"Miss Wabash wouldn't do that to you." Amma sounded desperate. "She gives you those extra maths problems. I know you like those. On back-to-school night she was so welcoming. You're lying." Perhaps Amma was thinking of all the times over the last few months when she'd caught me stuffing cookies into my mouth because I'd missed lunch, hiding in the bathroom. I'd lied then, in spite of the crumbs around my mouth.

"I'm not lying!" I insisted, frantic now. "Why don't you believe me?"

I could imagine it so clearly, standing in the garbage can, my feet hidden by five crumpled papers, two apple cores—one red and one green—the stink of half a tuna fish sandwich. Half of a one vibrating. "It happened over and over. And she makes me recite the times tables while I stand there. Because she thinks I'm a show-off." Of course, it was freckle-faced Bobby Jamison and a band of boys who'd called me a show-off at lunchtime while making me recite the times tables, which I'd known for years, and mimicking my accent, but this fact was only a trivial detail now, as were the after-school games of cops and robbers Bobby and I played after we arrived in the States. It seemed truer that it was

Miss Wabash who never said anything when they teased me about my lunches, Miss Wabash who made me feel forgotten because she was in charge.

"I thought she was trying to help you with maths? You love numbers," Amma said. The rain pelted the windows.

"No, she just wanted to make fun of me." I pushed away the memory of Miss Wabash recommending a novel about an Indian girl she thought I might like to get from the school library and the mixed feelings it stirred in me, both gratitude for the gesture and resentment that she assumed I'd only be interested in Indians. I plunked down on the hard cot in the living room where I slept and flipped through my numerology book as the cook prepared dinner.

When my father returned from visiting his old IT classmates, I ran to hug him. As I wrapped my arms around his neck, Amma emerged from the kitchen and told him what Latha had said.

"The world has gone mad," Appa said. He pulled me from his neck and studied my face. "Is this true?"

I bit my lip. "Yes."

"No, I can't believe Miss Wabash could be so cruel," Amma said. "Americans know that Indians are not behind that attack."

"White people know no such thing. Anyone dark could be a terrorist in their minds. And at work, there's been a chill for the past few months. I've told you that."

Amma looked away, and then she said, "Well, that could be anything. Maybe it's just a bad fit with the office."

I had heard them talking about the chill my father experienced at work before that night—although we'd all lived there the same amount of time, they saw two different Americas. Amma with her fawn-colored skin believed that the white graduate students saw her as their equal and that they made a place for her, while Appa with his blue-black skin was convinced that a number of white Americans in his program were racists who saw him as inferior. Later I would look back and realize I had taken something away from my mother that night—a confidence in the dream that brought us to America—and she never quite got it back again.

At the dinner table that night, Thatha asked, "Why these long faces?" He looked right at me.

I wasn't sure how to answer. My grandfather had criticized my parents over the last few dinners, telling them they shouldn't have moved to the States, and that they should come home.

Amma answered for me, "We're just talking about how the world is a mess." Before she hid her face inside a teacup, I saw her blanch with anxiety.

Appa began talking quickly about the terrorist attack at the Parliament House in New Delhi. Later I would understand that they were trying to avoid getting another lecture from my grandfather. "We're discussing the suicide vest and these morons that blow themselves up for ideological reasons."

More talk about the rise of terrorism and violence in the world today, the clatter of their voices rising as they momentarily forgot about me and what I'd said. "You ignore the way America bullies other countries, the way it has supported fanatics for its own ends," my grandfather said. "No country deserves 9/11, but as Noam Chomsky said, it is only in children's stories that power is used wisely to destroy evil. I'm not looking forward to living in a country like that."

"What would a professor of linguistics know about terrorism? And if you would take better care of your health, you wouldn't have to," Amma retorted.

While mopping the spicy orange molaga podi with my dosa, I read the numerology book again. I brought the book with me when we went to have snacks and tea with my father's sister, and when we went to an older cousin's wedding on the penultimate day of our trip, but no matter how many times I reread the book, there seemed to be no numbers to explain my lie, or what would happen because of it.

* * *

We brought my grandfather with us when we returned to Pittsburgh. This was just days before the Indian government announced it would lay landmines along its border with Pakistan. In America, pundits were exploring who was to blame for missing all the signs that 9/11 would occur. We were detained longer than other passengers at customs in the airport, and I caught Appa looking at Amma as if to say *I told you so.* "Where you coming from?" asked the rough-spoken blond man at the counter. "No trips to the Middle East while you were there?" He dumped out the bags of clothes from the tailor's, my mother's turmeric creams and gold jewelry, the cowrie shell souvenirs they'd brought for friends, the sealed bags of seedai and jars of Latha's homemade lemon pickles. He searched thoroughly, and then we had to pack everything back in the bags while the passengers behind us grumbled.

In front of our tiny rented house in Squirrel Hill, the pale January sky burned whiter than it had in Mandaveli, and my red plastic boots sank deep into the snow on the front lawn. I walked into the foyer and set down my suitcase. It looked exactly as we left it, furnished entirely by our American landlord because my parents were too busy working on their graduate degrees to make it feel like ours. But the rooms smelled strange, like a doppelganger family had been living there in our absence, cooking their curries and burning our sandalwood incense.

"Very nice house, very nice," Thatha said, sounding impressed. He poked his head into the dining room. "But I am feeling a little faint."

My mother helped Thatha settle in, and by next morning, when I woke up, the smell had vanished, or perhaps I'd grown used to it.

Usually my parents drove together to the university. But on that day, my mother called my school's principal. They parked in the school parking lot, my mother commenting on how dangerous it was that children were dropped off and picked up in such chaotic conditions. At the meeting with the principal my mother repeated what Miss Wabash had done and my father, zippered up in his stiff green winter jacket, watched the principal's face remain stiff and unmoved. Above him, the minute hand kept ticking and each tick forward seemed like a stab: ten minutes, eleven minutes, twelve minutes. But when my mother spoke, it sounded like she was telling a true story about another girl who was being humiliated and I flooded with anger on her behalf.

"I'm sorry, but that's difficult to believe," said the principal. He rose from his seat and smiled at me. "Come now, Miss Wabash isn't cruel. She's new, but she's a very good teacher."

A faint pink flooded my mother's cheeks. "Hagar doesn't lie."

That was true, or at least it had once been true, which seemed like it could be the same thing. I hid my ice-cold hands in my pockets.

"There must be some misunderstanding," the principal said. "I'll investigate. I'll speak with Miss Wabash, but I'm sure this is some sort of mix-up or … exaggeration. We're in the midst of difficult times, as you know."

I said nothing. It was too late to say anything of significance. Amma paused, her face tightening like she didn't want to say what she said next. "It's not like we're Muslims."

"Do you want to take Hagar home for the day?" asked the principal.

My father had been silent the whole time, sizing up the principal—I had seen him do this in many other situations, erupt with anger after a few minutes of observing a person to see if he or she understood the moral gravity of a situation. I slouched deeper into my chair. "Miss Wabash should be suspended," he said suddenly. "Immediately."

"Afraid I can't do that," said the principal.

"She made my daughter feel like trash." Amma's voice trembled, and my father rested a hand on her sleeve. I'd never seen my mother cry before.

Appa said, "If you don't discipline this teacher, we'll go to the press, to the school board, to anybody who will listen to us."

The principal frowned and removed his wire-rimmed spectacles. He rubbed the scabby red skin under his glassy eyes and said, "Hagar, I'll ask you this once. I want you to tell me the truth now, hear? Is what your parents said true? Did Miss Wabash put you in a trash can during the lunch hour? Did she call you a terrorist?"

"Yes," I whispered. "All true." I willed myself to cry to add a much-needed emphasis to what I was saying, but by now, I was too anxious, distracted by the need to survive, and my facial muscles wouldn't let loose any emotions.

"All right. I will talk to Miss Wabash. If there's truth in what you're saying, I will suspend her. Until I get to the bottom of this, we'll put Hagar in the other classroom."

After my parents left, the principal took me down the breezeway to the other classroom and whispered to the teacher. Thirty-one students stared at me. "Why are you in our class now?" asked the girl who sat next to me during social studies. I didn't answer.

"Terrorist," whispered a boy. He'd built Lego castles with me after school two years before.

That day, I sat alone in the cafeteria rereading my numerology book, but the magic had already started to leech from the pages, and I was filled with dread. Picking at my rice, I counted each grain, feeling the gravity of those 137 grains. I noticed Miss Wabash, wearing a dazed expression as she glided down the breezeway toward the cafeteria with the principal. Her fine red hair unspooled, slipping out of its clip.

"I didn't do anything to you, Hagar. You know that," said Miss Wabash when they reached me.

"You did."

"I know you're having a hard time with the other kids. That's why we work on those extra problems you love so much. I'm trying to help you. Why are you lying?"

"Nobody loves extra work." I covered the book's title with my hands and felt my front tooth sinking into my bottom lip. "You put me in the garbage can. You wanted me to be embarrassed."

"I swear I didn't do anything." Miss Wabash turned to the principal with her palms turned up. "Let me meet with her parents."

When I returned home, Amma was waiting in the foyer. "Your teacher denies it. They're asking other students if they've seen anything."

I shook my head. "She just doesn't want to be punished."

"They'll start the paperwork for your transfer to the other class in any case." My mother went into the kitchen.

I thought she would come back and accuse me again, but instead she called my father and said I was going through such a tough time, there was no way to force me to take back what I said. "Latha called to check on Hagar," Amma said. "I told her we don't know what will happen. Maybe my father is right. Maybe this isn't the right place for us."

I wondered if we would move back to Chennai, into my grandfather's house. I'd see my friends at the convent school every day again. We'd be next door to the Kumaraswamys again.

Thatha walked slowly downstairs, clasping a book of mathematical puzzles to his chest. He caught me standing just outside the kitchen door. "What are they saying?" he asked.

"Nothing," I said. "I was just counting cracks in the wall. Twenty-three." I pointed at the plaster where a mysterious web of cracks spread.

"I count, too."

"You do?" I'd never noticed him counting.

He beckoned me over to the dining room table, too far to eavesdrop any further on my parents. "I'll show you something else. Maybe it will help." He turned on the television, handed me a pencil, and opened the book to a puzzle, which he placed in front of me. Thinking about the difficult abstract problem took me away from Pittsburgh and all my troubles for a few moments. "See, isn't this better than that numerology book?"

But just then, on the television, a platinum blonde anchor was talking about how war clouds loomed over India and Pakistan. Both countries were mobilizing their offensive army formations along the border and had conducted nuclear tests. "Secretary of State Colin Powell has issued a warning to Pakistan to rein in two militant Islamic organizations. The United States is trying to reduce tensions between these hotheaded nations," she said.

"Hotheaded nations. Such condescension from the superior

West. So rational! So righteous!" Thatha scoffed. If my mother had been with us when he went off on his tirade, she would have chided him. She was forever telling him he shouldn't talk that way, and every time, he would respond there was no point in coddling children and that I was smart enough to understand. But I could hear the quiet hum of her voice—she was still on the telephone—and he kept going. "When it was convenient for Americans they allied themselves with militant Islam. Just to fight the Soviet Union. That's how these bloody fanatics have flourished."

A chill rippled through my body as the blonde anchor kept talking in her easy, lukewarm voice about nuclear war and terrorists. Outside, snow fell in great white drifts, and the warm golden lights of the other houses were blurred. "Is there going to be a war?"

"Maybe."

"Where will we go?"

"If it's up to your parents, we'll stay right here." Thatha rubbed his leg.

"Is it safe here?"

Thatha didn't answer. After a moment: "What I like about numbers is that they are eternal. People are the opposite. Inconsistent. Fickle. Things with people are always changing, and what's the right answer with people one moment is not the right answer the next. But you can have faith in numbers, in their steadiness. Here, let me explain the sultan's dowry problem to you."

* * *

Every student in Miss Wabash's fifth-grade class was called to the principal's office that week to ask if they'd seen anything. At lunch on my second day back, Anne stared at me from across the cafeteria. She said something to the group of girls sitting with her, and then they all looked over with accusing expressions. It was the eighth of January. The book said eight had the worst vibrations. Eights were heavy karmic debt. That meant I had to accept whatever happened, swallow it whole as I had the truth. Outside the cafeteria, rain and snow battered the school. I ran out of the cafeteria and took shelter in a bathroom stall, waiting for lunch to be over, for the truth to come out.

On Thursday afternoon, the principal phoned Amma. They were not quite finished with the interviews, but the principal wanted all three of us to meet with Miss Wabash.

"Why are you agreeing to go?" Thatha said in a belligerent tone. By then, my parents had explained to him what was happening. "Why do you let these Americans push you around? You believe Hagar, don't you?"

"Of course we believe her."

"This is just how things are done here."

My parents looked at each other.

"We should move," Thatha said. "It's not safe for Hagar here."

On our way to meet the principal the following day, I kept track of the numbers of the houses and apartment buildings. On one stretch, an anxious 4000. As we rounded the corner onto another road, the angry, scornful vibration of 881. The car skidded on a patch of black ice in the neighborhood by the school. Appa struggled to regain control of the car, pumping the brakes as the vehicle careened toward the sidewalk. Nobody was on the road, and in a few moments, the tires found purchase, but we arrived at the principal's office badly shaken. Miss Wabash and the principal were already seated inside, talking.

The principal made small talk with my mother, who was trying to cover her agitation from our near-accident. After a few minutes, he said, "Three other students have said that Miss Wabash was inappropriate or tried to embarrass them, too. One said she made her stand in the corner the whole day. Another said she used the n-word around her."

"I admit I may have, on the rare occasion, used excessive punishment," Miss Wabash said. She avoided making eye contact with my father or me and looked straight at my mother instead.

"I apologized to those students. But I didn't do what Hagar says I did." I felt amazement, believing that perhaps I was right to accuse Miss Wabash—she was guilty. If not of the trash can incident, then something else.

"Why would she make up such a thing?" Appa asked.

"You hate me," I said in a quiet voice.

Something must have snapped inside Miss Wabash, because her calm tone disappeared. She turned to my father in a rage. "How should I know what your daughter's motivation is? I can't stand you people. You come to our country, you take jobs from red-blooded Americans, and then you have the gall to complain? You should be grateful, Hagar, to be getting an education in the best country on earth."

Appa jumped up as if he were ready to fight Miss Wabash. "Are you going to let her talk to our daughter like this?"

I opened my mouth to confess. I didn't want my father to get in trouble.

But then the principal intervened. "That's enough, Miss Wabash. Hagar, why don't you step outside." I waited in the hall, thinking about what Miss Wabash had said, that I should be grateful.

My parents emerged. "I'm sorry I didn't believe you." Amma hugged me. "They're firing Miss Wabash."

Over the weekend, during the lulls in rain and snow, I took Thatha around the neighborhood for his afternoon walk. One fox lurked by the skeletal rose bushes and one red-breasted robin hopped through a shimmery brown puddle. One deflated balloon hung from a sycamore tree in the neighbor's yard. There was no real pleasure in counting. There was only one of every living thing in the winter snow.

"But she wouldn't admit it?" my grandfather asked. "If she was willing to admit to some of those things, it seems she would admit to the others." He pushed his glasses up on his nose and peered down at me as we shuffled down the street. He waited, breathing heavily, but I said nothing.

Thatha complained that his chest hurt, and went inside, but I stood on the front lawn for a long while, my feet cold and moist and tender inside my soggy sneakers. I tried to reignite the old feeling of excitement when I accounted for things. It wouldn't catch.

The next week, there was a substitute teacher in Miss Wabash's place, a gnomish man named Mr. Kaplan who had hair growing in thick tufts from his ears. During the math hour, he assigned the same problems to everyone. He did not use colored chalks. Everybody worked alone and there were no advanced problems, nothing to keep my interest. Frustrated, I chewed my cuticles and made up fraction problems to keep myself occupied. I remembered what my grandfather had said—that numbers were eternal, trustworthy.

At lunch in the cafeteria, Anne passed my table, and unexpectedly, she paused. "What is that?" She was chewing on the end of her wispy blonde braid and staring at the black numerology book.

At first, I was too startled to answer her. She hadn't spoken to me in months. Finally, I said, "It tells me about people based on their birthdate." I told Anne about her personality number and then her karmic number.

"That's not anything like me." Anne wrinkled her nose. "I'm not peaceful." All the kids at the table pressed in close around asking me to calculate their numbers. Flustered, I started to count in Tamil. The kids stared at me with uneasy expressions, and with a start, I realized I was so upset I was speaking in the wrong language and began counting in English again.

After I gave them each the number from their birthdays—not the right ones—everyone agreed I was wrong, and the chorus of their voices in agreement was like the black whirring of wasps. I closed my eyes and opened them again. The vibration that numbers had always possessed—the special thing that connected me to the invisible sense-making structures of the world—was gone. Instead, the world buzzed with energy entirely unresponsive to me, and the group, an unknown number of children, stopped talking and stared.

"That's so dumb," said a boy who had once thrown me against

the wall. "You can't tell the future with a stupid book. Dummy."

"Yeah!"

"Yeah!"

After school, I spotted Miss Wabash with her familiar shock of red hair walking with a cardboard box toward the parking lot. "Miss Wabash!" I called. It wasn't too late. This time, I would tell the truth. This time, I would say how sorry I was.

But she didn't respond to my calls. I screamed "Miss Wabash!" again and again as I ran across the frosty field, my backpack bouncing off my spine. I slid on a long patch of ice flowering the lawn and fell and scraped my knee. I jumped back up and raced past the other kids as they strolled toward the street where the school monitor was directing traffic. By the time I reached the parking lot, Miss Wabash was already ensconced in her Volvo, pulling out of a spot.

"Miss Wabash, I'm sorry," I screamed at the car, and beat the car windows with my fists. "Sorry. I'm sorry!"

Miss Wabash looked past me with bloodshot grey eyes and the car kept rolling backward, until it couldn't any farther, and then it lurched forward. I ran after the car in the icy lot. I slid on a patch of ice and steadied myself, and started running again, but Miss Wabash was determined to escape from me. The car picked up speed as it screeched around a turn. Up ahead, the school monitor was turned the other way, directing kids across the crosswalk.

Meanwhile Anne was galloping through a snowdrift in the lot, her blonde braids bouncing. In a moment's miscalculation, she lost her balance and dropped to her hands and knees in the car's path. Miss Wabash swerved. The scream of brakes, metal on metal. A quiet thud as the corner of the bumper hit Anne. She landed on her face on the cold asphalt. My heart stopped. All around me, I heard screaming and wailing and crying. Horrified, I froze. How could I have missed it? Somehow, I'd failed to read the signs that somebody could be hurt. Nothing in the numbers of today's date, nothing in the world around me, had suggested this possibility. There was no order to the universe after all—everything was random.

Parents and children were running toward Anne, running and falling on the ice. In all the commotion, there was the sound of a woman screaming, *Get help, get help.* Bobby Jamison stood on the sidewalk, watching. He caught my eye and narrowed his gaze before turning back to the gathering mob. Before the crowd in dark overcoats surrounded Anne, I saw a streak of blood, a cardinal feather lost in the grey slush.

* * *

Thawing ash-colored snow coursed in streams in the gutters alongside me as I trudged home. The ambulance with its bright red lights hurtled past, and then the fire truck. The air was warmer than it had been and carried the smells of wet concrete and fresh yeasty bread. I started to count the snowdrop shoots in a neighbor's yard, but when I got to seven, I stopped and shook my head. Numbers would do nothing. Counting was futile.

Near my house, I stopped and opened my backpack and took out the numerology book. I threw it in the gutter. It sank for a moment, the thin cheap paper dissolving almost immediately in the murky swirling water. For a brief moment, hope rose up in my chest. I was tempted to retrieve the book, yank it out sopping wet, and study it, lay bare all the mysteries of this new and vicious life. I would discover the eternal wisdom that the first pages of the book promised, the secret answers that had eluded me thus far, for reasons I didn't yet understand. Just because it hadn't worked before, that didn't mean it wouldn't work this time. I followed the stream as it carried the book. In a moment, the stream quickened, and the pages were caught in an eddy, which flung it over the metal grates and down into the dark sewer.

It began to rain. A sudden downpour. From the sidewalk outside I could see my grandfather and my mother through the living room window, fighting in raised voices about something, perhaps his heart pills, perhaps the war, perhaps me. Through the glass came the glow of the fire they'd lit in the hearth, the shower of blue and gold sparks. I hoped to go inside and receive the sole remaining comfort I knew existed in the chaotic, terrifying world we had come into—that my mother would run her gentle fingers through my hair and tell me everything would be all right. But I was afraid there was no coming back from what I'd done, so instead I just stood outside, watching firelight animate their faces until I was drenched. Black smoke unfurled from the top of the chimney and died in all that rain and wind.

WILD THINGS

The first day Siena invited them up for chamomile tea, Malik held one of the fragile, downy white hatchlings in his hand. Jenny never wanted to hold them. Siena and Malik would gaze at the finches with wonder as they hopped on and off the millet spray, their red and orange beaks pecking eagerly, but the finches were something foreign to Jenny.

Siena stands in the apartment doorway now, showing off her belly again, interrupting. Jenny had been writing her latest erotic encounter—a man and woman painting each other in gold and jade green, sinking into the dark abyss of each other. Stretched out on ivory silk sheets with the trade winds blowing. She hasn't written the ending yet, and barricades the entrance with her body, but Siena scoots past, oblivious. "Sure you guys don't want some finches? When Malik stopped by yesterday, he was playing with the nestlings again." Siena pats her swollen belly and glances at the pumpkin velvet couch before sitting down, legs crossed, on the hardwood floor.

"All that warbling might drive us crazy," Jenny says, and resigns herself to Malik's plush russet armchair.

"Shane didn't like them much at first either. Thought they were too neurotic, but now we let the adults fly all over the apartment. If you change your mind, they're constantly mating. Eight eggs in this last batch and more of them all the time."

"Can I get you coffee or something?"

"No, no, no. I just had my carrot juice upstairs. The other reason I came down is to see if you and Malik wanted to go camping with us in a couple weeks."

Siena is a transplant from the other coast. Jenny suspects Siena only pretends to like raw carrot juice and transcendental meditation and psychics. Probably she secretly binges on Oreos like everyone else. "Thanks, but we're city mice."

"Oh, there's no such thing! Camping's for everyone. It'll do us all good to get out of this pollution." Siena slides her alexandrite pendant back and forth along the slim silver chain around her neck so that it blinks in the afternoon light, first mossy green, then raspberry. She fashions crystal jewelry for a living, wrapping gemstones in silver wire, sometimes adding beads, and she wants to move her miniature business and Shane to the Siskiyous.

After the Fourth of July fireworks in San Francisco, two months ago, they had strolled back to the train station. Siena, stroking her bulging belly, looked around at the littered streets, the greasy bits of fried calamari, half-eaten hot dogs and fluttering bubble-gum wrappers, abandoned light sticks, and confetti. "Who will clean this?" she asked Jenny, who was unsure of whether Siena intended the question as a kind of polemical opening to an argument or whether she wanted the kind of technical response that involved knowledge of the city sanitation. Nobody answered.

"You see, this is why we need to move back to nature," said Siena, clarifying the intent behind her question. She poked Shane.

He laughed. "I'm an architect, not a forest ranger, Siena."

Siena smiled, and wrapped an arm around her boyfriend's waist, nestling against his chest. Jenny was sure it was an act. Shane said, "How about a compromise? I'll take my vacation time next summer. We can travel around America together like outlaws, hopping freights, hitchhiking, walking."

As they'd boarded the train, Malik whispered to Jenny, "See, they're not so bad." All Jenny could think was that it was astonishing they chose to couple. Surely Shane would crush Siena. A skyscraper sinking down. In Pittsburgh, where Jenny's parents live, some people have insurance for their houses, just in case a mine beneath the house opens its hungry steel mouth to swallow the lumber, the bricks, the furniture.

Siena continues to talk about camping in an insistent, high-pitched voice. She explains how difficult it was to convince Shane to go camping when they first got together, but now he loves it. She asks Jenny what she thinks about natural childbirth in the forest. "I know I don't want to go to a hospital, but Shane doesn't think that he can handle delivering the baby by himself. Do you think midwives will go into the woods for a delivery?"

"Honestly, I have no idea. It doesn't sound safe." She tries to imagine wanting to do Siena—those thin Puritan lips opening, snake-tongue darting out, lids shutting over sapphire eyes—and decides that a facsimile of Siena will be featured in the next erotic encounter she submits to her editor.

Siena cocks her head to one side. "Are you and Malik ... ?"

Jenny jumps up quickly. "Oh. Who knows? Life's tricky." She strides through the hall into the kitchen. Siena follows. Jenny dumps pink, brown, and white wafer cookies onto a plate and pours two cups of coffee. "Sure you don't want some coffee?"

"Caffeine can cause a miscarriage."

Malik's keys jangle at the door, and Jenny brings the snacks to the living room coffee table. "Hey you," she says, hugging him. She's glad of his physical presence, for his sharp, clear outline. The faintly roast-beef-sandwich smell of his breath, his relaxed tone of voice. When he's not there, he blurs, unreadable, in her memory of him. "How were the new kids?"

Malik teaches fourth grade at an elementary school in Albany, and classes started today.

He drops his beige man purse and plays with the hair at the nape of her neck. "These kids are a big handful. One of the kids from last year, Jude, I told you about him, right? He had to stay behind and has become the coolest kid in the class. The king."

"That won't last after the kids decide it's dumb to stay behind a year."

Siena emerges from the kitchen. "Come here and you can feel the baby kick, Malik."

He concentrates, placing a hand on her belly, fingers splayed over her brown peasant skirt. He draws in a breath.

"Jen, did you check this out yet?" He and Siena smile, so she's forced to smile, too.

Siena asks Malik, "Does Ivory know about the crush?"

"Oh, Evan keeps throwing tanbark at her during lunch, so I imagine she thinks he hates her. Isn't that what little girls think of boys who beat them up?"

"I always thought it meant they wanted me," Jenny says, handing him a cup of coffee.

Siena shakes her head. "Terrible! I hope you disciplined Evan. It only encourage violence against women to allow him to think that's okay."

"Oh, it's harmless," Jenny says. "Well, not harmless, but it's not as if he's actually beating her up, right?"

"I made him take a time-out today. This little girl, Ivory, is adorable. She'll probably be gorgeous when she's older. And she's so smart! Today, when I was giving my overview of fractions, she volunteered for a whole bunch of them. But she doesn't do it in a know-it-all way. All the boys like her." Malik nibbles at a wafer.

"Why is it that people are so impressed with math? I don't get it." Jenny's coffee is still too hot to drink. There is an annoying conversational pause, as if she has said something obscene or petty.

"All right, I should go upstairs. My finches probably miss me." Siena forces herself up over her abdomen. Malik walks her to the door, but Jenny waves goodbye from the armchair.

"Because math is fundamental. Duh." Malik slumps into the couch and eats more heartily now that Siena has left.

"No, I mean, why is it impressive that Ivory can do math? That's what some people are naturally good at."

"Why are you being defensive? That was just an example, Jen. During writing time, she wrote this amazing descriptive paragraph on an old, abandoned carousel. It's a metaphor for the end of childhood. She's wise." Malik pulls her on top of him as he lies back on the couch. She can't taste him—her tongue is dull from the coffee and she is curiously annoyed at this precocious little girl who makes metaphors about childhood even before she's left it.

"Just wait till she hits puberty. It'll be all over then. She'll lie around all afternoon watching soap operas and talking on the phone about makeup and how god-awful ugly she is instead of reading books and solving math problems." Jenny pulls her face away, unable to resist deflating him. Malik scowls and pushes her upright.

"You can't just agree, can you? Just fucking agree for once." He stands, grabs his man purse and goes into the bedroom. "And don't think I didn't notice you were faking excitement about Siena's baby. If you're jealous of her pregnancy—"

"You're the one jealous of her pregnancy! You're the reason we're trying to have a baby," Jenny calls after him. Malik pads back into the living room.

"Okay." He brushes hair away from her face. "But think about how it felt to feel that kicking inside Siena. That kicking is going to be a baby—a person! It's going to learn to play basketball and eat chocolate and have sex. It's made of your insides and mine, the stuff of the entire universe. How wonderful is that?"

She's heard these tender appeals before. For the past five months they haven't been using condoms. Two weeks after they first met, they talked about life over cappuccinos and Malik called marriage a "stale, artificial state." Now, he proposes anytime Siena's belly makes a performance. "You sound all pro-lifey. It's going to be a person. It's not one yet."

"You're impossible. How can you like sex as much as you do, without wanting to have kids? Evolutionary psychology went wrong somewhere." Malik picks up the plate of wafers and the coffee cups and returns to the kitchen. He turns on Thelonious Monk's *Straight No Chaser*. Jenny closes her eyes. Carried away in the percussion and angst, filled with dread at the thought of trying to reconstruct their sexual role-play for her porn stories.

She thinks of the pregnancy test that Malik brought home the night before. She waited for the results as he brushed his teeth and pretended to be disappointed and surprised when it showed she wasn't pregnant. Malik looked at her suspiciously. Not suspicious of her, it turned out, but of her knowledge. "Sure you were ovulating?"

"My period's next week. And you can tell anyway from the thinness of the mucus. When it's clear, it's time."

He reaches inside her open robe and pulls her to him, his rough sweater scratching her breasts and face. She could tell him about the doctor's appointment years ago. She'd been sitting fully dressed in the doctor's office, yet utterly naked. The doctor in her white jacket over a beige silk blouse spoke to her, compassionately, deliberately. She explained Jenny's sex life as a nasty joke—all those frantic early-morning trips to get the morning-after pill, banter with boyfriends about what they'd name their children, the prolonged delays in getting her period and the futile, meaningless worry those delays engendered. Speechless, Jenny looked at the doctor. She would sit the same way, starving in her living room for the whole day, watching the hours tick by. She'd dropped the news to her then-boyfriend over egg-flower soup the following night. But she can't tell Malik so lightly. He'll suggest all kinds of technologically advanced methods of having children, he'll so kindly, so gently take over her body, over their life, and she doesn't know what's wrong with this, if she loves him.

Shouldn't she be able to remember him clearly, when he's not there, to have children with him? She wants him branded into her memory, she wants to be able to touch something of him on her own mental flesh, burned and discolored, so she can believe there's no way to truly extract him from herself. But he is, as he always will be, entirely separate.

After dinner she paints Malik up—gold mascara, black eyeliner, lipstick, foundation, powder, the works. He bats pretty eyelashes at her. "Just for that, we have to go outside now," she tells him slyly.

"What?"

"Come on, sugah. Let me take you for a little walk on the wild side."

"You bitch! No way." He laughs. But he can be persuaded, after she coaxes him with a few more drinks. They stumble, drunk and happy, out of the duplex, and ramble toward the park at the Rose Garden. In the dark, the playground structures look like beasts slumbering. They climb on top of one. Above the trees, the universe zings with stars and they are two mites, two nothings. Malik points out some constellations, instructive even with Flame lips. She listens. She leans over and covers his mouth with a kiss. Long and hard, vicious even.

* * *

Craigslist is a deep hole of disappointment. She has been to five job interviews but has been too embarrassed to admit to prospective employers that in order to move to California she spent the last few years writing Internet pornography, and that she's not even very good at it. Before that she'd worked as a journalist for the small Pittsburgh paper she'd grown up reading, but that still leaves two years of her life missing. Perhaps she can claim she's been researching freelance articles on zebra finches.

She's observed Siena's birds, in four wood and chicken wire cages around the otherwise empty living room. The grown finches hop up and down the branches slung through the wire, tapping on cuttle bones in a blind search for calcium, and pecking voraciously at carrots and lettuce, millet spray, seed. The males compete by serenading the females with long, loud warbles and hopping, tails in a furious vibration, on the females' backs. Jenny has seen them take quick, joyous baths, splashing water, seed, and shit on the pages of the Utne Reader that line their cages.

New babies arrive with some frequency, first peeping, later squawking for food. Siena loves observing them, loves waiting to see which ones develop gaudy cheek patches so she can determine their genders before selling them. The nestlings grow into fledglings. The newest fledglings have names that Shane chose and Siena approved: Truth, Beauty, Charm, and others. Jenny can't remember them all.

On the Friday when they leave to go camping, Siena stops by while Shane carries their orange tent to the car. "Camping is good for the soul. You really don't want to come?" Siena lingers in Jenny's doorway, clapping her tiny mittened hands together.

"Are you in good enough condition to go camping? Particularly since, well, look at the weather."

Shane enters and stands behind Siena. "I'll take care of her, don't worry," he says, enfolding Siena in his thick overcoat. Even from a few feet away they smell like Pittsburgh in the autumn—dead leaves, freshly baked bread, the possibility of rain. "It's not that cold."

"Besides. I want the baby to feel grounded," Siena explains.

"Considering we'll be living in the city for quite some time," Shane adds. They drive off in the truck, heading north to the Siskiyous.

Jenny returns to the bedroom with her laptop, thinking about how she met Malik at a furniture store on San Pablo, a few blocks from her old apartment. She'd been carrying a bag of groceries, contemplating loft beds, leaving after learning the store didn't sell them. Even though Malik was lugging a large plastic bag stuffed with a king-sized down comforter, he held the glass door for her—she'd observed that since coming to Berkeley, no man had held a door for her, and said words to that effect. "Maybe they think you'll be offended," Malik said. They made small talk as they stepped into a drizzle, moving past the parking lot into the busy thoroughfare. His glistening black eyelashes as he asked if she wanted to be walked somewhere out of the rain, the green delirium of trees blowing in the wind, the scent of wet peaches as she took them out of the paper bag at home, the way a peach tanged differently in his mouth than in her own. The memory somehow does not translate to anything usable as pornography.

Jenny hears finches warbling. Malik's grandfather clock continues ticking. Words that once excited her now seem to be merely marks. Warble, warble. She can't stand the sounds! Squeak-squeak-squeak. The finches chortle continuously.

She stuffs gloves and keys in her pocket. She walks outside, hurrying around the duplex to the side alley where they keep recycling and garbage bins. She creeps up the cobwebbed outdoor staircase, avoiding dead roses and moths. From the landing, she climbs over the railing and onto Siena and Shane's window ledge. She peers through the kitchen window, between the potted plants.

She slips on her gloves, pulls the screen out carefully, and hoists herself through the window, into the kitchen sink, and then drops noisily down to the yellow-tiled floor. She tiptoes into the living room, even though nobody is home. Fortunately, Siena has left the living room window open, probably to air out the finch-smell.

Jenny takes the end of the millet spray slung through the black wire and waves it around. The birds twitter at her, trying to catch and tame the millet, usually getting swatted by it instead. Jenny cackles out loud, trying to imitate a noir villainess, perhaps Ava Gardner, sporting a vivid dress and skinny, lacquered nails. One red-cheeked male hops on the branch and Jenny swings him around on it. Jenny pushes the cage closer to the window, lifts the thin wooden latch slowly, although she knows she won't change her mind. The finches don't move toward the large open cage door, so she reaches in and they flap around the cage in a frantic flurry.

"Look at what a great day it is!"

Outside the window, clouds move almost imperceptibly over the neighborhoods on the hill below and she can see the San Francisco skyline, across the bay. Suddenly in a fury of feathers, one finch flies out. "Go on, pretty thing." The others follow his hesitant lead onto the window ledge. For a moment, she panics, lest they don't know how to fly yet. But at the sound of a car honking, all take off, flapping wildly, then gracefully as they swoop past a eucalyptus grove and toward the vast bay. Soon they're out of sight.

Two are left behind. In one cage, a mother and father snuggle religiously on their eggs in the dark, cave-like hollow of their nest. She searches the abandoned nests. They also hold eggs. She reaches into one nest and touches the egg, which is not like a chicken egg at all, as she had expected. Instead it is as cold and silky smooth as a pebble, and between her fingers, it feels as if it could be used in sacred rituals or magic spells, if she believed in that sort of thing. Jenny closes the cage door, deciding to pretend she didn't know that these two devout parents stayed.

She thinks she should make it look a little more like a break-in, but there is nothing with which to make a mess. Also, it's even quieter than it had been in her apartment before she'd heard the birds. She hears a slight rustling and the expectant father pokes his head out of the nest. He jumps to the edge of the cage, preening his feathers with his beak, seemingly aware of his own dapper charm.

On impulse, Jenny opens the cage door and he, too, glides across the sky like a feathery comet. She closes the cage door. The expectant mother finch stays sitting on her eggs.

When Jenny returns to their front door, Malik is unlocking it. There is something downhearted in his kiss, or is she imagining it? His lips taste salty with sweat, but there is also something else. "We should talk," he says as he pulls away.

"What about?" Jenny asks, pushing past him into the living room. She pulls off her finchy-smelling gloves, throwing them in the corner so Malik won't smell them.

"I think we should both get checked out to see if we can even— if we can have kids." He clasps her hands, drawing her down next to him on the couch. His hands weigh on hers like sandbags heated under the sun.

Trying to conceal her anxiety, she says, "Are you joking?! We've only really been trying for a few months! Let's give it some time."

"Listen, Sam and his wife went to a doctor when they were trying to conceive and he said it was really helpful." Malik looks so earnest that she almost believes it is a brilliant idea. She wonders, for a split second, what their future baby would look like. Perhaps it would have Malik's eyes, his mouth, her eyebrows and cheekbones. Perhaps it would combine them so closely that nobody would be able to distinguish or assign features.

"No! I said give it time." Jenny reaches back down for her gloves, avoiding Malik, who reaches for her. If she waits long enough, perhaps Malik will change his mind.

She buries the gloves in the laundry basket at the end of the hall, under their other clothes, and glances back. Malik is rubbing his temples. Jenny closes the bedroom door behind her and hunches in bed with her laptop. She hears the front door close quietly. Again silence. No finches, no clock ticking, and the light fades. She squints at the words of her story as if it is a kind of steganography, a series of marks that mean *help wanted.*

Opening the window, she listens to the blue static monotone of crickets chirping, the only sound in the sleepy residential streets. She trembles for a while and then she falls asleep.

* * *

Morning sunshine runs across the room. Blessed silence. Malik is lying asleep beside her. Jenny leans over to kiss him, then stops, remembering. Siena and Shane will come home from their camping trip today. And yesterday she released their finches.

Jenny decides to go to the library to plan her job search. As she walks to her car, she imagines the look of horror on Siena's face, those thin lips pulled downward. Somehow, it bothers her. She considers buying some more finches. But it's too late, and they would notice the difference. They probably stared at those stupid birds all day long.

* * *

Malik tells her that someone has broken into Siena and Shane's apartment. Had she seen anyone? No, she'd been in bed most of the day. "But you were just coming in when I ran into you outside the door," he interrupts.

"Oh, I just went for a quick jog. I wasn't paying attention to anything."

According to Malik, the mother Jenny left behind sits on her eggs alone, only leaving the nest for more food. She has started pecking out her own feathers, and balding. Siena has mentioned that she doesn't think the babies will hatch. This bothers Jenny more than she thought it would.

A month passes before Siena knocks on her door again. "Wow, you're almost to the finish line, huh?" Jenny looks at Siena's belly to avoid her face, which is red and puffy from crying.

"Do you think I could stay here for a few hours?" Tears slide like small mirrors down her cheeks.

"What's wrong?"

"Shane left."

"He what?"

"He doesn't want to raise the baby with me. No explanation. Well … I mean, I can think of ways this has been coming for a few weeks. He had cold feet about being a father and then the camping sent him over the edge."

Jenny pulls Siena down next to her on the couch. She wonders if releasing the finches caused Shane to leave. No, that makes no sense. It's totally absurd.

"How could camping make it worse?"

"Remember how I told you I want to raise the baby in a forest? It freaked Shane out. Maybe I could live in a city if it meant Shane would stay with me, but he doesn't want to do that. He says he doesn't want to be responsible for my decisions. I said, 'We're having a baby. Of course you're partially responsible for my decisions,' and he said, 'Well, I don't want to be.' The baby was an accident. We didn't plan it or anything."

"Um, maybe he'll change his mind?"

"No. When he gets like that, there's no changing anything. He might change his mind months or years from now, but I don't want to wait until then."

Jenny listens silently, patting Siena's arm. Siena says, "And the finches are gone. Did Malik tell you? I haven't been down here because Shane and I have been fighting so much. But somebody broke in. We think maybe, because there was nothing to steal, they just opened the cages for spite."

"But, uh, Malik said they left the mother."

"Yes. But she's mentally ill now. I'm probably going to have to move, so I'll give her to an aviary or something. Rent's too expensive here if Shane's not paying for it."

"You could stay down here temporarily, if you want. Malik and I could help you."

"Really? But you don't even like me."

Jenny's stomach flips. She examines her chapped hands, tracing her life line, her head line, her heart line on the palms. Siena had shown her these when they had first met. "Of course I like you."

"Do you?"

"Stay here at least until you figure out what you're doing."

Siena sleeps upstairs for the following nights, but during waking hours she crochets in the living room. She teaches Jenny to crochet, even though Jenny thinks it is one of the most boring activities ever, calling to mind log cabins cradled in snow and stern, industrious women sitting primly in rocking chairs beside kerosene lamps.

Later Siena tells them that Shane came back to pick up the last of his things. "He didn't leave a phone number but said he would call to check on me and the baby later. When we first started dating, we had a long conversation about flying buttresses. Well, I guess it wasn't a conversation, because Shane talked more than I did. He can talk for hours. Have you guys noticed that? He told me that he used to win awards for the sandcastles he built in elementary school. Who wants to bet that even back then he would give acceptance speeches? He won an award this year and almost left the audience snoring, the self-centered bastard. We didn't have anything to talk about when he came to get his stuff, though."

To Malik and Jenny, Shane always seemed more work-obsessed than anything else, but they nod sympathetically.

They look for apartments for Siena that night and the next and the next. They stop having sex or talking about kids. Siena calls the local zoos, but most of them aren't interested in taking a single zebra finch and suggest she take the bird to an animal shelter. Finally, they transport the bald mother finch to a nonprofit conservation aviary an hour and a half away, across the bridge, in Los Altos Hills. The director, Lucy Yang, asks Siena questions about the mother's health. "I'm not sure we can put her in with the other birds," she says to Siena's stomach. "I'll have one of our vets examine her."

"She's just depressed because she's alone." A hint of despair creeps into Siena's voice. Malik massages Siena's shoulder. Lucy nods, her eyes cloaked in pity. Jenny looks away, staring out the plate glass windows at the lush gardens adorned with whimsical sculptures and fountains made of rainbow mosaic tiles, the bright and cloudless blue sky.

The apartment seems naturally quiet now, as if neither Shane nor the finches had ever taken up residence upstairs. Every night, Malik's eyes are shadowy as he narrates stories of the schoolyard. Ivory has mercilessly bullied Evan ever since Malik explained Evan's crush to her. Jude's kingdom has rebelled and he's found himself divested of his riches, a serf once more. The other kids ignore him on the playground and he rambles around the outskirts of the field alone as he chews a sandwich. Now Malik regrets keeping him back a year.

One night, as they're washing dishes, Siena calls out to them from the living room. Malik trots off to see what's wrong, coming back to announce that her water broke and that he's going to bring the car around.

Jenny picks up the phone. "Call my midwife," Siena insists. But the midwife doesn't answer. Jenny pages her. She doesn't answer the page. Through the window, Malik's car is waiting, light on, engine running. He gestures at Jenny.

"We have to take you to the hospital," Jenny says. "We don't know what else to do."

"I could walk you through it?" pleads Siena. But Jenny helps her up. They struggle across the lawn, through fallen leaves, to Malik's car. The hospital isn't too far away, but Siena cries during the ride. Jenny holds her hand.

"Remember how you told me that your heart line was long and deep? Doesn't that mean you have a strong heart?" Jenny tries. Malik stays silent.

"That was total bullshit." Siena cries harder, holding her belly.

Malik shakes his head at Jenny in the rearview mirror. Every once in a while, Siena stops sobbing to wince with pain during a contraction.

"Do you have a number for Shane? I'll call him when we get there."

"No! He's not coming. He left. He—"

Malik parks and helps Siena through the glass doors of the hospital. Jenny follows behind, feeling uncertain and useless. She stays in the waiting room while Malik, without even being asked, helps Siena in the delivery room. Some volunteer spreads a fresh batch of magazines on the table, but Jenny stands by the window, staring at the city, all shadowed toy buildings and random spots of light, dark hills that almost blend seamlessly into the night sky.

She waits, it seems, for hours, but neither Malik nor Siena emerges. Something dark begins to swallow her up from the inside. How long can she keep up this wait, and why has she been waiting? This hospital with Siena in labor is where Malik wants to be. But she is not this sort of person; this is not her life, or at least it shouldn't be. She takes an Uber home and stands in front of the apartment for a few minutes, uncertain. Through her apartment window is the old familiar pumpkin-colored couch and the television in the living room, the computer in the corner. They look like someone else's belongings. Upstairs, Siena's window is dark.

Jenny wanders uphill, meandering through the quiet, winding shadowy streets. She finds herself at Codornices Park by the rose garden. She climbs the forty-foot concrete slide, and her throat starts to burn from the exertion of going up the incline. At the top of the slide, she chooses a big cardboard square from the stack people have left behind. She sits down on it and closes her eyes. She tries to feel a kiss from Malik, a kiss from before Siena and Shane moved in, from before there was any talk of babies, when love, luminous as amber, swam and splashed around her insides. Nothing.

After a few minutes of silence, Jenny feels his breath over her lips, but she can't quite taste or smell it—she can't describe a smell in words, the way she can describe the color of lipstick or the sky. Instead she thinks of the smell in layers of tangible things—first, just a liqueur haze from his mouth and her own, then closer, a more blistering scent—salty, stinky, delicious oysters, maybe a trace of cinnamon because Malik gnaws on whole cinnamon sticks.

Jenny wonders how Malik became the Malik he is now, and how it could have happened without her really noticing over a period of years. Maybe he was always gentle and kind, boring and staid. Maybe he always wanted children, domestic bliss, to settle down, and the memory she has of another Malik, the more liberated, bohemian Malik who'd hang out with her in the playground at night, now represents some other, less important part of him, a minor note.

Jenny imagines Malik and Siena raising the baby together. She's never sensed sexual attraction between them, but that doesn't matter, maybe. They could see the same thing in those birds. They could see something she couldn't. They could gaze at those finches for hours.

She looks up. Clouds quilt the sky in shades of grey. No constellations. She pushes off and begins the fast descent down the slide, her breath catching. As she slides down the steep slope, eyes closed, hands outstretched, fingers treading air, her heart jumps in her chest. That's when she remembers. Nothing but the softness, the fragile featheriness of the baby finch, as if its heart is pulsing in her own hands. It lay on its back, quiet and still resting on Malik's palm, and when he released it into the cage, it flew around like a wild thing.

THE ART OF LOSING

After a flamenco show, they picnic on the villa rooftop, eating knobs of hard cheese and tart apples, and drinking straight from a tall bottle of sticky port. They toast to enduring love, their two beautiful children, and how happy they are their children have grown up. The Andalusian sky is the same as the one at home, she thinks, as they stumble drunk to their rooms, yet somehow going abroad has made the sparkling covey of stars appear closer and brighter.

It also makes the cell phone's midnight bleats more alarming.

Maisie's hand closes around the tiny cell phone on the nightstand. Perhaps a friend has simply forgotten they're on a trip for their anniversary. It's midafternoon in the Bay Area.

"Hello?"

"Mrs. Turcotte?" The voice is tense, slightly fearful.

This is the call. This is the call she's been waiting for and imagining and dreaming and dreading for her son's whole life. After a few moments, she understands the call is real.

"We're sorry, ma'am. Your son's been in a terrible accident."

* * *

They wait for a taxicab in the darkened alley next to the spice market, the cold night air sweet with vanilla, peppercorn, saffron. Maisie is suffused with dread. Her earlobes are icy cold and she keeps folding them, tucking them inside her ear for comfort as she had as a small child. Bran sets the rolling suitcase upright and sits on its short side. He's stout, barely balancing. His eyelids flutter down, his sleek silver hair gleams by moonlight.

She doesn't understand how he can be so calm, so callous, but after a while, she thinks it must be all the years of struggling with Drew—they forced him to resign himself to the possibility of disaster at all times. But if that's the case, why can't she be as stoic as he is?

Maisie lets go of her ear and fishes through her purse. She will scroll through her cell phone contact list and determine which of her friends still owes her a favor, which of them might be willing to check on Drew at the hospital. Beneath the litter of receipts, her hand closes around an oddly shaped metal talisman.

A toy Maserati Gran Turismo, cherry red in the dim light from the street lamp. Drew's favorite toy as a child. When she'd packed up her office earlier that year, after selling the daycare franchise she'd built from nothing, it had been secreted away in one of the particleboard desk drawers, and she dropped it in her purse before throwing away a champagne bottle and bidding farewell to her staff for the last time. She rotates the car in her palm, trying to remember how it ended up in her desk, whether she'd taken it away from Drew as a punishment—likely.

* * *

Drew was difficult from the start. During pregnancy, hyperemesis gravidarum rendered Maisie wildly nauseous, vomiting several times a day. As if this weren't enough, her joints relaxed excessively. She could barely walk for the last two months of the pregnancy and needed to keep a crusty blue vomit bucket on her side of the bed. During labor, Drew flipped into a breech position and started to have trouble breathing, and she needed the doctors to C-section him out of her. When they pulled him out, faintly bluish and screaming bloody murder, he wouldn't latch on to nurse.

Trouble flooded his childhood. He was adorable, by far the funniest child she would ever meet, but he didn't listen, and he found rules irrelevant. Maisie appreciated his unique sense of humor, his unprecedented generosity, but she fretted that he flung himself headlong into danger. He'd repeatedly pry the light-socket covers off the wall and dismantle the second-story window screens and climb out onto the roof, and stand there, victorious and cheering after he'd been told not to. He ran screaming around and around the room of the preschool during circle time, completely incapable of calming down. When he was four, he struck a preschool teacher hard in the face and would later claim she was making fun of him, but he couldn't remember specifics. Maisie didn't quite believe it at first, but then he clobbered a little boy who made fun of him for making a buzzing noise and was kicked out of preschool. "You can't hit people because they say something you don't like."

"Why?"

She struggled to come up with an explanation that would satisfy Drew. He poked holes in her half-hearted sermon about respecting authority, sensing that she secretly found his behavior amusing. "But what if they tell you to hurt someone? Then should you do it?" His resistance to authority was what Bran later reminded her of when Drew's kindergarten teacher suggested they take him to a psychiatrist.

Maisie wanted to wait and see. The son she knew was high-spirited and sweet and resourceful. If he was challenging, wasn't it a teacher's job to straighten him out? Not the job of prescription drugs? "I don't want to crush his spirit, I love his spirit," she told

Bran. He nodded, but she could see from the way he turned away and pursed his lips, he didn't agree.

Gwen was born four years after Drew, plump and big-cheeked. It was a delayed revelation to discover parenting didn't have to be all tears and sleepless nights—it could be shot through with incandescent sunshine, joy. Gwen was funny and bold, too, but she could follow rules and pay attention. Before, Maisie hadn't believed her girlfriends genuinely enjoyed their lives as stay-at-home mothers. She believed they must be at least half-lying, just as she was, to survive it.

When Drew got kicked out of kindergarten, Maisie relented and took him to a psychiatrist. For all his fancy degrees and the $250 she paid per hour (more than she'd ever paid to see a doctor in all her life), the psychiatrist had no answers, but he recommended a childhood behavioral research group in nearby Menlo Park. At the group's offices, the researchers put Drew in a soundproof room with a secret window and, from a clandestine vantage, observed how he played with toys. That was where he'd gotten the toy Maserati. A friendly Asian researcher had given it to him because he wouldn't relinquish it after the observation. Mine! Mine! he'd shouted when they tried to take it away.

Afterward, he was prescribed Ritalin, but the other children still didn't want to play with him. It broke her heart when nobody came to his birthday parties—he entertained a bunch of imaginary characters and Gwen with fizzy bottle rockets on the front lawn instead. "Look, Wennie, wouldn't you like to go to space, too?" The next psychiatrist diagnosed him with pediatric bipolar disorder comorbid with attention deficit disorder and added antipsychotics to the mix. The medications had an effect for a period, but then after a year, they inexplicably stopped working, and he received a new diagnosis. Narcissist. Antisocial behavioral disorder. Intermittent explosive disorder. Labels that seemed to mean nothing and everything at once.

Whenever Maisie cheerfully advised the parents of difficult children at her daycare to stay positive, that all of this would pass too fast, she reminded herself of the same thing. Maybe these new pills would be the magic bullet. Maybe these would fix whatever was broken inside her son. But by the time he arrived at his teen years in a dark fog of testosterone and licit and illicit psychoactive chemicals, Maisie understood there was no repair, and there never had been. He would be who he was.

* * *

As befitting an airport named after a poet, the ticket counter clerks are quirky and disorganized, all chunky jewelry and lilac lipstick. Finally, one of them, a woman with a severe hooked nose, finds them a flight with two stops—Madrid and Los Angeles—before it flies into San Jose. Six hours until departure.

"Should we call Gwen?" Bran asks. "She can get there faster than we can."

"What could she do?" In her last conversation with Gwen, a month before, Gwen had informed Maisie she'd moved to Boston in order to escape the permanent drama of her brother, that his problems had defined her childhood and adolescence, and that she was too old to allow them to define her thirties, too. Maisie hasn't yet told Bran about the fight—Gwen has always been her father's daughter.

"Well, talking to someone in a coma improves their chances, doesn't it?"

"Vivian's there. She wasn't hurt in the accident."

"Why? Wasn't she driving?"

Maisie shrugs, but is wondering the same thing. Vivian is a redhead in her thirties who works as a server at an upscale French bistro in town and is quite fond of the Renaissance Faire. According to the browser history on the computer in their living room, she special-orders custom corsets on a regular basis. She's been Drew's girlfriend for five years and might be the first girlfriend of his who has been a good fit, and yet, what makes her right for Drew—tolerant, mellow, regularly stoned, young, intelligent but not too intelligent—is probably also what led to her not being the one to drive even though Drew was high and buzzed. Side by side, she and Drew look like Jack Sprat and his wife in reverse—she's tiny and angular, and he's huge, overweight, and diabetic.

As Maisie shakes her head, his one other serious girlfriend comes to mind, some Indian girl. Gwen would correct Maisie in an exasperated tone, she's a woman, not a girl. A lawyer, uppity and mostly aloof, but occasionally too familiar, upsettingly familiar. Not right for Drew.

Bran liked her and said privately that an Indian girl like that would look out for Drew for the rest of his life, and they'd never worry again. But Maisie was suspicious—what did this foreign lawyer want with Drew? He was loveable, yes, but Maisie harbored no delusions that he was a catch or a status symbol or the sort who'd have success the way other people defined it. There had to be something wrong, deeply wrong, with that girl. And in fact, the Indian girl had emailed once, explaining she was worried Drew was an addict who needed help and revealing he'd borrowed thousands of dollars from them under false pretenses, solely to finance his habit. This shocked Maisie, and then it made her furious that the girl had dared butt into their family business as if she were family! Just a year later, she'd broken up with him for reasons Drew did not divulge, and Maisie had breathed a sigh of relief.

After hours of waiting in an uncomfortable bucket seat, they are called to board their row at the back of the airplane. Maisie squishes into the middle seat because Bran has prostate problems and will need quick access to the bathrooms. Once the plane is aloft and she hears the loud ding that permits removal of seatbelts, Maisie requests a shot of whiskey. She notices Bran's mouth is moving. He has been speaking to her, but she hasn't heard a word, and when he asks if she's listening, she shakes her head. "I think my friends are tired of me coming to them about Drew."

"I'll call Gwen from Madrid. One of us should be with him."

This time, Maisie doesn't argue. A gnawing sensation in her stomach—she is here and Drew is there, and the ocean between them is more than physical. She's never believed in God because what God would have given her the life she had before Bran?

* * *

Before Drew was born, Maisie had assumed her little sisters in Kentucky were simply lazy. They live in mobile parks with their husbands and one works in a hair salon and the other is on welfare. Their boys joined the Army when they were grown. Their daughters got pregnant and married as teenagers. They don't care for Maisie's new accent—an accent that in Silicon Valley means she doesn't have an accent. They don't like that she got out of their way of life. They don't like that she's rich, and they think it means she believes herself to be better than them. Maisie tries to feel okay about this—maybe if she'd gotten stuck there, she wouldn't like herself either. But, uncomfortable with the possibility that only luck separates them from her, she reminds herself she'd always worked much harder than they did. They were lazy, and she was not. It's that simple—or it was until Drew was born and turned out to be just like them.

She'd trained the Appalachian, the color, really, out of her voice right after she moved to the Bay Area. It was clear right away that the NPR liberals where she lived looked down on her for the accent, and before she reinvented herself, it was impossible to get investors for the daycare. But every time she calls her sisters to check in, hears their beautiful, rolling, lilting voices. it feels like a punch in the gut. And it's almost too easy to blame her father and his raging alcoholism for Drew's problems, even if it's true, if there's something in the blood—or in the genes as they say now.

Her earliest memory is of her mother shucking peas and cooking grits in a cast iron skillet over an open flame, the grits sizzling, the smell of hot fat in her nostrils. A fan set in the window over a bucket of cold water to cool the room down. Her mother humming to herself.

"Who moved my typewriter?" Maisie's father shouted. He fancied himself a novelist and believed if he could just get some quiet time away from his girls to write, just get enough money to get the damn coal company off his back for a couple weeks—he'd be rich and famous, and then they'd all see. She'd moved the typewriter from the living room the day before because they were expecting guests, but she knew better than to say anything. Her mom continued to shuck peas, but her father must have seen a trace of guilt in Maisie's expression. He picked up the skillet and advanced toward her. She backed up, screaming, knowing and fearful of what was coming next.

Her mother turned, shouted at him to stop.

He grabbed Maisie's mousey ponytail and swung the skillet sideways and low, as if he were swinging a softball bat. Heavy skillet. Pressed against her thighs for only a moment, but oh, the intense hot pain of it. She can't remember the pain in a visceral way, but she remembers flashes of the aftermath. Picked up by her mother and run outside. Dunked in the watering hole, the mossy, decaying stench of the watering hole. Deathly cold washing over her face.

It was sixty years ago, but she still has a red mark shaped like a banana slug where the hot iron seared her flesh.

As she grew bigger, she got better at avoiding him. One night he'd chased Maisie and her sisters out of the double-wide and into the watery starlight. He was drunk, armed with his shotgun. Maisie sprinted through past the watering hole and into the forest, pulling her sisters behind the trees, inhaling the sharp resinous pine and trying not to breathe too loudly. He couldn't catch them because he kept tripping. By the time he entered the forest and stopped in the clearing ten feet from them, he was out of breath and panting. He smoothed his chestnut brown hair back from his sweaty forehead. Maisie clapped her hands over her sisters' mouths. They all stopped breathing, huddled together, mesmerized by the chilling, bluish-green glow of nearby foxfire.

"I put you into this world!" he hollered. He waved his shotgun. He fired into the air wildly and stood there for what seemed like hours. Finally, muttering to himself, he turned and staggered away.

Early the next morning, they snuck back inside the trailer. Her father had gone to sleep, her mother was cooking bacon. Looking back, she can't remember where her mother was while her father was chasing them, but that morning, fixing breakfast for herself and her sisters, Maisie realized she couldn't depend on her. Thin mountain air, the night scents of pine and freshly mowed grass, still turn her stomach.

* * *

In Madrid, Bran calls Gwen, and although Maisie can't hear her daughter's side of the conversation, Bran repeats several times that she needs to take a flight home to be by Drew's side. "Don't worry about the money. We'll pay for your direct flight. Somebody needs to be there for him." His voice, usually smooth, cracks. Maisie looks away. She doesn't want to witness him begging.

"Do you want to talk to Mom?" Bran asks Gwen at the end of the conversation.

From force of habit, Maisie reaches out to take the phone, but Gwen's already hung up.

Bran looks apologetic. "She was upset about having to go. Did you guys fight about something?"

Maisie considers making something up, but admits, "She thinks I always paid more attention to Drew."

"Well, you had to." He's covering for her, as is his wont. "He needed you more."

"She said she needed me, too."

Bran throws his arm around Maisie, and faintly reassured, she sits quietly for a moment before deciding to call the hospital for an update. The girl who answers the phone says there has been no change.

"Is Vivian there?" Maisie asks.

The nurse is summoned. She says, "The young lady who came in with him was discharged."

* * *

The last time Maisie felt alone, truly far from everything that mattered, was when she was twenty-three and her first husband, Jefferson, came home to their apartment in Knoxville from Vietnam. He was discharged from the Marines after losing his hand—he never explained how, and where it had been was a curiously silky, pinkish smooth stump. It pained Maisie to look at it, thinking of how he'd once thrown footballs with it. After a long struggle, she forced herself to look and to touch it, mainly so she didn't feel awkward.

They'd been high school sweethearts, married just a year before he shipped off. He'd been gone for three years while she went to college and started working as a receptionist at a construction company. To her new friends, Maisie described him as a bit of a clown, noting that he was MVP of the football team his senior year, that his family was rich, or seemed richer than hers at least, that what they both loved to do was go driving, long drives, fast drives through the sinuous curves of the mountain roads with his father's car, pressing the accelerator down hard, going so fast downhill that it felt like free fall, their hearts flying up in their chests in defiance of gravity.

For his homecoming party, she'd baked from scratch a yellow cake with fudge frosting, his favorite. There were two six-packs of cold beer in the refrigerator and a meatloaf in the oven. She'd turned on the record player, and her friends filed in, eager to meet the man they'd heard about. The little celebration she'd planned with so much care was punched through with sullen silences and gaping holes. Jeff didn't like cake anymore. He didn't come out looking too wonderful in front of her friends, and it was unsurprising because he was a completely different person than the one she'd described. At some point during the party, he'd flown into a rage and locked himself in the bedroom. After Maisie's friends had left, she and Jeff had nothing to say to each other.

The polite way to put it, the way Maisie put it to her mother, was that he was different when he returned. "Different, huh?" her father said as he walked to the stove and started laughing. "Well, you never was good at sticking with things. Why should this be any different?" She hated him in that moment, a fierce hate. When that passed, she started to feel grief, mourning what could have been and what would never be. Everything was out of her control, but she did what she could to put a positive spin on it. At least he was home. At least he hadn't been killed.

One night, about two weeks after Jeff's return, they'd had sex and gone to sleep. After midnight, Maisie woke to a strong hand clutching her throat, sharp nails digging into her skin. Airless. She could hear crickets chirping merrily through the open window. She thrashed, but he slept through it and kept cussing. She pushed against his chest, fighting him off, realizing as she struggled to get her breath he was going to kill her in his sleep. With one swift movement, she'd kicked him in the balls. Startled, he awoke. He said he was sorry several times, but it was like a stranger who apologized for bumping you on a bus but was secretly angry with you for calling the bump to his attention. Eventually he grabbed his pillow and stomped out to sleep in the living room for the rest of the night, and Maisie lay there stunned. They didn't talk about it the next day. It happened again, once more, and then she moved out with nothing but a suitcase full of clothes—she wanted nothing to remind her of that life—and took a bus to stay with a girlfriend who she wasn't sure was happy to have her. Anything not to go back to her father's house. When she told the story to her friends, she tried to relay it in comic terms, describing the one-handed stranger choking her while she slept. She tried to make them laugh, but once they laughed, she started crying. She filed for divorce, wondering, *Is this how it's going to be from now on?*

Maisie met Bran a month later. He was a civil engineer and his brother Cadfael was an architect who owned a share of the construction company where she worked. She was helping one of the other girls at the company host a weekend barbecue when a sturdy man, older than her, with an unusual accent, approached her with a glass of punch. He and his brother were recent Welsh immigrants who'd moved to Knoxville for work. On their first date, he brought Maisie a bouquet of red and pink gerbera daisies. Nobody had ever brought her flowers before. A great weight lifted from her, and she stepped into a dazzling fairy tale with a handsome, chivalrous prince whose mellifluous accent and stable job kept her from ever looking back. They married a month later, honeymooning by the river near where she'd grown up and moving into a butter-yellow cottage. Bran made so much money—more money than her family had ever seen since she'd been born—they could afford to hire a girl to clean. Shortly thereafter, she realized she was pregnant with Drew, and while perhaps, technically, it might have been her first husband's son, she always considered him Bran's.

* * *

En route to Los Angeles. The whirring of the air conditioner annoys Maisie. She huddles under a blanket with headphones on, watching a funny stand-up routine on the tiny overhead screen. "Damn Wi-Fi connection is so spotty. I should get a refund," Bran says as he sips his coffee. "Goddammit! I burned my tongue."

"They can't predict whether a Wi-Fi connection will be good in the air," she says. Bran's an engineer, and he probably knows this, but it makes her feel better to contradict him, to suggest he's being irrational.

"I don't understand what happened." Bran looks angry.

"With the Wi-Fi?"

"With Drew."

"I told you, he was racing someone in the mountains after a few beers, and a semi crashed into him."

"No, I mean, we managed to keep him alive all these years, but it's always been hard. Where did we go wrong?"

"We didn't. No parent can predict this kind of thing." She pats his arm.

"I want to travel back in time. I want to see what we could

have done differently." He has tears in his eyes. She's never seen him so distraught, and perversely, this makes her feel less alone.

* * *

When Drew and Gwen were small, Maisie had driven them to the aquarium in Monterey. It was summer, and in the spacious aquarium children and tourists walked shoulder to shoulder. Drew wanted only to stare at the octopus turning a florid reddish-purple as it oozed over the glass wall, while Gwen preferred sitting in the dark room with its wall-length tank, full of green sea turtles and blacktip reef sharks and hammerhead sharks in their slow, surreal exploration. They stayed in front of the octopus for fifteen minutes before Maisie noted that they needed to take turns doing what they wanted to do. Drew flung himself on the floor, screaming as she dragged him toward the room with sea turtles. He kicked Gwen, and she howled. A few families turned and stared. They were thinking what she would be thinking, that she was a bad mother. She had a brief vision of simply walking away from Drew and Gwen, of pretending she didn't know them. She would just disappear into the crowd.

On the way back from the aquarium, driving north through the mountains, all three of them were hot and tired, and Drew and Gwen were fighting in the back seat. Drew had taken his seat belt off so he could torture his sister with a rubber toy he kept snapping against her forehead. "*Drew.* Put your seat belt on!" Maisie had shouted repeatedly, glaring into the rearview mirror. "Put your goddamn seat belt on!"

Drew turned and climbed into the front seat and began snapping Maisie's forehead with the toy and laughing hysterically. Gwen started crying. There was nobody behind her on the road, and something came over Maisie, a blinding pressure behind the eyeballs, maybe the same rage that drove her father to drink, certainly the same species of rage that emerged when her father was drunk, and she slammed on the brakes as hard she could.

Squealing tires. The car skidded into the shoulder, toward the guardrail, her heart jumping into her throat before the car came to a complete stop.

Drew flew over the center console, and his head slammed into the front windshield. Stunned for a moment, he then threw himself back in the passenger seat and wailed. Under the flop of his chestnut brown hair, he had a large purple welt on his forehead.

Maisie collected herself. A truck whizzed by. "Put your seat belt on!" He did so, and she slammed her foot on the accelerator.

* * *

At LAX, the flight to San Jose is delayed due to engine trouble. "We could drive," Bran says. They nod in agreement, and head toward the Hertz rental car counter. A whole day has passed, but it is still light out. While Bran secures a car, Maisie calls Vivian. She wants Vivian to know that she knows Vivian's not there. She wants Vivian to experience something of what she is experiencing, the despair, the loss, the realization that every hope can be extinguished in a flash.

But Vivian doesn't answer her phone. Ring. Ring. Ring. Maisie finds the sound immensely frustrating, and calls her again, and again, Drew's girlfriend doesn't pick up. Vivian must know it's her—she must be screening her calls. Maisie is livid. She thinks with fury of all the Christmases to which she's invited Vivian, all the summer barbecues where she'd whip up her special black barbecue sauce for mutton, and Vivian can't even be bothered to call back?

"Who are you calling?" Bran folds the rental agreement as they walk out to the rental car.

"No one." As she sits down in the rental, Maisie draws the tiny red toy car from her purse. She slides her fingernail into one of the skinny dark grooves on its side, and pries open its two delicate doors. Open and shut them, open and shut them, like the song her teachers belt out to the kids at daycare.

Just south of Bakersfield, driving alongside the dry gold hills, victims of the drought, the whiskey Maisie has been drinking all day comes up. "Pull over, pull over!" Bran pulls over. She opens the door before the car stops on the shoulder, and unfastens her seat belt, almost falling out of the car as she vomits onto the concrete. Twilight. The top of the sky takes on a violet cast, the air sulfurous, hellish. Bran pats her shoulder sympathetically.

The phone rings. Without looking at the ID, Maisie answers.

"This is Vivian's mother. You need to stop calling my daughter."

Maisie is startled she has taken such an aggressive tone. For a second, she says nothing but then the surprise passes, and she says, "My son's alone in a coma." She climbs out of the car, careful not to fall in the beige puddle of vomit. Cars burn by on Highway 5 with their headlights on. Tractor trailers rumble past, blocking the orange light of the setting sun with long violet shadows.

"He nearly killed my daughter."

"Please, I just want to talk to Vivian and find out how this happened."

There's a sharp bitter sound, apparently a laugh. "Have you met your son? He's an entitled menace. Viv's lucky to be alive. No thanks to your awful parenting."

With that, she hangs up.

Maisie wipes her mouth with the back of her hand. As she steps back into the car, she forgets about the puddle, and sinks into it. She cries out, and then removes her shoe and flings it toward the hills. She removes her other shoe and throws that, too. The toy car had fallen when she opened the car door. She picks it up, thinks about chucking it.

As her hand moves behind her head, she thinks of Drew at age five, racing it around the room, persisting in being himself, shouting *Mommy, Mommy, Mommy* and making a weird buzzing noise with his lips drawn in a grimace, his hair too long because he refused to let anyone cut it. She would give anything to be in that moment again instead of this one.

The last time Maisie went back to Kentucky, she went alone to say goodbye to her dying father. She took time off from running the daycare, leaving her second-in-command in charge. Bran couldn't stand the man, and so she'd let him off the hook. Drew and Gwen said they were too busy with work, but she knew they simply didn't feel any warmth toward their grandfather, and who could blame them?

The old man lived in an old single wide that smelled like cigarette smoke, weed, and dirty laundry. Maisie's mother was long gone from cancer. In addition to the unwashed clothes and dingy streaked towels strewn everywhere, including the couch where Maisie was supposed to sleep, there were towering, messy piles of old unread local newspapers and yellowing issues of *Penthouse*, which seemed to Maisie a fire hazard. Her sisters were supposed to be taking care of him, but it was clear from the thick coat of dust and the horrifying odor of dirt, sweat, tobacco, and piss that nobody had cleaned the place in years.

"If you're so worried, you clean it," her sister Raeanne said. She'd brought over a pot of burgoo and corn muffins, and they were eating together on the couch, light sliding through the slats in the jalousie windows, licking crumbs from their fingers and gossiping, just as they had as teenagers.

Maisie said, "I'm not worried. I just thought I was sending you money to make sure Daddy was all right." The air grew thick with what she hadn't said, the light more stark.

Raeanne snorted. "Your precious money goes to pay doctor bills. Listen, you move back here and deal with that ornery man, then you can worry about cleaning."

Their father lasted one more week, and Maisie spent that time trying to put out fires at the three locations of the daycare by telephone. "You're right successful," her father said admiringly when she finished a phone call. He was fully bald by then, and his skin, unevenly sprinkled with pale brown age spots and freckles, showed his aging. His lips were chapped and bitten a candy pink. His nose had enlarged. Maisie could see a blue vein throbbing in his forehead. He still had the thick crust of sleep in the corners of his eyes. In the memory Maisie had of him brandishing the gun by moonlight, he was movie-star handsome, all frontiers still open to him in spite of the alcohol, in spite of the violence, but in the trailer, he smelled final, like sweat, dirt, and yeast.

"I'm not that successful."

"How did your mom and me have a girl like you?"

Maisie didn't respond partly because she didn't know what to say, and partly because he still enraged her so much she got a lump in her throat and the sensation that a fat man was sitting on her chest. Instead, she texted her assistant, who was in a panic over mandatory reporting procedures.

"I love you," her father said. She paused and considered all the things he'd ever shown love toward—his whiskey, his typewriter, his gun collection, his slippers, those damn magazines. Then, she replied that she loved him, too.

She decided to get his lunch ready. Soft slices of Wonder bread and Kraft cheese, slathered with mayonnaise. She pushed the slices together gently, and she supposed she should stop protecting him, finally, and remind him of all the nightmarish things he'd done to her growing up. She rubbed her scar and fought back tears. But perhaps she would thank him, too, because if it weren't for all the shit he'd given her, she might never have had the intensity, the drive it took to get out of that town, out of that life. If it were up to him, and not her, she would have been stuck with Jeff forever. She shook her head hard and took a deep breath. She placed a couple of sweet pickles in their brine on the side, careful to make sure the brine didn't touch the bread, as he'd always been fussy about keeping his foods completely separate.

When she returned to his bedside with the tray, her father was dead.

* * *

After midnight, Maisie and Bran finally reach the university hospital. Drew is still comatose, still in critical condition. Gwen is slumped on a chair by the bed. When she wakes up, her turquoise eyes are puffy, shot through with red. "His girlfriend just left him here in a coma. Who does that?" She hugs Bran immediately, long and hard. Almost as an afterthought, she turns to Maisie, placing her arms around Maisie in a pantomime of a hug—her arms are too light to qualify. Even in her leather jacket, Gwen feels like a sparrow. They release each other and Maisie stands over Drew. It seems that he's merely asleep, a big-boned giant stretched out on a hospital bed, waiting for true love to find him. When she leans and kisses his freckled cheek, he doesn't move. Both Gwen and Bran have rivulets of tears running down their cheeks, and they look at her like she's crazy. Maisie realizes it's because she's not joining in, she's not crying. This is inexplicable to them.

Soon they start talking about Spain. Maisie tunes them out. She feels entirely disconnected from her daughter and husband. Andalusia is a fairy tale next to the reality of the plastic tubes running into Drew's nose, and it seems like this is the life her father had expected for her, had primed her for. These little ugly plastic tubes. Well, she used to think of the way she and Bran came together as a kind of enchantment.

* * *

Drew remains unconscious for months, as spring shades into summer, and summer turns into fall. Lying there, being fed intravenously, breathing with the help of a ventilator, he shrinks. Soon his body looks oddly frail, his skin loose around his bones. A body no longer his. Maisie and Bran don't talk about unplugging him, even though the doctors have said people rarely wake up from comas that last this long.

One hot day, Gwen is in San Francisco for a conference and Maisie comes to meet her on Haight Street for lunch. They amble through

Golden Gate Park discussing Drew's condition, and they are closer than they have been in years. Maisie feels a stirring of relief when she expresses to her daughter how difficult it's been, how she doesn't know what the right thing to do is. Maybe there's no right thing, and the ambiguity, the open-endedness bothers her even more. Gwen looks troubled, and doesn't say much, doesn't judge.

Ten feet away from the sidewalk, in a playground, Maisie spots the Indian woman Drew used to date, standing with a teenager under a tree. The two are a mismatched pair—the woman has put on some weight, and the teenager is long and coltish, wearing a shirt that says Si si puede on it. Maisie stops. The woman stares back at her, and their eyes lock.

"Do you remember her?" Maisie asks Gwen.

Gwen nods, and wrinkles her nose in distaste at the pair. Years ago, when Gwen had heard about the woman calling about Drew's problems, they'd agreed the woman had crossed a line. Who did she think she was? "Let's go. I don't want to talk to a stranger about Drew."

"Wait a second."

Beyond the woman, a colorful whirl of dogs and roosters and tigers—the carousel spinning. Before Maisie can decide whether she really wants to talk to her, the woman approaches her, holding the teenager's hand, and bringing him along with her. Maisie struggles to remember her name, which is not an Indian name, running through the possibilities: Sharon, Sarah, Susie ... Susannah.

"Hi," Susannah says. "This is Jude, my son." She introduces the gangly teenager.

At first, Maisie doesn't think much of it. She registers only that Susannah is even darker than she remembered, and her son is white with freckles. Perhaps he's adopted? They make small talk, and then Maisie tells Susannah about Drew being in a coma. She hopes that, unlike Vivian, this girl who used to love her son will care. As Susannah listens, a pitying expression comes over her face, and her eyes start watering. She's clearly trying not to cry, and Maisie is about to join her, relieved somebody besides her remembers that whatever his faults, Drew is basically good.

A small flash goes off.

Susannah and Drew broke up around thirteen years ago. The boy's light freckles remind Maisie of Drew's freckles, and Gwen's, too, and her father's for that matter. His eyes are not as dark as his mother's, but a luminous hazel or greyish hue that shifts with the sunlight through the eucalyptus branches. Maisie wonders how to ask; she opens her mouth and shuts it.

The boy is looking at her intently, but Gwen looks irritated. She says impatiently, "Pleasure seeing you again, but we should go, Mom."

"How old are you?" Maisie asks the boy.

"Thirteen."

Susannah puts an arm around her son protectively. But at that moment, a tiny golden-brown girl runs up and grabs Susannah's hand. "Mommy, Mommy, push me!" Maisie is struck by how much darker Jude's sister is, and desperately wishes she could ask the question on the tip of her tongue.

"She needs me," Susannah apologizes before Maisie can even approach the question. She touches Jude's shoulder for a second as if she's about to pull him along with them but seems to think better of it. She races with the girl to the swings. It must mean something that she trusts Maisie and Gwen alone with her son.

"What kinds of things do you like to do?" Maisie asks Jude, hoping to catch some vestige of Drew in this boy.

He shrugs and looks around, clearly embarrassed to be talking to two older women, two strangers.

"Do you like cars? Going fast?"

"They're all right." He blushes.

"Mom, that's such a stereotype," Gwen says, and tugs at her hand.

"My son loved cars. He wanted to be a race car driver when he was your age."

Jude looks uncertain.

"Jude!" The little girl is calling from the swing. "Look at me!"

Maisie thinks she will go through Drew's things to find Susannah's email address later. "Wait." She pulls the tiny red race car from her purse. "I have something for you. It was my son's, he loved it."

Gwen's face is incredulous and confused by her mother's behavior. "What are you doing?" she asks her mother. Maisie doesn't reply, focused only on standing back, on not taking this boy and crushing him in her arms.

The boy takes it and examines it. Maisie wishes his face would transform with delight, as Drew's used to, but he stays perfectly neutral. He's too old for the toy, but he seems to understand that it's important to her to give it to him. He starts running, yelling over his shoulder as an afterthought. "Thanks!"

* * *

Maisie and Bran obtain a court order to remove Drew from life support.

They all say their farewells. Gwen, returned from Boston, strokes her brother's hair and whispers in his ear, *something something, Major Tom*. Bran says nothing, eyes watering, but kisses his son's forehead. Maisie looks at the machine to distract herself from crying. *Iloveyouiloveyouiloveyou*, she whispers into his soft freckled ear, the same delicate ear she kissed every morning when he was a baby and she was bringing him into the bedroom to nurse. She's trying to be grateful that she has this moment to say it out loud to him. She holds his hand, and feels it twitch, but thinks, this is not your hand, this is not your life, and lets go.

Once Drew is unplugged, it takes time for him to pass. The nurses put him on a morphine drip because he seizes. Maisie sits by his bed, holding Bran's hand, watching life abandon her son, wondering how she is surviving this. After many hours, he makes a wet-sounding expiration, a death rattle. She understands now why people believe in an afterlife. They have to.

She didn't think she would cry, because as still as he was, he simply wasn't Drew. He wasn't the boy who wanted to be a race car driver, who wanted to ride the roller coaster at the Boardwalk fifty times at a stretch all the way into his thirties. In spite of herself, in spite of her unwillingness to give herself over, her unwillingness to admit he's already left the earth, she heaves with sobs.

Afterward, every fiber of Maisie's body resists saying goodbye to Gwen, and she holds tight to her. Gwen extricates herself, and Maisie gets into the car, and closes her eyes. Bran starts the car and rolls out of the parking stop. Soon, he steps on the gas to merge onto the freeway. Soon, they are taking the exit toward home, and they drive back into hills and as ever, she's reminded of the hills back home in Kentucky, and the man she left behind, and the baby boy she took with her to start over in California.

For a moment as the car rounds the bend, she can still feel Drew there in all the things around them, in their spirit. Wind runs cool over her face like water, the loud whir of cars rushing by, the blur of oleander and sunlight at speed. This is what he loved.

RAMPION

It was early spring in Paris and our yearlong efforts to get pregnant had failed. The fertility clinic tested Connall and the problem wasn't his sperm, so that left me to measure my basal temperature, take pills, inject myself, explore homeopathic cures. Relax, the doctors said. *Relax*, my acupuncturist said. You're wound too tight. I had always been tense, but I was pretty sure the problem was my eggs, or the lack of them, not the whorled knots in my shoulders. Nonetheless I rented us a Parisian apartment in the Latin Quarter, hopeful the city of light and love would work its magic.

We decided to spend our first afternoon at the Pompidou. "The trees should be just starting to turn," Connall said. As a landscape architect, he was always attuned to what was growing, even in the heart of a city. "Maybe we'll catch some of the blossoms on our walk."

At a corner market, I bought a baguette and a round of chevre, which Connall stored in his backpack. I tried not to bring it up, but after the third perambulator, I couldn't contain myself. "Do you think it will work?" I asked.

"What?" He was looking down at his city map and I took his arm to keep him from bumping into other pedestrians.

"The IVF."

"Let's not think about that. We're not there yet," he said. "Let's just enjoy Paris."

"I would so much like to have a tiny child."

"Me, too, but let's be patient."

We arrived at the Pompidou, its splendor made up of hard metal bars and cold rainbow pipes and phallic glass tunnels in the midst of the elegant architecture of Paris. Connall insisted on seeing the entirety of the museum, for fear we would never be here again, so for what seemed like hours, I stood and stared at Yayoi Kusama's obsessive dot works. So many dots, an ocean of dots, and a quiet chamber of mirrors and bliss teeming with candy-colored LED lights and reflections of them and reflections of reflections—on and on, through time forever.

We emerged from that metal and glass behemoth into what we thought would be the vast light of that day, but the buttery light had been replaced with silver clouds and a fierce, howling wind. I turned on my phone and tried to provoke Connall by videotaping him. "You like it, don't you," I said, gesturing at the Pompidou.

"It's fantastic."

"It's a monstrosity."

He put up his hand, so I spun around to find another subject through the lens. Far across the plaza by a set of large white tubular structures, a group of vagrants played music on trash can lids and drums. Their front woman, desiccated with thick platinum gold hair blowing around her face in the wind, was screeching The Police song *So Lonely*. One of the boys in the group was lighting scraps of paper on fire, letting them fly away on the wind.

"That's right," Connall said. "Shoot someone else."

We walked toward the ragtag group. Connall took the baguette out of his backpack, tore off a hunk, and slathered cheese on the soft side with a plastic knife. The white of the bread caved so that there was nothing left of the soft insides, only the crust and the cheese. We stood a safe distance from the group and when they finished playing music, the woman pushed back her thick platinum hair. She looked like a fox, with luminous ice-blue eyes and a red furry face. As I approached, I said, "I'm sorry. I liked your song so much. Is it okay that I took this video?"

I played the video back for her and as she studied the screen, I studied her cheeks. They were draped in hair, her nose smooth and wet. Her breath smelled dark, like onions and root vegetables. It was impossible to tell her age—her hair up close was baby-fine and flax-bright like the palest part of a flame, but the smudged skin on her hands lay soft as worn suede.

"I'll trade you," the fox-faced woman said in English. "Seeds for that." She gestured at the baguette.

"What kind of seeds?" Connall asked. He could never resist new seeds. He had built and grown a garden out back of our house. Full of rarities, he would say, like our love. Oh, he wasn't perfect, but he was so kind and good-looking that even among pessimists like me he could get away with his sunny disposition.

"Rampion," the fox-faced woman said. She grinned and the inner rim of her lips disclosed her darkness, her needle-sharp teeth. "Try it, you'll like it."

Connall handed her the loaf in exchange for a small brown paper packet. The woman ripped into the baguette with her teeth. We turned and strolled toward the Seine. "Be sure to water it," the woman called after us as her group resumed their trash can lid jamboree.

"Do you know if those seeds will translate to American soil?" I teased Connall.

"*Campanula rapunculus*—I can make it take," Connall said with his usual cockiness.

On the bridge, we paused to watch the sun sizzle near the horizon, turning the walls by the Seine, where people were eating ice creams, a warm pink. Connall handed me the packet of seeds while he fished for the apartment keys. I could have sworn the seeds vibrated in the packaging.

* * *

The doctor told us that the IVF hadn't worked. There would be no tiny baby, no smell of milk and powder, no petal-soft skin, no first teeth. We drove home in silence and I trudged upstairs and crawled back into our large bed, flinching from the feel of the cold sheets against my skin. Outside the bedroom window, crows circled the sky. A breeze fluttered through the little green fans dangling from the gingko trees. The odor of garlic and cucumber blew off the rampion that Connall had planted. He held my hands in both of his as I cried. He didn't cry, but the edges of his lips went hard and they stayed that way.

* * *

"We've got to get away from Dennis and Linda," Connall said when he got a raise. Dennis and Linda Trueblood were our new neighbors. "They're standing in front of their house trying to decide whether to put in Astroturf." He was shaking his head, deeply offended. "Who puts in *Astroturf?*"

"And that Chihuahua. It's always barking. All day, every day," I said.

"And little dogs live a long time."

"They do?"

"Well, too long for us to live here next to it yapping anyway. We've always wanted to live by the ocean."

"When California breaks away from the nation in an earthquake, people who live by the ocean will lose their homes."

"We'll float away. We'll be our own island."

"Hmmm. That could be all right."

Although we could not find an island, we bought a stone cottage overlooking the Pacific where we would one day retire. In a burst of romanticism, Connall resolved to construct a stone tower in the backyard, a place where we could look out at the immense ocean, the better to imagine our adventures. We spent every weekend for months holed up in the cottage, away from our annoying neighbors, secluded from society, while he built the tower. I worked on the website for my online children's bookstore on the cramped loveseat, my back to the ocean view. Next to the cottage, there was a second garden, blooming and giddy with the scent of roses and lilacs and salt. In one corner, a patch of transplanted rampion flourished.

Seagulls alighted on the top layer of stone and their harsh cries sounded ever more distant as the tower reached toward the clouds. On slick black rocks jutting from the ocean, velvety brown otters sunned themselves, watching my husband and the other workers lay stone. Within a few months, the tower proved to be immense and imposing against the moody coastal sky. Three stories tall with a narrow interior staircase spiraling up the center of it like a warped spinal cord.

On the day Connall set the last piece of limestone, he brought me out to sit at a teak garden bench beside the tower. "Here's to you," he said, pouring pink champagne into two flutes. Bees were buzzing, flecks of gold around the heliotrope.

"Me?"

"Yeah, you."

"Couldn't be."

"Then who?"

We toasted.

The violet shadows of twilight crept up on the cottage and we walked out onto the beach. "It's marvelous," I said. Connall took my hand in his, and we walked across the sand.

"It's a kind of consolation, isn't it?" he said. "That we were lucky enough to find each other. Do you want to go for a swim?"

I shook my head no, and I could tell he was disappointed. I was no fun.

"All right, I'm going in." He took off his clothes and ran across the hard-packed sand. He swam into the ocean. I could see the gleam of his muscular back in the moonlight, and the shimmer of the moon reflected in the dark water. Far from shore, he stopped and began waving at me. The sound of the waves crashing was monstrously loud. I wondered if he was saying something, and I waved back. He kept on waving. "Come back! I really don't want to come in," I shouted back at him, on the off chance he would hear it. Still the roar of the waves. I walked up to the edge of the water, the foam lapping my toes, squinting at Connall. He wouldn't stop waving. Foam churned all around his head. My whole body stiffened—something was wrong. In a moment, he disappeared under a wave, and I waded into the ocean, and soon found myself waist-deep in the dark, icy waves. I swam to the spot where he'd been waving, but when I reached it, there was nothing to suggest what had caused his disappearance. I looked down, but only my own face looked back at me. I swam and swam, but I couldn't find him.

* * *

Later, they found his body. They told me a flash rip current must have pulled him away farther out into the ocean, that he must have drowned. No baby, no love, no life. I woke every day with my mind on fire and my body scarred and bruised. My hair turned white almost overnight. I didn't bother to dye it. I stopped returning telephone calls. I stopped going to bars for drinks to catch up with friends. I wished for death that night in the water. Why hadn't I just stayed out there?

I wanted to shout *How does this work?* to everyone I knew, but instead I did everything you are supposed to do when death comes. I notified everyone. I cremated Connall. I held a memorial service. His ashes sat in a metal urn on our coffee table. I never had the heart to scatter them.

"Hello!" shouted my neighbor Linda. "And how are we today?" She was standing next to the garden wall in her hot-pink yoga pants on a stepladder, plucking nearly black avocados from the tree. It was many months after the funeral, but the funeral was still all I thought about.

"Fine, never better." I was sitting at a bench by the koi pond watching three enormous koi swim round and round, their golden and crimson and ice-colored scales glimmering in the sun. Rampion had taken over the yard, intermingling with the sweet peas, parsley, sage, and marionberries. I remembered that in the months before his death Connall used to pull the little purple rampion flowers out by their roots so we could cook them in butter with other vegetables and reminisce about our trip to Paris. The hope we had, the fox-faced woman. *So lonely.*

"Well, if you need anything, don't hesitate to ask." Linda descended the stepladder with her wicker basket overflowing with avocados. What I needed was for her to stop talking to me. Every time I sat in my garden, she seemed to be climbing into her fruit trees to hunt persimmons, oranges, pomegranates. "Oh, and guess what!" she shouted. "Dennis and I are expecting."

I tried to smile. "How lovely," I said. Why them? Why not us? Who decides who gets to be happy?

"We're having a barbecue to celebrate with the neighborhood association. Why don't you come?"

I smiled and nodded. Linda climbed back down the ladder. The abundance of the garden—its shiny vulvar blossoms, its constant reminder of how easy reproduction is—taunted me. A menagerie of bars and gaudy flowers. I sat there for hours, but the sticky-sweet fragrance of jasmine and honeysuckle were choked by the rampion, and only grew more nauseating.

* * *

The barbecue happened on a humid Sunday night. All the usual suspects were at the neighborhood community center. A woman artist whose paintings were all white canvases with white numbers on them. The professor who studied whether Kanye West was a feminist, and his husband, a flamboyant stockbroker. Soccer moms with blowouts and tech entrepreneur husbands I didn't know. The elderly couple with matching prosthetic limbs. At most of these neighborhood get-togethers, the elderly couple would propose an hour of square dancing that concluded with them removing their limbs by the end of the night.

Children were eating in the corner and there were red balloons and giant blue paper letters on the wall spelling "CONGRATULATIONS." I sidled up to the meringue plate.

"Those are for kids," one of the little girls advised me as I reached for a meringue. She was wearing roller skates.

"I'm a kid at heart," I said.

The little girl reached out with a black plastic fork and rapped my knuckles as I took a chocolate-chip-flecked white meringue. I smiled politely and started eating. Suddenly I was surrounded by a mob of children with plastic forks, all pricking me with sharp tines. "Stop eating the kids' cookies, stop eating the kids' cookies," they chanted. I looked up and a number of adults were staring at me. My cheeks were hot.

"Stop it," I said. Quietly and then more loudly. Suddenly, I couldn't take it anymore and I was shouting. "Stop, stop!" The professor rushed over and took control of the ringleader, the little girl with the glittery roller skates. Once she had been shunted away, the other children stopped. They walked backward, still eyeing me. By then, my mascara was running. I went to the bathroom to fix it up. When I was done dabbing under my eyes with a cold paper towel, I went inside one of the stalls. I was inside the stall, sitting on the toilet lid and waiting for my heart to stop beating so hard, when I heard two women come in, talking and laughing.

"You know why she was so weird about that, right?" asked one of the voices. It sounded familiar. I peeked through the crack between the metal door of the stall and its frame. It was Linda and one of the soccer moms.

"No. What do you mean?"

"She can't have kids. She and her husband tried for years," Linda said, her voice dropping an octave as she reapplied her hot-pink lipstick.

"Oh, that's so sad."

"It is," Linda said. "But I'm not sure what kind of mom she'd be, honestly. Can you see someone who is so fucking uncomfortable in her own skin taking care of a child? She'd probably starve it to death. And you should see how she looks at my belly. I told her she could rub it, and she *wouldn't*."

The other woman clucked. "God, yeah, she's definitely hard to be around. Her husband was all right though. Rest in peace."

"All right? I'd watch him any time—" Linda started to say. Someone opened the door.

"You ready, Linda? Time to cut the cake," one of the neighbors said.

When the women left, I stayed inside the metal stall, my palms pressed against the door. I stared at the nails I'd painted lilac, my stubby nails, their cuticles peeling back, red and raw. My heart rate had not gone down.

I unlatched the stall and walked out into the main recreation room. People were laughing and stuffing their mouths with big hunks of a vanilla sheet cake with pink and blue fondant roses on top. Their mouths were smeared with white frosting and somebody had turned on happy fiddle music. The couple with the prosthetic limbs were already dancing. "Do-si-do, people!" Tiny white lights blinked around the mirrored room, a chamber of empty silver reflections and reflections of reflections that made my head spin. I was oozing tears.

"Can I get you some cake?" the artist asked as I staggered past her to return to the safety of my house, away from the sounds, the scarlet and turquoise and gold of that room, the scent of Chanel No. 5 and champagne and the tartness of the lemonade.

＊ ＊ ＊

One night, not long after that, I heard a sound. It woke me, the sound of something scritch-scratching against stone. I got up from my four-poster bed and looked out the window. From that vantage, I could see the garden by moonlight, gleaming and bright. Dennis, in his pajamas, was straddling the wall with a wicker basket. He looked up at the house and I moved behind a velvet curtain. When he was satisfied nobody was there, he threw the basket down and dropped with a soft thud into my flowerbed. He crept toward the rampion. He dropped to his knees and began yanking up the plants, working quickly and quietly. For about twenty minutes, he hovered over the plants, carefully pulling up the blue-violet flowers by the roots.

He stuffed the bounty into his basket, looked around, and ran back to the wall. He tossed the basket over and jumped a couple of times, finally getting a footing and throwing himself over the top. He was paunchy, more plainly so in his nightshirt than he was while wearing business clothes because the thin cloth failed to disguise his girth. I was surprised he could make it back over. He lingered at the top of the wall, panting, before dropping to the other side.

The next night I heard it again. The scritching. This time I pulled on a dressing gown and walked down. I wanted to give him a scare. I quietly opened the sliding glass door beside the garden. He was breathing heavily as he gathered the plants into the basket. He didn't hear me at first. His tawny hair was sticking straight up atop his scalp like fur that had been petted the wrong way. I approached slowly. "Dennis," I said as I came up to him.

He dropped the plant he had been pulling and blanched as he turned to me. "Oh, hi," he said. "I'm so sorry. I'm so sorry."

I stared at him. He looked vaguely pathetic, but I didn't feel any pity. All I heard was *She'd probably starve it to death.* "Hungry?" I said.

He gave that weak weasel smile people get when they fail to apprehend a situation and aren't quite sure where they stand, when they think you might be joking, but you are deadly serious. "It's Linda. She craves this stuff. She absolutely craves it."

"Rampion?" I asked.

"God, it's good. And you know how pregnant women are," he said, shrugging. I wanted to say no, I don't know, but I still felt humiliated thinking of Linda and the soccer mom in the bathroom. The hair on the back of my neck in a ponytail was prickly. Fear and rage. "We would have asked, of course, but we didn't want to bother you ... after that party, you know?"

I thought about the fox-faced woman who had given us the seeds. About the way we had believed we would one day be parents and how romantic it had seemed, the rosy future that lay in front of us versus the one we had, filled with pills and injections and surgeries and so-called consolations that were not enough. "This is unacceptable," I said. I felt like I had floated out of my body and was looking down at myself saying words I would not normally say.

Dennis was pale by moonlight. "I'm so sorry. What can we do? Come on, tell me. We'll do anything."

"Your baby, your firstborn," I said. "Give it to me."

He laughed. "Good one," he said. "All righty then, I'll give it to you." He kneeled down and put the plant he had dropped into the basket. "Only if we can have some of this stuff every night, though. Linda loves it."

"Done," I said. I pulled at the sash of my mauve dressing gown and swept back into the house and up the stairs. When I looked out my window, he was climbing back over the garden wall. After that, he came every night, leaving bald patches in the wide swath of rampion.

During the day I would avoid going outside when Linda was there, wobbling through her yard with her enormous distended belly. Night after night, Dennis took more and more of the rampion, leaving only a little bit of it, a few plants in the back. Fairness, I knew, had nothing to do with the reality of a situation. What was fair to them was not what I thought was fair. I kept thinking about the supposed joke, the promise of a firstborn in exchange for an all-you-can-eat rampion buffet—it rattled around in my mind as Linda approached her due date, the sound of our words getting louder and more dissonant with each passing day.

After the baby was born, I could hear her cooing every day through the screen door while the nanny cleaned their house, but I did not visit. I knew that my absence, my failure to pay my respects and meet the baby, would lead to more gossip, but I couldn't bring myself to visit, and several months went by. One afternoon, I could hear Linda screaming at the nanny, and the sharp sound of the baby screaming. A few minutes later, Linda arrived on my doorstep, bouncing the baby in her arms to keep her calm. She claimed the nanny had fallen ill and had to go home and wanted me to watch the baby. "Can you believe it? She abandoned us on date night!"

I nodded in faux-sympathy, but she mistook it.

"Thanks," she said, and paused. I wondered if she was debating how much money to offer me. "You never go out anyway, right? So this will work out nicely." I was about to change my mind, but she was already turning and stomping down the path. I could have said no, I suppose, but instead I was thinking about the agreement. I slipped on my flip-flops and followed her back to her house.

I had been inside the house once before with Connall. We'd privately mocked the blotchy pastel landscapes that looked like they belonged in a motel room, the sickly stench of synthetic plumeria, the expensive lime green curtains—lime green was trending that year. After Linda and Dennis left, I shuffled around the living room with the baby in my arms, feeding her from a bottle and remembering the looks Connall and I had shared about our neighbors' tackiness.

The baby was six months old and already terribly alert. She smelled of spit up and milk, but underneath that newborn scent, I thought I could smell something abiding—the smell of rampion in spring. She had platinum-gold hair—flax-bright like the palest part of a flame—and roses in her apple cheeks. Her eyes were black, beetle-black, stormy black, perplexingly so since both her parents had blue eyes. After I fed her formula, she fell deep into sleep in my arms. Her tiny delicate nostrils quivered with every breath. I turned on the television. A reality show was on. I started to think about why Dennis believed it was a joke, instead of a contract. Surely, they were not entitled to everything. Nobody is entitled to anything.

It happened so quickly, I hardly thought about it. I picked up the sleeping baby and nestled her in a car seat in the back of my car. It's just a little drive, I told myself. I drove past the thick poisonous pink oleander in the center median of the highway and up through the mountains, and gradually wound around until I was at sea level, driving along the gold-beige dunes at the coast. In a few miles, I pulled into the rough dirt driveway of the beach property.

In the many months since I'd been there, rampion had spread across the garden, plush and meandering over the rocks, over the alyssum, over the pansies, over the hyacinth, suffocating and burying everything within its reach like a sandstorm. "You're home," I said to the baby, whose eyes were fluttering open as I unbuckled her car seat. I swaddled her in a yellow cotton blanket and put the bag of her things over my shoulder. We trundled to the ocean. Bright green-blue surf crashed against the jagged rocks and the horizon line burned with the setting sun.

We climbed the steep staircase of the tower. The steps were made of stone blocks. I held the baby tightly as I climbed the narrow steps, and each step seemed taller than the last, and the curving walls seemed suffocating as they closed in on me. The bag kept falling off my shoulder and I kept heaving it back onto my shoulder. I was panting and breathless by the time I reached the porthole at the top landing, far above the ground. I looked down at the baby. She was awake, but quiet. She watched my face intently with alert, luminous eyes. I unlatched the door to the roof. "Look," I said. We looked out into the ocean. I remembered that sometimes dolphins migrated past, their silvery backs shining for a moment before they submerged under the dark ocean waves. But now I could not see dolphins, only the faraway boats.

"See the ships? We could take one of those ships and travel all around the world." The baby gazed back at me and puckered her lips a few times. I thought of the quips Connall would have made if he were here. I sat cross-legged on the stone surface, cradling her and feeding her the rest of the formula from her bottle. In the corner were a few dead succulents in terra cotta pots that he had probably bought to make the rooftop nicer for me. I resolved to revive them, now that everything was, for the moment, as it should be.

As the baby suckled at the bottle, I could almost sense Connall beside me, the salty, musky smell of him after gardening, the worn softness of his flannel shirt on my arm, even the warmth of his hand. The baby surveyed the sky through the turrets and ran tiny hot, sweaty fingers over my toes—I did not know that babies were so damp, all of them water babies. She tickled my toes, but I stayed perfectly still and content, feeling those delicate fingers and how little she knew of what the world held.

In a few moments, violet-tinged stars started to prick the sky, a misty halo circling the full moon. The distant hum of the highway came as if through cotton. Gulls were crying. Otters squealed and the waves were hard crashing. The baby whimpered. It was well after eight. I was searching through my purse for her pacifier when I came upon a compact. It fell open in my hand.

By the light of the moon, I could see it was not my familiar face looking back at me. There was a redness to my cheeks, a hairiness, and my white hair looked platinum blonde. I touched my face softly, marveling at my suede-covered cheeks. And the smell—garlic and cucumber—the smell of rampion was all around me, or perhaps emanating from me.

The coastal summer air was still warm. Minutes passed, or perhaps hours. The baby was sleeping, her eyelashes invisible and her tiny nostrils quivering almost imperceptibly as she breathed in and out. I took off my sweater and wrapped it around the baby to keep her warm in the night.

Later, the high-pitched whine of sirens would sound, and my skin would be ice-cold. I would see a peach-pink blot just above the bit of ocean between the turrets. After the police took the baby back to her parents, after they told me that the Truebloods would not press charges, I would sit in the tower alone for hours, gazing out at the cold grey waters, the thick soft whiteness of fog hanging over everything like wet cotton or memories. I would light the scraps of paper in my purse with a lighter and fling the little flaming beacons out toward the ocean on the wind. Some of them would float away, on and on over the water, and others would lie flickering and burning on the stone. Smoke would surround me as the day wore on and still I would sit there alone.

But in that moment, the baby gurgled in a deep sleep and I was looking up into a million points of light.

SWANS AND OTHER LIES

Leda meets Patterson in a dive bar named Three Thimbles, just past Atascadero. She is hitchhiking south to Indio for a music festival during a drought, and the gentle hills along Highway 5 are barren and grey-brown like donkey skins. She last traveled this route with her parents as a small child, and without their bickering or the blaring of Carnatic music, the ride is strangely bleak, the cobalt sky unexpectedly vast and cloudless. The truck drivers who offer her rides are entirely taciturn or they regale her with explosive tales about their lives—an unstoppable gush of molten words. She smiles to be agreeable, but stays silent, unsure which of her stories to offer in response.

She is drinking a Sidecar and reading Nietzsche's *The Birth of Tragedy* when Patterson approaches. On the side of the bar, patrons tack business cards as they pass through town and in front of her is a waxy paper cup full of brass tacks. Patterson tacks a card on the bar right next to her, taking a moment to screw it deep into the wood. She side-eyes the pixelation of the hokey music-store logo on the card and wonders if it's even real. He asks whether she wants to join him for a round of pool. "Can't play," she says without looking at him.

"Now how are you going to know that if you don't try?"

She looks up solely to tell him to fuck off, but he smiles.

He points to her book. "I've always been partial to Dionysian art myself."

Leda graduated from a college in Eugene two weeks ago. Over the course of her years there she came to realize there are a number of folks who not only prefer wild debauchery, but also look down on those who don't. She believes—because of the tattooed tendril making its way out from under his long-sleeved shirt—that admitting she prefers the order and clarity and light of Apollonian art and that left to her own devices, she blasts Katy Perry, not The Velvet Underground—would sound uncool and bourgeois. It would be even more uncool, perhaps, to acknowledge she prefers both art and the world to be orderly so that she knows how to react, so she isn't confronted by the disorder, the utter aimlessness inside her. And, of course, there are Patterson's murky green eyes and his slightly crooked teeth. She has learned to nod to avoid judgment, and she does so almost reflexively.

Patterson buys Leda another Sidecar. The bartender, a bald, potbellied man in dungarees, shakes his head, presumably at her choice in drinks, but sugars the rim of the glass and goes strong on the cognac.

Later, they stumble onto the sidewalk. He carries his bass guitar case, and she remembers she has forgotten her book on the barstool, but lets it go, uncertain it would provide the road map she's looking for. Stars above, mica sparkling below the street lamps. She has rented a room at the Shrinking Violet Motel for the night and she spins around to find her bearings. Nobody else is out at this hour. The streets are wide, stygian, infinite. She turns again and one of her tan suede boots falls down around her ankle. Patterson drops to his knees and slides the suede up her shin back to her knee, slowly so that the callouses on his palms caress her shin.

"I'm not sleeping with you tonight," she says, pretending to be certain.

Within the hour they are kissing in her motel room. He sets his bass guitar down by the bed. She reaches out to touch its glossy lacquered surface, but he quickly moves it out of her reach. "Got that as a gift while I was in the band, maybe twenty years ago." He draws her to him. She tugs at his boxers, lightly snapping their elastic. When she comes with a savage shudder, he enters quickly and finishes, lets out a long sigh as if pushing a last squat beneath three hundred pounds.

Patterson sleeps into the early afternoon and she sits on the floor, beside the bed, and fingers the glossy finish of his bass guitar. He wakes and catches her turning it over in her hands. "Curious, aren't you? Haven't you heard what happened to the cat?"

"I've got nine lives," Leda says, shrugging.

His tone shifts as he tells her he is traveling for the thrill of it and invites her to go with him. "Open road—who knows what we'll find?"

She thinks of the pixelated business logo for a moment, but he is pulling her into the bed, and by the time they're finished, she's put away the nagging sensation that something is out of place and agrees to join him.

They fuck each other in seedy motels with names like Watering Hole Inn and Afternoon Delight Motel and Seven Brides. The sheets on the beds smell like wet dog and cigarette smoke and bleach, odors that cleaning crews attempt to mask with cloying air freshener in scents of pine and rose. The first night on the road and the second and the third, he serenades her on his bass guitar. Later, she won't be able to remember what the song was, but she will remember the quality of his voice, its high-pitched jagged tenderness, and the way he looks down while he plucks the strings, as if he's fingering an old girlfriend.

Patterson has sleeve tattoos on both arms, intricate jewel-toned illustrations of dragons and griffins and albatrosses, all elongated necks and enfolding wings, and surprisingly masculine. His muscular back has no tattoos, just a long, thick jagged pink keloid running like a highway from the place on his back where a wing would be if he had one to the top of his hipbone. "How'd you get that?" she asks, pointing. At first his silence seems like a slight. Most people would think he's out of her league—she is dark and stubby, and he is vaguely leonine, all jalapeño greens and burnished gold. He should compensate accordingly. As the days pass, however, the ugliness of that long scar makes her feel closer to him, like they are more alike than she originally thought.

* * *

They wind their way through the Grapevine, driving from Los Angeles to Tucson, where Leda learns Patterson might be psychic. They are sitting in a blue vinyl booth. Overhead is a row of lamps, each shaped like a blowfish. He points out a couple sitting at the bar. The woman has dyed blonde hair with black roots showing, and she is wearing corduroy pants and a hoodie covered with tiny grey dog hairs. The man has a shaggy beard, sideburns and earlobes sagging with wide black gauges. The woman runs her hand across the man's arm, reassuring him. Then the woman's hand melts into the man's arm, disappearing and then reappearing as it moves back and forth. The couple is talking about where they should go to dinner that night.

"They're from the Bronx," Patterson says in a low voice. He claims he can do this trick because he toured around the country with a metal band in his teens, hopped freight trains in his twenties. "I've been everywhere," he says. "Go ask them where they're from." Leda raises her eyebrows. "Just ask! They won't mind, people like to yammer on about themselves."

He drags her over to the couple and they say they're from the Bronx. The four take tequila shots together. Patterson raises his eyebrows and smiles as if to crow *I told you so*. At the end of the evening, the man realizes he's left his wallet somewhere and Patterson pays for the drinks. Everyone is having such a good time that Leda suppresses her suspicions.

* * *

They travel to Las Cruces and then Houston, occasionally taking detours to enjoy the bone and gold desert, the boundless blue sky, and every night they drink at a different dive bar. He teaches her how to play pool. They spend leisurely mornings swimming in motel pools and sampling gas station pastries.

Patterson accurately guesses a white man with dreadlocks doing tequila shots at a restaurant in Ciudad Juarez is from Ukiah. A woman wearing a violet cloche and walking her dog around the park in a small town just outside Big Bend National Park is from Ann Arbor. He guesses the bald, black bartender in San Antonio is from Murfreesboro. "So where am I from?" she asks him.

"I'm guessing Cupertino," he says.

"Because there's a big Indian population there? Well, you're wrong."

* * *

They are mostly out of money by the time they get to Houston, and they start sleeping in the back of his pickup, parked off the highway, laying their heads down on his rolled-up sweatshirts and wrangling both their bodies into a single sleeping bag. In the black exhaustion of those hours, fucking loses its sharp wild intensity and she wants to be cutting, she wants to say, *If you're so psychic, why are we scavenging trash behind bakeries?*

They veer off the interstate and start running scams in small inland towns. The first scam involves the bass guitar. Patterson researches the town's restaurants ahead of time by asking the local bartenders about the best places to eat and what the owners are like. He gets people to chat, and then picks their mark. It is a simple plan. Leda enters a fancy restaurant with the guitar, wearing a red sticker pottu—nobody will suspect a traditional young Indian woman of anything, Patterson explains as he sticks it in the center of her forehead.

The dining room is paneled in warm brown oak and a fire roars in the brick hearth. She lingers over the possibility of a medium rare burger and a beer, but decides it might blow her cover, and orders a mixed green salad, a coke and a slice of yellow cake frosted in chocolate buttercream.

Heavy barrels of wine line the back wall. She flirts with the waiter during the hour she spends eating. At the end of the meal, her heart pounding and a ringing in her ears, she pretends she forgot her cash back at home. The waiter waves over the plump restaurant owner, euphoric and distracted from a recent lotto win—or so a bartender a town over told them. She shows the owner how valuable her 1960s bass guitar is on a website accessed on his smartphone. He is genial, lets her leave the bass as collateral for the meal. When she leaves, Patterson swoops in and offers the owner $20,000 for the Fender Jazz bass guitar in the corner, telling a story about Jaco Pastorius's Bass of Doom and the sweet focused sound of the instrument—he even plays the owner a tune to demonstrate—and when the owner demurs, explaining the bass isn't his, Patterson leaves a business card from when he worked at a music store. Leda returns thirty minutes after he leaves, and the owner offers her $5,000 for the guitar.

Leda telephones her mother from the swanky Shreveport hotel where they stay that night. Fingering the complimentary vanilla-frangipani lotions on the oak dresser, Leda tells her it will be at least another month before she comes home. Her mother, a practical engineer, expresses concern that Leda has no plan for her life, no concrete job in the wings. In the background, Leda can hear the familiar sound of her father listening to NPR, the wheezing and barking of the French bulldog they bought after she left home. She tells her mother that it's a long life, and there's time enough for all that when she returns home. "Love you," she says, and hangs up.

Patterson is busying himself unpacking his clothes and putting them in the mahogany dresser. "Won't you miss your guitar?" she asks Patterson, realizing suddenly that he must feel unsettled without it. He looks a little sad, and says he'll buy another one when he has more money. He doesn't offer to split the money with her, although he does pay for anything and everything she wants. She thinks of bringing up the inequity but decides not to say anything since, after all, it was his bass they used.

Other scams follow, crafted while lying in hotel room beds, lying face-to-face, or while hiking through the green humidity or while drinking Fernet or absinthe at upscale bars. The liqueurs leave Leda dehydrated and dizzy. The scams prove to be the inverse of his other trick. Persuasion requires almost as much observation as divination since the things that convince people to trust you are bound up with who they've been, what they've seen, where they want to be.

Patterson says this trick is new to him, too. Just think, if they make enough money with these tricks, they will be able to travel abroad.

* * *

Everything changes in Mobile, three weeks and five days after they first meet. They are visiting Patterson's redheaded aunt, his mother's youngest sister. She lives with her son and his family in a planned community where occasionally an alligator comes up from the creeks and attacks a toddler. The son's wife cooks a Southern feast on the night they arrive—fried okra, grits, fried chicken, a ham, and pie. After putting her grandchild to bed with Gillian Welch's lilting *I'll Fly Away*, the aunt notices Leda's sweater and asks what designer it is. Leda shrugs and says it's second-hand, but the aunt's eyes are glinting.

The aunt smokes pot on a front porch lit with fireflies and Patterson joins her in a folding chair. The aunt asks Leda, "You ever tried chewing tobacco?" Leda shakes her head no. "Next time y'all visit, we'll get you some." The aunt notes briefly that Indian girls like Leda are quiet, and she teases Leda about never having eaten potted meat. "Spam's a delicacy," she says. Leda likes the aunt. She is mesmerized by the cold blinking lights, the croaking of the frogs, and the rattling thrum of the cicadas. The aunt explains that they emerge from their subterranean burrows every thirteen years. "We know lean times are on their way when we hear them rumbling up through the earth," she says. The screen door creaks slowly open and then slams shut. Patterson has gone inside.

After a few minutes, the aunt starts talking about her childhood. She tells a story about her crazy father, Patterson's grandfather, and how he had once chased his four children through the graveyard with a rifle at midnight. "Annie pulled me behind a headstone and we hid there all night." Annie is Patterson's mother. Leda's parents have dramatic tales too—about village life in Tamil Nadu, the southernmost state in India, about unrequited love and tigers attacking babies and corrupt police—but they would never share them with a random stranger.

The aunt's generosity is warming. Leda hugs her before turning in for the night, and she feels herself dissolving into the aunt's tough bony shoulders, melting into the smell of marijuana and spring lilac perfume. When she pulls away, she has left something behind—all that had been orderly about her has sunk into the woman's shoulders, never to reemerge.

The next morning, the aunt and her daughter-in-law take them on a tour of the grand antebellum mansions of Mobile—white Greek Revival homes with plain pillars and white porch rails. Leda is covered in angry red insect bites from the night before, and she's trying not to scratch her arms and legs raw.

They are stalled in front of one of the mansions, fantasizing about the chandeliers and the circular staircases inside, when the aunt drops the n-word so casually that Leda thinks she has imagined it. But then the aunt drops the word again, and again, a grenade each time. Leda is surprised and uncomfortable. She looks at Patterson in profile, and sees that he is not shocked at all. The aunt and daughter-in-law continue their conversation about the interior of the homes. Leda wonders how the aunt will talk about her when she is not there. She knows the word was not directed at her, but she worries over it, turning it over, considering it in different lights, wondering if she is overreacting—she cannot banish the word from her thoughts. It occurs to Leda that an elaborate show is being put on for her, a California girl, a dark foreign girl—the food, the music.

The aunt turns around and looks into the back seat at Leda and Patterson. "I used to ride bikes with my older sisters in this neighborhood when I was a little girl. One time, they went ahead, and I just walked into the house through the servant's entrance. Nobody was there, so I climbed up the circular staircase to the second floor. The chandelier overhead was so big and bright it was like a snowball made of stars and fire. I thought I could touch it, and I leaned over the bannister, holding my hands out. I reached and reached, and almost fell over the railing when a little boy who lived there pulled me back. I ran right out of there as fast as I could."

Leda nods. She can see this in the aunt: the ghost of that young girl reaching for a ball of stars on the ceiling, the little boy pulling her back so she wouldn't fall.

Later that night, Leda and Patterson lie in the narrow guest bed together, uncomfortable under the nubby sheets, the mosquitoes devouring them. Above them is a needlepoint wall hanging that depicts a house. Over it in pastel pink script it says, *Be it ever so humble, there's no place like home.*

Leda asks whether they can return to the Left Coast.

Patterson turns to face her on the starched pillow and the cold moonlight backlights his blond hair. His face is in dark shadow so she can't read his expression. "You don't really want to go back, do you? We're having so much fun on the road."

"You've done all this before, and you'll do it all again," she says and hides part of her face in the pillow.

"I don't know what you're talking about. Go to sleep." He turns over and he throws an arm around her. That business card Patterson gave the restaurant owner. Her original take on it, banished by lust and adrenaline, returns to her. Is it a genuine business card from a music store sales job as he claimed, or was it a card manufactured with Photoshop to create an elaborate illusion, a scam he knew in advance he would run and has run many times before with other girls in other places? Patterson's arm is heavy on her chest, and she stares at the curved shadows on the ceiling, listens to the cicadas until dawn.

* * *

On the following night, Patterson's gaunt cousin, who drives a big rig, takes his mandatory rest break. He gathers the family to play pool in the basement. The basement is mummified in cobwebs, and stinks of mushrooms and standing water, and its periphery is piled with a jumble of cardboard moving boxes. The aunt thuds down the narrow stairs, carrying a six-pack of Coors and a jumbo bag of Fritos.

She pulls rolling paper out of her pocket and shakes some bud into it as her son sidles around the table, racking up the balls. "I got something from one of the guys at work to make this more fun," the son says.

The aunt laughs. "You do have that bonus coming due." Patterson grabs three cues leaned up against a cobwebby corner of the basement, and hands two to his aunt and cousin.

Leaning the cue on the table, the cousin sprinkles some crystals on the green line and rolls it up, licking the edge of the paper to seal it. He lights the joint.

"Your son wanted to come down to get his goodnight kiss," his wife calls as she lumbers down the stairs. His son—tow-haired and already in his powder-blue pajamas, exuding sweetness and milk—pads toward his father, and the father swings him up and kisses all over his head, then swats him on the bottom, pushing him toward the stairs.

"Don't do anything I wouldn't do, kids," the wife says, gesturing at her husband's anemic pink lips as the smoke swirls between them.

"Too late," he says, exhaling, and takes another drag before handing the joint to his mother. A faint aroma—acetone and doughnuts burning and cat piss—floods the basement. He looks around the room after the wife and son are gone, and notes that Leda's hands are empty. "Grab a cue." He won't make eye contact with her. Unnerving. She floats through the dust motes toward the fourth cue, still hanging in the dark corner.

"Oh, she can't play," Patterson says.

"What are you talking about?" Leda asks. "We've played a bunch of times."

"Well, all right, I didn't want to say it straight up, but you're not very good." He turns to his cousin and says, "There are times she can't even make contact."

"Like my wife," the cousin says.

"You can play on my team, honey," the aunt says to Leda.

They play eight-ball, and as the night wears on, the mood is increasingly raucous, and the basement is smoky. Nobody is tired except for Leda, who is thinking about a few snapshots Patterson has in his wallet of playing his bass in a band. She has never bothered to compare the real Fender Jazz bass to those pictures to see if it was the same one, or a replacement. She takes a handful of Fritos and a sip of her beer.

"She's not that bad," the cousin tells Patterson. He is bouncing on the balls of his toes and drinking his fourth beer.

"I can't believe you would say I can't play," Leda says. "And truth be told, your aunt's better than you."

"She is that," Patterson admits.

"We're leaving tomorrow."

"Gonna let your lady talk to you like that?" the cousin asks, taking his shot.

"We'll see," Patterson says, with an edge in his voice.

Leda smiles and sets down her cue. "I'm beat," she says. "Thanks for the game, guys."

When she gets upstairs, she opens Patterson's wallet. She looks at the snapshots of Patterson with his band. They look like real aged photographs, but the bass, the one he had for so many years, looks different—blond wood instead of a deep red and black finish.

At daybreak, they head along the coast toward Biloxi, steaming down the I-10 in the pickup. Patterson doesn't turn on the radio or put in his CDs. They drive in an oppressive silence. The beaches are flat and paler than sawdust, a little ugly, with long docks running out into the placid waters and an array of gleaming sails rising from the boats moored there. "I'm feeling lucky!" he says as they start to approach the bright, hulking casinos. "Let's hit the tables and go to the beach." She is pretty sure he would want to hit the tables whether or not he was feeling lucky, but she mumbles her assent. Maybe the philosophy, the art, all of it, is a long con because he has intuited that her parents are rich, maybe he read her the way he reads their marks.

They stop at a casino that rises above the ocean, plate glass windows gleaming like a wide silver spacecraft. Patterson has a craving for crawfish and they find a restaurant that sells them boiled. She orders a diet root beer, and sips it slowly, trying to make the sweet sassafras taste last. A waiter brings Patterson a plate of crawfish. They lie there with their bright red shells and necks intact. He offers her some crawfish, but she shakes her head and watches him dive into the plate, twisting the heads off the necks and sucking the juice from the opening. Next, he cracks the shell on the tail and stuffs the meat into his mouth. He sucks the claws. "Sure you don't want some?" he asks. "It's stupendous." She wants to vomit.

They hit the blackjack tables. Patterson likes blackjack because the only person he has to read at the table is the female dealer. Easy. "Do you want to play?" he asks. He hasn't asked her what's wrong, or what she's thinking, or what she'd like to do. When she shakes her head, he asks if she wants to go to the spa and hands her a hundred-dollar bill. She can hear him flirting with the dealer as she walks away. She doesn't visit the spa, but wanders in and out of stores, eying the merchandise and thinking about how much it would cost to buy a plane ticket home. Certainly more than one hundred dollars, but that might cover the cost of economy train fare or a bus. She thinks of all those days on a bus, backtracking to her ordinary, sterile suburban life, the life she grew up in and grew out of, and the idea of going on, the way she always has, disappearing into her childhood room with its framed Degas prints and Andrew Lang fairytale books and white writing desk, seems simultaneously comforting and horrifying. She could take the elevator upstairs and ring her parents, ask them to wire the money for airfare—they wouldn't make her beg or anything—but she feels too ashamed to explain that her adventure has turned sour, just as her mother feared it would, and to return home defeated.

She returns to the hotel room, and flops on the bed, burying her face in the pillows, and takes a long nap, her sleep suffused with dreams of Patterson's tattoos unpeeling from the skin on his arms, lifting off his body and flying away, leaving only that ugly pink keloid behind. When she wakes her mouth is bone dry and her head pounds from sleeping too long. Patterson is changing into clothes. "How'd you do?" she asks.

He takes out bills, unfolds them and swats at them with his hand. "We're goin' big tonight," he drawls.

They hang out in an old-fashioned bar, draped in crimson velvet with a zinc bar. Roy Orbison's voice plays on the jukebox. *Crying over you*. Patterson orders a top-shelf habanero pepper margarita and turns to her. "May I have this dance?" he asks.

They revolve around the center of the dark room, the only ones dancing. The wall behind the zinc bar is backlit with violet light that makes the bottles of spirits shimmer, and slowly that wall, all the walls, recede into the distance. As she presses against Patterson, she feels her feet softening, losing gravity. He's embracing her, willing her, the her that is her and not somebody else, to disappear, swallowing her. Her arms pressed around his shoulders sink, disappearing into the red and white checks of his shirt like butter in a hot pan, into the smell of his damp hair, like wet hay, and the zingy spiciness of his shaving cream.

* * *

Leda wakes before Patterson, as she always does after a night of heavy drinking. Her thighs are sore. She can't sleep, and she feels grateful for that. He sleeps soundly and quietly, naked under the single white sheet, his blond hair gleaming against his neck, and she tugs a paisley comforter over him. She pulls on her T-shirt and hoodie and slides her jeans over her hips, the clothes she wore when she met him. She steps into flip-flops she picked up at a drugstore and leaves her suede boots and the new clothes she bought along the way, hoping that by leaving the illusion of her return she will buy more time to run.

On the dresser is Patterson's brown leather wallet, and the corners of bills are poking out of it. The air conditioner is on, but her palms are sweating, moisture collecting in the whorls on her fingers. She carefully slides most of the bills from the wallet and folds them and pushes them into her jeans pocket.

A sound from the bed and she turns, her skin burning hot. She opens her mouth to explain. But he has only burrowed deeper under the covers. She worked up the marks too and should have been given half the spoils. She can hear her own heart gonging in her chest and is surprised that he doesn't sense anything is amiss. She tells herself that, Dionysian that he is, it could very well be him sneaking out and abandoning her in a hotel. With her backpack, she slips out of the hotel room, and releases the handle slowly. It makes a quiet clicking sound.

The sun is warm and the air like wet cotton and salty. A bracing sea breeze swirls up toward her face. Leda convinces a businessman loading his suitcases into a yellow taxicab to let her share the cost of a ride to the airport. The sugar beach and warm waters of the Gulf of Mexico stretch out, deep and boundless and sparkling through the scratched cab window. She imagines for a moment that Patterson will come running after the cab, screaming that he's been robbed, perhaps crying and heartbroken, but just as quickly she realizes this would be ridiculous. It has only been a little over a month, even if it feels like a lifetime. Far more likely—he will wait for a while, and then he will understand what has happened. She glances through the back window of the cab. The silver casino is shrinking into the middle ground, and then disappearing into the distance. Noting his plush, dark red leather briefcase and his elegant, burnished cufflinks, Leda turns to the businessman to make light chitchat about where he is from and where he is going. Patterson read her after all, and surely, he must have guessed she was capable of this.

THE LOOKOUT

Even from one hundred feet up, the air smells of dust and dirt. The sky is bone-dry blue over land as barren as burned flesh, and in the orchards, the fruit trees are pale and skeletal. Industrious farmers scurry over the fields, hand-watering crops with the last of the reservoir water. Pine trees break the horizon like crooked teeth. She scans the inside of the observatory, adjusts the baby on her hip.

Double-paned windows run nearly the length of the pine walls on all four sides. Nestled in the one corner of the observatory is a small kitchenette with a toaster oven and a hot plate, its base covered in black drips. In the adjacent corner hangs an old pink shower curtain that hides a flush toilet. The lookout is supposed to call the scientists and inventors from a rotary phone on a table in the center of the observatory if she spies anything resembling a cloud, so they can seed it: rockets filled with silver iodide shot into the cloud, the iodide wrapping itself in moisture until it can no longer hold the water. This is what they tell her.

No television. The radio mostly comes in as mumbling and static. The baby cries with hunger. Otherwise, cool silence inside the observatory. She reminds herself that she should name the baby soon, but for now, she sits by the window and latches the small mouth to her breast. She searches the horizon for clouds. There are binoculars next to the rotary phone to help spot faraway clouds in a pinch, but most days all she witnesses from the windows are shades of blue: a bright blue, a powder blue, an eggshell blue, a grey-blue, a lunar blue, a midnight blue, Delft blue, aquamarine. She grows so attuned to the subtlest differences she does not need the binoculars, and as days pass, the minute shifts in hue become a kind of drama. If she stares too long, she starts to perceive differences in the blue of the southern sky and the blue of the eastern sky. Other times, she is convinced the changes are just her imagination finding ways to create and articulate differences, the way a couple with all the same interests and similar personalities eventually, through the depraved power of monogamy, start to believe they are wholly different sorts of people. Some days the shades of blue compel her to write poetry, almost. Some days a hawk floats by or a crow smashes headlong into the glass windows. Passerines circle the observatory, hovering on the wind with wings raised. Perhaps they are searching for a perch. The lookout likes to think they find a home on the top of the observatory where she can't see them.

The baby learns to sit up and cloud gaze. She wobbles and squishes her nose flat against the glass for hours. Then she learns to crawl, and day by day her laps around the periphery of the observatory increase in speed until she is crawling the length of the four glass windows as fast as she can, crawling as if she is looking for some means of escape from all the blue.

Every week, one of the scientists' assistants climbs the staircase that winds its way to the observatory. Bearing a sack of groceries and the local newspaper, he pauses to huff and make breathless small talk, then trudges back down the steps, hauling away garbage and recyclables. At first the lookout can rely on two or three hothouse apples in the sack, but eventually, the produce stops coming, and there are only powder mixes for Wacky cake and bread and corn muffins, and the eggs and oil with which to make them. The newspaper carries profiles of terminated and obsolescent weathermen, and an article about how the old weather station has become a factory that produces waterless bath powder. Eventually the newspaper stops reporting the drought.

A year passes with no clouds.

The baby learns to toddle. She learns to sing lullabies, eliding the l's and w's. Every night, she counts stars, and although the lookout doesn't know the names of any of them, she starts to point out the same ones, noticing their different arrangements against the sky. The baby stops nursing, and the assistant brings glass jugs of milk. The milk is bluish—it doesn't taste the way the lookout remembers.

Sometimes she unlocks the door and stands at the top of the staircase with the baby, looking down from a vertiginous knotted pine step. The air is still, smelling of dust and dirt. She imagines what it would be like to walk all the way down these steps to the yellow weeds and brown earth below.

Baby claps her cheeks with tiny palms and says imperiously, Inside, Mommy!

* * *

While the lookout is making Baby a sandwich one afternoon, she sees something white whirling by the glass.

Later, after she has called the head scientist with the coordinates, they hear the rocket rumbling below. This is it, Baby! she says.

This is it, Baby says. This is it Baby!

Baby takes her peanut butter and jelly sandwich apart with the absorbed curiosity of a mechanic. She pulls the edges of the white bread this way and then that on her plate. A cloud.

Around twilight, something smacks the glass. A drop of rain and then many and fast. They crawl into the puffy sleeping bag on the futon, but the warmth and the synthetic scrunch of the fabric is not comforting. Lightning strikes a nearby skeletal tree and a bare branch flies off and thwacks the rain-coated window. Water swirls on the glass and oozes away. Through the water, blue moonlight. A crash—the world cracked open.

Late that night, masses of people congregate in the violet darkness of the fields below. Baby listens carefully to the horns and noisemakers. Cheering and dancing as thunder roars. The glass drizzles away, leaving only the pine platform in the wind. The lookout wraps her arms around Baby like a mantle, and all through the night she sings songs of dust and dirt. *Remember?*

ACKNOWLEDGMENTS

"Deception" appeared in *Juked* under a different title; "Elephants in the Pink City" appeared in *Joyland*; "Hema and Kathy" appeared in *The Normal School*; "The Logic of Someday" appeared in the *Stockholm Review of Literature*; "Everywhere, Signs" appeared in *Kweli Journal*; "Wild Things" appeared in *The Doctor T.J. Eckleburg Review*; "Rampion" appeared in *Strangelet Journal*; "Swans and Other Lies" appeared in *The Rumpus*; "The Lookout" appeared in *Necessary Fiction*.

I wrote the first story of this book, "Wild Things," in a workshop with the late Beat poet and novelist Ron Loewinsohn at UC Berkeley in 1998. During the two decades since then, scores of readers have offered comment on earlier incarnations of these stories, and some are bound to be lost in the slippage of my memory. For forgetting or not acknowledging someone formally, I apologize in advance.

Thank you to Porochista Khakpour for selecting this collection and opening a door.

Immense gratitude to editor Blake Calamas of Stillhouse Press for completely and wholeheartedly engaging with another writer's stories, asking such smart questions, and trying to help make these stories the best versions of themselves, draft after draft after draft—and also, for the gift of a sequence that felt right. Many thanks to all the good people of Stillhouse Press who believed in this collection, and put their valuable time, energy, and resources behind it, including Meghan McNamara, Michelle Webber, Marcos Martinez, Douglas Luman, and Scott W. Berg.

Thank you to Beth Parker for PR help and kindness to a lit-world outsider.

Thank you to the journals where these stories first found homes, and the readers and editors who selected them: Ashley Farmer at *Juked*, Helen McClory at *Necessary Fiction*, Casey Brown at *Strangelet Journal*, Sofia Capel and Ted Greijer at *The Stockholm Review of Literature*, Randa Jarrar at *The Normal School*, Sarah Lyn Rogers at *The Rumpus*, and Lisa Locascio at *Joyland*.

Thanks especially to these incredible teachers: to sharp and insightful Rae Bryant of Eckleburg Workshops, without whose phenomenal editorial feedback and strong sense of aesthetics I might not have understood in what direction to take this collection. To generous and wholehearted Laura Pegram of Kweli Journal whose emotional tuning fork and dedication toward writers of color is everything. To Chris Abani of Voices of Our Nations Arts Foundation (VONA), for lasting wisdom, vision, and survival skills.

Thanks also to workshops taught by Lan Samantha Chang, Gary Soto, Eric Puchner, Katherine Noel, Tom Jenks, and Lynn Stegner.

Over twenty years, many lectures and books have infiltrated my subconscious, but I'd like to cite, as factual research indispensable to writing this collection, Sumathi Ramaswamy's *The Lost Land of Lemuria: Fabulous Geographies, Catastrophic Histories* and *Passions of the Tongue: Language Devotion in Tamil India 1891-1970*, as well as Jennifer Cole's *Forget Colonialism? Sacrifice and the Art of Memory in Madagascar*. Any interpretive errors or alterations to their research and ideas in the service of fiction are mine alone.

Thank you to Ina Roy-Faderman, a sister from another mother, for understanding these stories right away, and championing an earlier draft of this collection. Thank you to the astute readers of one or more drafts of these stories (or either of the novels that were abandoned and transmogrified into these stories): Karin Spirn, Phoebe Kitanidis, Sarita Sarvate, Vidya Pradhan, and Jo Greiner. Thank you to literary agents Victoria Sanders and Deborah Jayne for reading this collection, and taking me on as a client.

Thank you to Elisa Cheng, Kerry Guinn, Nalini Rao, and Athena Wong for listening to my stories for decades and for such staunch friendships.

Thanks to my parents for spending time with my small children while I worked and for handling with equanimity and grace my lifelong compulsion to write all the things that good girls don't. Also in particular, thank you to my father for patiently teaching me to read when I was four—this remains the most important thing I've learned how to do.

Eternal love to my trio—Illyria, Kavi, and Beckett—you will always be my North Star. Love and gratitude to Steven, a true believer, for recommending all the best existentialist and magical realism books for the last seventeen years and for being my first reader. I couldn't have written this collection without you.

ANITA FELICELLI's short stories have appeared in *The Normal School, Joyland, Kweli Journal*, and *Eckleburg*, and have been finalists for Glimmer Train awards. She's contributed essays and reviews to the *New York Times* (Modern Love), *Salon*, the *San Francisco Chronicle, LA Review of Books, The Rumpus*, and elsewhere. She is the recipient of a Puffin Foundation grant for poetry and two Greater Bay Area Journalism awards. Her work appears in several anthologies and has been nominated for Pushcart Prizes. She holds a B.A. with honors in Rhetoric, English and Interdisciplinary Studies (visual art) from UC Berkeley and a J.D. from UC Berkeley School of Law. She was bitten by the travel bug, and has never recovered—she's visited all the continents except two. Born in South India, she lives in the Bay Area with her family.

This book would not have been possible
without the hard work of our staff.

We would like to acknowledge:

BLAKE CALAMAS   Managing Editor
MEGHAN McNAMARA   Director of Media
DANIELLE MADDOX   Intern
SARAH LURIA   Intern

Our Donors

ANONYMOUS

THERESE HOWELL

DALLAS HUDGENS

WAYNE B. JOHNSON

WILLIAM MILLER

stillhouse
press

CPSIA information can be obtained
at www.ICGtesting.com
Printed in the USA
BVHW071104261118
534009BV00006B/524/P